IN THE WOODS
MURDER IN THE NORTH EAST
KINGDOM

A novel by
Elisabeth Zguta

COPYRIGHT

All rights belong to Elisabeth Zguta
ISBN-10   0-9894946-9-1
ISBN13   978-0989494694
Library of Congress filed 1-5919043851

Book Designer: EZ Indie Design by Elisabeth Zguta
Publisher: EZ Indie Publishing by Elisabeth Zguta

OTHER BOOKS BY ELISABETH ZGUTA FOR YOU TO ENJOY!

Curses & Secrets Serial:
>   Breaking Cursed Bonds
>   Exposing Secret Sins
>   Seeking Redemption

Here's what some readers say about Breaking Cursed Bonds

Awesome!!!!!
"This book was very enjoyable I could not put it down! I am looking forward to future projects from this author!"

A race against time to break a family curse.
"Fear of an old family curse was intertwined with more earthly greed and sprinkled with unexplained deaths. The main chcracters were interesting and Zguta used the psychology of fear, betrayal and insecurity to give them depth and kept them constantly moving the story on. The descriptions of the various places the book was set, the UK, New Orleans and Florida were excellent and gave a good flavour of the atmosphere. An enjoyable read."

Learn more at EZIndiePublishing.com

Contents

ABENAKI PRAYER

Prayer Translation:

With we who visit ghosts from
The sun star of our birth and in our
Infancy which is from the Land of
The rising star, as long as the deer and moose
Shall run free and the grass shall grow
And the rivers run swiftly; the Abenaki shall survive
The white man's wickedness.
Again our Grandfathers' spirits
Have given us guidance and wisdom to
Rise and come together to dance.
We have been taught
To Love Mother Earth and to respect her.
We are the Children of the Dawn, the People
Of the East. May the Great Spirit and
The Great Creator bless us and smile upon us.

Written by Chief Edwin "Joe" Pero,
Coos (Cowasuck-Koasek) Deer Clan

1 - Stranger Danger

Jessica edged her way into the room, turning her gaze left then right, trying to make sense of the place. The glow from the candles threw shadows of twisted shapes onto the opposite wall, distorted silhouettes of the furniture. The dreary incandescence faded to darkness, the room's corners became sullied and obscure.

An uneasiness twisted in the pit of her stomach. She sobered up quickly when she stepped foot into this house, despite the numerous shots of bourbon she had downed an hour earlier. Fear rose within her as she moved forward, looking for the guy who had brought her here.

It was a cold night. Jessica had drunk too much, using the weak excuse of keeping herself warm, but the truth was she had wanted to get wasted.

Only now, she wished that she hadn't taken off her jacket. She couldn't remember where she left it. The guy who picked her up had insisted that she wear this damned pink sweater as part of her costume, and somehow she never put her jacket back on.

When they had met at the rendezvous earlier in the night, Jessica initially thought the guy seemed cute and wondered if he was the same person her friend had met a few months ago. The stranger was tall and had a lean body, as her friend had described, but it was hard to tell if he was cute. He seemed her type, but she couldn't see his face because he wore that damned mask.

She had flinched when she first saw his disguise, scared from the unexpected face of the mask, and Jessica expected Donnie Darko's apparition to announce that she only had twenty-eight days left. She laughed out loud at the awesome costume and at her genuine reaction to the gruesome mask. The stranger had joined in, his laughter sounded credible, and she anticipated a great game was in store for her.

Jessica wanted to experience the fright night to its fullest potential, then she could tell her friends all about it. The suspense of it all would make a great story. But now she wasn't so sure this had been a good idea. As the evening wore on, she started having doubts.

At least the stranger had been a gentleman and had invited her to drive his vehicle for a while, that was a blast. The trail was lit only by the dim headlights of the ATV with only ten feet of visibility.

She zoomed through the woods regardless and experienced such a rush from the danger of it all. It had grown cold fast as the brisk night air breezed against her face and burned her cheeks until they were raw.

The stranger had suggested that they go inside to warm up, but it didn't feel right even though her cold hands felt like Popsicles. Reluctantly, she had agreed, but internally she cringed.

The inside of the house wasn't very warm nor much to look at, as she poked around his shabby place. The eeriness and desolation of the house alone was alarming, add to it the tattered furnishings, and she was pushed beyond her tolerance, standing alone, waiting for him to return. Something scampered across the room, a mouse or rat. She recoiled.

Jessica looked for her host. He had sidled into a back room, so she crept through the dreariness and peeked around the corner. She noticed the outline of a table and a few chairs around it and figured it was a kitchen. Something smelled horrid in there.

Repulsed, Jessica pinched her nose. She turned around to go back into the living room and almost slammed into the stranger. He was right there, almost on top of her, still wearing that disturbing costume.

Jessica jumped, a shiver ran down her back, and she involuntarily shuddered.

"Don't be scared it's only me."

Jessica placed her hand on her chest and bent over to catch her breath. Then she looked up and watched as he pulled off the weird rabbit mask. He smiled down at her. Instead of being comforted by a human face, the sight of him sickened her. It wasn't that he was bad looking—it was his smile—it was off. The guy looked demented.

Jessica stepped back. She retched and covered her mouth.

He stepped closer and reached his hand down.

"Get away from me, you creep."

She batted his hand away but felt his searing glare and so looked up. She had never seen such hatred. His eyes were torrid pools of evil.

Deep regret worked its way up to her throat and threatened to make her sick. Gagging again, she covered her mouth.

Drinking all that liquor had been a terrible mistake. Frightened, all she wanted was to get out of there.

He grabbed hold of her arm.

Jessica flinched.

"Let go of me, you creep. What? You like to pick on helpless girls? You chicken s-s-hit." Her words slurred.

She was drunker than she thought and should have kept her mouth shut. Despite her tough talk, the creep must have sensed her alarm because he stepped even closer. In a split second, he had his arm around her waist. She felt the sting of a bee just above her breast and wondered if a nest in the house. Had a window been left open?

She wiggled away from his grip and let out a small screech. He reached and grabbed her, pulled her body close to his, and held her in his firm grip. Warm air washed across her face as he exhaled heavily. His breath smelled of rotten eggs and repulsed her. She dry heaved.

He dragged her over toward the sink. Did he think she was going to puke? All she wanted was for the creep to get his hands off her. She scratched at his hands and tried to pull their grip off her.

There was a shadow in the far corner of the room; someone was sitting in one of the chairs watching. They might help to control this guy, but the fleeting thought vanished when he took hold of her head, pushed down, and submerged it into a sink full of water.

Shock and pain surged. The water was ice-cold, and her brain experienced a sharp, intense ache. She screamed, but it only intensified things for the worse. After she exhaled all the air in her lungs, they filled up again with the freezing water.

Pulled in by her breathing, the coldness burned her from the inside. Her tongue tasted soap. Another bolt of throbbing agony shot through her like a gripping vice, screwing her head tight enough that she thought she'd burst. Her lungs felt a horrid spike poking her from the inside-out, like steak knives stabbing through her chest.

Her head moved back and forth frantically, instinctively searching for air. She raised her arms up to grab hold of anything above her to help break herself free. She used every muscle in her body to get away from this crazy creep, but it turned out that her attempts were only thoughts and images of wild movements. All her efforts fell short of reality.

Her struggle only incited him to hold her head down deeper into the water.

In her last attempt, she opened her eyes looking for anything that might help to free herself, a knife or fork at the bottom of the sink would have been useful. Instead, the cold rush of soapy water stung her eyeballs, and she was blinded.

His hand pushed hard on the back of her neck.
Her forehead bumped the sink's bottom. Then Jessica lost all ability to move. She couldn't budge as much as she strained, something blocked her. There was nothing left for her to do except to give up.

2 - The Loon

Samantha Tremblay sat at a weather-beaten picnic table situated in the carved out beach area of Maidstone Lake, watching from the shoreline. She focused on the center of the pond. A family of loons swam on the icy water, the little ones bobbed and weaved close to the parents and splashed wildly, exercising their new wings.

The cooler northern climate had proved to be an excellent habitat for the loon. They were thriving again after having been endangered, near extinction. Listening to their eerie calls carry across the water in the early morning stillness gave Samantha a sense of accomplishment. She worked hard along with other volunteers on the LoonWatch, a program assisting the Vermont Center for Ecostudies, by monitoring the bird's activities on the lakes. Combined efforts and awareness management saved nests, nurturing the climb from seven loon pairs three decades ago, to now over seventy known breeding pairs in Vermont.

Despite her gratification from the recent new numbers, unhappiness echoed in her heart. The hurt originated from a more personal matter, and it was an issue she preferred to stuff away rather than face.

A nippy breeze caught her off guard as it swept across the gray lake and chilled her to the bone. She shivered and drew her arms around herself to keep warm, it was a brisk spring morning in the North East Kingdom.

A flock of geese flew overhead, Samantha looked up and followed their gray trail against the pale blue sky. Their honking noise faded as the flock landed in a nearby field, ready to eat whatever they could uproot from the desiccated grass. She marveled their journey embedded into their instinct, they were obliged to follow nature's call.

The sun's rays were inching over the tree line and energized a soft glow of yellow on the horizon. The sheathing mist hovering over the lake's glassy surface had begun to evaporate. It promised to be a warm day like the weather station had predicted. Soon the cool morning would transform into a heated afternoon, though high temperatures were uncommon for this time of year, recent cycles have seen raised temperatures.

Samantha sipped her coffee appreciating the warmth of the cup against her cold hands, as well as the caffeine boost she needed so early. She wasn't by nature a morning person but had awoken early this morning without objections to witness the sunrise. She was thankful for her job with the Vermont State Park Service especially since assigned to the North East Kingdom where she worked at Maidstone Lake, a small park but filled with natural wonder and her paradise. This area she called her home.

The job was a dream come true and the only sliver of happiness in Samantha's twenty-six years of life. Well, there may have been one other sliver, but that chance had come and gone, over before it had even begun. Years ago she thought she had found her soul mate, but then Zach left. She couldn't blame him. *He had dreams*. Still, they had connected and experienced something special, at least she had thought so. Whatever it was they had shared, it slipped away like water through her fingers. Zach was gone, and she was still here, living in a podunk town.

Samantha drew in a deep breath and closed her eyes. The smell of the dark green pines invigorated her especially near this lake. In a dreamy sort of way her senses were heightened here and she imagined how it all began, envisioned how the Maidstone area was created by a glacier, ages ago. The massive ice block tore at the ground, gouged the land and formed this deep cold-water lake and the surrounding terrain. She imagined the slow birth of the luscious North East Kingdom. A boreal forest surrounded the water-front and filled the air with a thick evergreen fragrance from the balsam fir and the red spruce which grew rampant.

Her eyes still closed, Samantha listened to the haunting loon's call. She heard a woodpecker's knock and the flute-like song of the hermit thrush, ringing in the air. She even heard the splash from a lake trout, as it jumped to grab an early morning meal of water-bug. Its tail slapped the water's surface with a plunk.

Bzzzt. Ugh! Samantha regretted not putting her phone on silence mode. She fumbled in her jacket pocket searching for her cell, once found she swiped its face.

"Tremblay," she said. "Yes Sir, I'm here at the beach front now."

Samantha tilted her head sideways, resting it on her left shoulder, and felt the weight of her long black hair as it cascaded down her back. She listened with her eyes still closed.

She would have liked to have stayed right there all day if she could, it was so peaceful. Her initial frustration with the disruption was replaced with her smiling approval.

"Yes, sir, I'll be happy to scout that area today . . . Yes, of course. Any dead trees will be designated to be cut . . . You can schedule the contractors to come tomorrow. Yes, sir, it's an excellent day for a trip up to the Springs."

Samantha hung up grinning; her day looked brighter. The new assignment was to drive up to Brunswick Springs and scout the area woods for dead trees and fire hazards. It was a welcomed change. She had never walked those woods before and only had a faint memory of being there once or twice when she was a child. Her pop had told her to stay away from the area, she had no clue why, but to keep peace at home, she had listened to him. Today was her chance to take a good look at the Springs. She had to, after all, it was her job.

She pulled back her long strands and looped them into a ponytail then she walked toward the parking area. Her two co-workers stood waiting for her to hand out the day's duties. Technically, she was in charge of her two friends, Josh Fayette and Kevin Rasle. She had known them forever; they grew up together, went to school together longer than she cared to remember. In the spring her friends were hired on as extra hands, and each year it was the same thing—the kidding around with small jokes—then they escalated into major pranks. That's when the unbearable horseplay began, causing trouble she would have to referee.

Last year when things got a little out of control, Josh ended up giving Kevin a black eye, and she had to fill out a mountain of required paperwork. But hey, they lived up here in the middle of nowhere. No place to go and let off steam except the nature trails.

Anxious by the thought of them standing idle for too long, her step quickened, her long stride brought her to the parking area in seconds. They stood near her old Jeep at the top of a small knoll. Plumes of dust from the parking area's gravel lifted into the breeze as Kevin kicked dirt out of boredom.

"I just got the word," she called up to them. "Change of plans, we have to check the grounds around the Springs today."

"Okay, boss." Josh saluted her with his long bony fingers and smirked. His sabel eyes beamed despite the fact that a nasty red bruise outlined his left eye, transforming his ordinary face.

"Had too much fun this weekend, I see," she said.

Josh laughed aloud.

"You should see the other guy."

He stood by her side, towering over Samantha, his scrappy demeanor matched his sense of humor. She had liked Josh since the first day they met in grade school. When they were kids, his playfulness cheered the dark mood that shadowed her since her mother's death. But lately, Josh only managed to get on her nerves.

"Like I haven't heard that before. You two, empty the trash barrels around the bathrooms and picnic area first. And clean up the mess an ornery bear left for us at the edge of the woods just south of the comfort station. Then use the machine and comb the beach area. When you've finished, follow me up to the Springs. Can you handle it?"

"Sam, why do we have to go up there?" Kevin asked, his voice a whimper.

Her friends had always called her Sam; often she forgot her given name was Samantha, even signed work documents as Sam. She preferred her nickname, not because she was a tomboy, necessarily. The name Sam seemed comfortable, like a well-worn favored shoe.

Only her Baptismal records listed her as Samantha Tremblay, a name her mother gave her in honor of her Native American heritage. The name Samantha meant child of the sun according to the Abenaki. Her mother had been a descendant of the original Sokoki Abenaki tribe of Vermont, who believed in the Sun God of the east. Sam didn't think the name fit her. She was dark-haired, strong and beautiful, but not what one might expect of a child named after the sun, and far from being cheerful and bright.

"Do we have to go to the Springs?" Kevin's voice sounded whiny. He stared at the graveled ground, then kicked stones around with his klutzy foot.

Samantha noticed his dark-framed glasses had plastic flip-ups clipped on top, which were entangled in his wavy ash blond hair. If the hot weather forecast was correct, he would need the shades later in the afternoon. His beak nose was steeply angled, and his glasses slipped down. Kevin pushed them up into place like he always did. Kevin stood inches above her, but he didn't have an elevated stance like Josh. Instead, Kevin wavered like a spindly tree, awkward and gawky. His over-sized baggy dark jeans hung on his hips and revealed the top of his blue boxers, not something she wanted to see. Add into the mix his red fleece shirt two sizes too big and it made the impression that part of him was missing, lost in the folds somewhere.

"We have to check the trail leading down to the spring and the nearby trails as well. You know the drill. If there's any dead wood it needs to get cleared away or marked to be cut," she said.

Sam explained with more details, hoping Kevin would accept the task with grace. She knew why he asked to get out of it. Kevin was squirrelly about the place, like many other local people, and she understood his wariness after hearing the tales herself. The town's gossip overflowed with local superstitions. Unfortunately, there's nothing else to talk about around these parts. So, the curse of Brunswick Springs became a legendary ghost story with many versions and liberties taken over the years. Sam never paid much attention to the embellished folklore, but Kevin had always been scared of the place, and never grew out of it.

"What? You afraid of ghosts?" Josh's voice rang sing-song. "Scared someone's going to jump out at you?" Josh lunged forward, his arms splayed out.

"No, of course not." Kevin spat back. "There's no such thing as ghosts. But the place creeps me out anyway." Looking at the ground, Kevin swung his head, mumbled to himself, then nodded. "Okay Sam, I'll go there, for you. After all, it's daylight. Nothing there but some trees. But I'm only doing it for you."

"Thanks, Kevin. Don't let Josh's taunting get to you." She nudged his shoulder. "Don't forget to bring your canteens to fill with spring water."

"Na, I'm fine drinking the well water from home. Have

you seen the spring? There's white stuff floating through the water. My mother says it will kill ya," Kevin smirked, and his eyes glazed over with a strange look.

Sam didn't get the joke, neither did Josh.

"Moron," Josh said. "I don't care what your mommy says. The health benefits of the springs have been proved time and again. They've even written about it. Why don't you try something healthy for a change?" He laughed under his breath and shook his head.

Sam knew as soon as she left them alone, Josh would be all over Kevin, teasing him with no mercy. As much as she liked Kevin, at times, he behaved as if afraid of his own shadow. She had felt sorry for Kevin when they were kids; he was always the victim of a joke. But they were adults now. *It's time to toughen up.* As soon as the thought entered her mind, another followed. She sounded just like her pop. *How can I be so judgmental?*

"Okay then," she said. "You two start here and then meet me at the Spring."

"Bye, Sam." Josh smiled waving, bending his fingers halfway down. Cute. Then he headed toward the picnic area to begin the duties.

Sure enough, Kevin followed Josh like a puppy dog. *I wonder if he'll ever get a spine. No, stop it.* Sam didn't like herself when she forgot to put compassion first. Lately, injudicious thoughts sprang into her head without her taking the time to curb them with patience, instead she reacted punchy and careless.

Something was absent in her life, she felt the hole it left.

The emptiness often spread to her expression, and she appeared stern and uncaring. Sam knew better, but still, she muddled through her days only half caring. She ached to find the missing ingredient, the mislaid piece of herself because the way she felt inside now made her anxious.

Perhaps someday, she'd find the answer that her soul desired, then her gentler side would win over her more cynical thoughts. Disappointed with herself, she left the men to their task.

3 - Nothing To Prove

Samantha jumped into her Jeep, a leftover from her pop. He can't drive any longer, the state took his license away for a D.U.I. and rather than selling it, Sam decided to make it her vehicle. She had the engine checked over, replaced plugs and cracked wires and had been driving it for four years now. She drove down Maidstone Lake Road, made of dirt but wide, leveled, and in good condition. The only thing wrong was the few missing road signs. They were artistic and comical designs, one of a Bigfoot crossing, another of a rabbit marking snowmobile trails. The signs most likely were stolen last fall by exuberant hikers who wanted to save a memento from their trip. At the end of the street, she turned left and headed north on Route 102 toward Brunswick Springs.

Brunswick was a rural area of twenty-five square miles of woodland. Barely over a hundred residents, the homesteads were spread out, most of the houses situated far back from the main road. It was a lonely drive with no traffic, only spring greenery flashed by as she sped down the highway. It didn't matter, Sam was accustomed to the solitude.

She unrolled her window a bit and let fresh air into the Jeep as she hummed to the song 'Honky Tonk' by the Road-side Graves, which was playing on the college radio station. It was the closest on the dial with a transmittable signal reaching this far. She leaned forward, turned the volume up, and sang aloud to one of her favorite tunes playing. "If I die in a honky tonk, lock me up and ship me home hmm hmm."

She turned left and parked the Jeep across the street from the original town building, an old white frame that was locked up and marked with a historical plaque. The old fashioned one room school house had stood as the only public building in the town for many years. Now, Brunswick had a single story town building across the street with a small parking area, her Jeep the only vehicle in the lot. There was no substantial village, just this building existing to support the locals for all its community needs.

"Yes, we're definitely in rural Vermont."

She harrumphed, knowing this was exactly where she wanted to be, despite the remoteness; she appreciated the beauty resting in these old woods full of life and mystery.

After scanning the area, she officially confirmed that not another living human soul was around. Sam cracked open her Jeep's front door. Listening, she heard the faint swooshing of rushing water in the distance. She hadn't been here in years but remembered Silver Lake was nearby, which actually looked more like a pond as she recalled.

A distinct memory came to mind of how, when the sunlight hit the water on one early afternoon long ago, the rays had bounced off the surface, shimmered, and gave the illusion of silver tinsel.

She knew from the map that the spring was farther away from the road, beyond the lake. It consisted of six spring feeds which unified at a point before falling down the steep rock embankment into an outlet situated below. The water from the spring fed the stream that then spilled into the Connecticut River, which lay a couple hundred feet away. When standing on the highest points of the riverbank, you can see New Hampshire on the other side. Technically parts of this bank were considered New Hampshire territory, the boundaries were peculiar.

To protect the area the Abenaki tribe from Swanton Vermont had purchased the land surrounding the spring through a nonprofit. But according to their beliefs, no one owned land, so the tribe sold the rights of development and conservation easement to the Vermont Land Trust knowing they would never allow new buildings or development per the by-laws, and they would protect the land. The Vermont Park and Forest Services were encouraged to keep the area safe for the hikers and tourists who visited the trails. All were welcome to sample the spring waters, which the tribe believed, had healing powers. The land still remained a sacred spiritual place for the tribe.

A memory of her mother's haunting voice stirred Samantha, the whispered words that had been spoken long ago, "Nature is for everyone to share." Samantha held on to her mother's voice which had inspired Sam's career choice. Her mother would have approved of Sam's caring of the parklands and forests, and helping with the ecology and wildlife projects like saving the loons.

An old folklore tale that her mother had told her when she was a child came to mind. It was a story about a loon, named Medawisla, which in Abenaki means spirit bird. The bird was friends with Gluskabe, a folk hero of the tribe. Gluskabe left the land of the Wabanaki people at the end of a mystical age, long ago, promising to return one day when the tribe needed him. Medawisla the loon was Gluskabe's secret messenger, and the loon spied on the people and then reported every detail to his friend, Gluskabe. The legend says the loud, eerie cries of the loon are the messages the spirit bird calls up to Gluskabe, informing him of the deeds of men.

Sam smiled as a warm feeling washed over her. There weren't enough stories or memories of her mother. Pop rarely spoke of her; Samantha imagined it was too painful for him to remember. Over the years, the crispness of her mother's image blurred, and it became difficult for Samantha to recall her mother's gentle touch against the skin of her arm and her mother's pure natural scent.

Samantha tried to make peace with her loss instead of letting it get the better of her like her father had.

Pop wouldn't speak of Brunswick Springs, either. It was as if he had had some personal tragedy done to him, right here in this spot. But no, how could he have, he never came here. He always stayed on the New Hampshire side, in Stratford, the small town across the river where they lived. He never put stock into hearsay of curses or ghosts, but something stopped him from coming over to this side of the river.

Perhaps it was the stories, and he didn't want to admit that he listened to such nonsense. Sam couldn't tell the lies from the truth, depending who's doing the talking, it could be a story of a curse wished upon white people by a native shaman, or it could be an evil spell contrived by a witch.

She smiled, thinking she'd take some of the spring water home and sneak it into her father's drink later tonight, without him being the wiser. Sam was skeptical of the claimed healing powers, to her knowledge, mineral water didn't cure people, though it was healthier than drinking tap that had been chlorinated. But the Tribe contended it wasn't the minerals that made the water worth drinking, but the spiritual qualities. Perhaps the natural powers are from one of the Lodges she had heard stories of. She remained open-minded about many of the Abenaki beliefs because she felt they were based on nature, and that she understood and accepted.

Still, she kept her opinions to herself, remaining quiet meant being unchallenged. Samantha refused to argue issues with Pop or any other person in her rinky-dink hometown. She knew some folks hated the Abenaki ideas, just for the sake of hating them. No sense in flaming the fire. A few Abenaki families remained in town but had kept quiet about their heritage to maintain peace in their lives. Sam's family had stayed.

Years ago when Sam was in grammar school, there had been many a fistfight over the tribe's legal rights. A Few local families had Native American blood, like herself, and they clung to their heritage, or what was left of it after years of melding in with the European cultures. Other residents had no attachment to the culture and feared that if the tribe flourished then, they might try to take back the land. Kids came to school with those preached ideas, and well, kids could be mean. Sam never wanted to argue with anyone about any of it. The idea of arguing had always seemed foolish to her.

Besides, she had nothing to prove to anyone.

Samantha walked into the woods, following a well-traveled dirt road leading toward the Spring. The timbers off to the sides displayed new life budding all around her. She noticed that the white blossoms of the Dutchman's Breeches had withered, the plant's spindly legs bent back toward the earth, their bright glory exhausted for the year. Nothing seemed out of sorts as she walked down the path, glancing down the off-shoots that ran deeper into the woods until she noticed a few downed trees far off in the horizon. They would need cutting so she would have to backtrack to mark the debris.

Passing Silver Lake, she admired the foliage along the water's opposite edge; it glowed bright green as the full-blown morning sun touched the new spring leaves, impressive with the darker green fir trees standing taller in the backdrop. She turned to her left and saw an old cement staircase embedded into the hill. Brown pine needles and a web of green ivy covered the crumbling step treads that led to a path at the top of the river's bluff. She added this spot to her mental list of areas that needed attention. Continuing up the path, she reached the top of the embankment. The Spring materialized below her, down the other side of the hill, just a staircase away.

Drawing in a deep breath, she inhaled the evergreens, closed her eyes, and took a moment for meditation. Then Samantha descended the old cement steps, part of the remains of the old hotel that had stood close by long ago.

4 - Area History

O ver a hundred years ago, a wealthy man had decided the spring was the perfect spot to build a hotel for travelers. There had been a small boom with the arrival of the railway. Timber and mill activity thrived, and people traveled to the area for business. Soon vacationing families followed, everyone captivated by the natural beauty of the spot. In those days, health conscious people from the cities boarded the new railroads seeking vacation areas offering fresh air to breathe, and a place to escape the smog from the city factories. The trend sprawled all the way to the North East Kingdom.

The original hotel owner had an ingenious plan to market the demand, unfortunately, before any guest could sign the register, the hotel had burned to the ground. Years later, the property was sold. The next owner built another hotel on the spot with the same vision—vacationers filling his pockets. The hotel burned to the ground again.

People talked, as they do in small towns. They claimed the place was cursed, but the stubborn owner refused to believe the allegation and rebuilt the hotel for the third time, only to have it burned to ashes. All that remained as evidence that anything had been built were the cement stairs leading to the spring and the ruined building foundations nearby in the woods, covered with leaves and with trees sprouting between the foundation walls.

Legend of the curse circulated in the area after the fires. Folklore of a curse, placed by the Abenaki, spread like wildfire. The first time Samantha heard the tale, she was just a child.

A fuzzy image came to mind of her mother's eyes, and how they had grown wide with excitement when she told Sam the story. Closing her eyes, she recalled how her mother's whispered words had felt warm against her neck and tickled her skin, making her giggle. She missed that simple pleasure.

Sam had heard more versions of the tale since, and also talk about what happened back in the 90's and how the Tribe marched for their rights. She had blurred memories of her mother playing a part in it all. But Sam's memory was faint and the more she tried to remember the weaker her mother's image.

It was more than curses and tribal disputes that complicated the area's demographics, though she understood the little nuances of the lines between the cultures. But there were also the misrepresented territory lines. Brunswick was, in fact, part of Essex County in Vermont and part of the North East Kingdom on the map. However, because Brunswick remained so remote with a small population, the census bureau lumped it within the Micropolitan Statistical Area of Berlin, New Hampshire.

Sam grew up in Stratford, on the New Hampshire side, just across the river. Both sides of the Connecticut River were remote natural wonders with only a few scattered locals who lived here year round. In the summer the population grew when tourists arrived to enjoy kayaking the pristine lakes and

IN THE WOODS MURDER IN THE NORTH EAST KINGDOM

rivers, hiking the forest trails, and ATVing along with the local rider groups. But even the tourism didn't boost the population enough to make significant changes.

This secluded paradise was Sam's home and the only place she had ever known. Surrounded by nature, she should feel happy. Instead, part of her was missing. Hollow inside, like the chocolate rabbit she used to get on Easter Sunday, she'd snap off the ears only to discover it was empty. Sam felt like that—vacant.

Sam never needed to leave like some of her school mates; her emptiness had nothing to do with the place where she lived, she was certain of that much. It had everything to do with questions pestering her about the past—her mother's past. She had questions and wanted the specifics of what happened back in 1994, the night when her mother died. Sam had been told that it was a car accident and the explanation had contained her curiosity for many years while growing up. Pop hugged her at bedtime, and she had a picture of her mother that she'd kiss when tucked into bed. Her nightly ritual since she was four was enough, until one day it wasn't any longer.

Pop was a weak man, sad and lonely, but at the same time, his tongue could be harsh when he had too much booze. She hated the idea of toppling the cart by asking him questions about her mother. So, she lived with unanswered questions. Somehow, Sam would find the truth, but she'd never get an answer from Pop, and she didn't know who else to trust or confide in with her questions.

Growing up in this small community, Samantha had noticed how others looked at her in a certain way. Not with pity,

35

exactly. Not anger or loathing either. But something was different in the way they looked at her. Their stare seemed guarded, offbeat, and different from how they looked at most other people. Did it have something to do with mother? Or was there something off with herself? Sam asked herself this question often.

5 - The Trail

S amantha held onto the rusty handrail and shuffled down the cement steps. Reaching the bottom she heard the trickling sound of the spring feeds gathering in the water pool. It was cooler here by at least ten degrees. Sam squatted, resting her weight on her legs, and leaned her arm toward the rushing stream. She situated her canteen under the running water. Her fingers froze from the ice-cold splashes that washed over her hand as the container filled. She took a sip, the refreshing water flowed down her throat, invigorating her. Time to get to work.

She stood and inventoried the area, as she screwed her canteen closed. The morning had grown brighter, and here on the thickly treed slope, she could spot the wildflowers sprouting up from the earth in clumps. Spring ephemerals are the first flowers to bloom in the woods, synchronized with the beginning of spring. Samantha spotted the Trillium first, recognized by its three white petals, tinged with pink, a brilliant show against the dark foliage. Random sprouts of Bloodroot also dotted the forest floor. Native Americans had used and shared the plant for red dye and respiratory medicine years ago, but today it's known to be dangerous. One of many fake and deadly miracle cures.

The early buds of the purple slippers peeked from beneath

piles of rotting leaves. Soft Lady Slippers had been her favorite for years. Once when Sam was a little girl, she had picked one of the blooms for her mother, so pleased with herself. But Mother scolded her. "Leave them growing free so others can enjoy their beauty, as well." Her mother had been right, of course. Working in the forest was Sam's way of keeping her mother's spirit alive.

Often she walked the trails around Maidstone Lake and used the time to clear her head. She cherished unexpected glimpses of a white-tailed deer edging from the forest's safety for a cold drink from a creek. Sometimes a glimpse of a red fox slipping out from its den in a hollowed tree or from a rock crevice near the stream. On a lucky day, she might spot a black bear wandering the wet areas for a meal of insects, or leftover nuts found hidden under a fallen tree.

But the woods surrounding the Brunswick Springs seemed different than at Maidstone. It was too quiet and sur-real—as if all the animals were hiding, burrowed deep into the earth, afraid of something. Even chipmunk chatter was absent.

Samantha dismissed her fleeting thoughts and climbed the hill. Taking the first trail to the left, she hiked the path, scanning the area for places that needed to be cleared. Spotting a large sturdy stick lying on the ground the perfect height and weight for a walking staff, Sam grabbed it up and rubbed it with her hand a few times, and decided to use it as she walked deeper into the woods and navigated the rooted terrain.

The sunlight filtered through the canopy of new leaves, the patches of light looked woven with the shadowy spots. A warm beam fell upon her face, she smiled and enjoyed its comfort, then continued walking deeper into the forest. After hiking thirty minutes or more, Samantha sensed a change in the air.

She stopped and realized how remote these woods stood, aware of an acute stillness. There weren't any human noises, of course not to be expected anyway. Sounds from the roadways never carried here, in the deep of the forest, and planes hardly flew overhead. But even noises that belonged in the woods, like scurrying squirrels rustling through the dried leaves, were absent. Nothing fell to the ground, like chestnuts left over from the last years' crop, dropping and thumping against the hard bark, or knocking on a stone. The sounds of the forest were absent.

A mist had risen from the rich dark earth. The peat had been warmed by the sun and now a fog formed and lingered in the lower ground between higher knolls. She stepped forward, kept her footfall soft and slow. A twig snapped to her right.

She froze and listened. Nothing. Sam continued walking, her steps a bit faster now but careful as her weight sunk into the spongy wet leaves beneath her feet. Something was out there, watching her, she felt it in her bones.

A cold draft shot up her spine and triggered shivers that prickled her skin like the sensation after a chalkboard was scratched. Nothing to be afraid of, she reminded herself as she rubbed her arms trying to get rid of the tingle. Sam squinted, trying to see her way through the fog which had gotten thicker. Only a few yards ahead were visible, she had wandered into a spot where the mist rose high around her, trapped between two mounds of earth.

At Maidstone Lake, Sam knew every path by heart, the rock formations, and where roots jutted from the ground. But this trail was a mystery to her. She cautiously stepped while wondering if someone was out there, turning her in circles, stalking her. A hanging vine touched her face.

Startled, she pulled it away and stopped to listen. Her throat tightened, her blood pulsed throughout her body, and panic gripped her. Twigs snapped again, louder, closer. She held her breath.

Another shiver ran down her back, now she was uncomfortable in her own skin. Samantha heard a soft sound rising from the woods, from somewhere in front of her.

The pattern began as a slight rumble, then it grew into a recognizable beat. The sound morphed into a repetitious drumming, vibrating the ground, like a pow wow drum, playing a ballad. Sam relaxed for the moment as if she had escaped to a peaceful place, sitting around a campfire. She imagined a tribe sitting around the fire with her, playing music, laughing and smiling. Was it a memory? It felt real like she had been there before.

The sound stopped, and she was jerked back to reality. Unsure of what was happening she waited a few moments, then Sam heard a buzzing drone, a much higher pitch this time. The irritating noise reminded her of the humming of a fluorescent light fixture, warming up, and perpetually increasing the intensity, tic-tic-ticking. A loud screech suddenly pierced the air. The pitch sounded like a whistle blown far off the chart range, elevated too high for the average human ear to hear. The ear-splitting noise was so extreme that it seemed as if it had been blown straight into her ear.

Sam flung her hands up. *Was it a scream from another world?* At that moment somehow she knew bad things were happening nearby. She let go of her ears and gripped both hands around her staff, holding it tight and ready to use as a weapon if need be. Willing to fight to protect herself.

6 - WALKING BLIND

Samantha found the direction she thought the noise originated. Without second thoughts, she hurried toward the piercing sound. Hastening through the woods, she pushed the low hanging branches back from across her path with the staff as she went. Leaves slapped her face, and a thorny vine scratched her cheek like a razor's edge.

She wiped the blood away with her fingers but never stopped running. She drew closer to the sound, then the noise stopped. Like a snap of the fingers, everything was quiet again. Taking cautionary steps, she turned, looked back and forth to her sides, and wondered, what the hell had happened.

Her skin prickled, a creepy feeling lingered, and she forced herself to stop. A sudden sense of bereavement overcame her, and she unwittingly began crying.

Wiping her eyes with the back of her hand she wondered what in hell had caused her to feel such deep sorrow. It came on as fast as the sound had, and left her just as abruptly. Was she going crazy? With no explanation for the weirdness, she turned and headed back toward the path, now hundreds of feet away.

Something caught her eye, a streak of sunlight hit a metallic object and glinted in the sun. Curious, she bent over to inspect. She saw a fragment of gold and brushed away some of the leaves until a watch was revealed—the time frozen at one o'clock—a watch still attached to a wrist. Exposed now, the visible dead hand looked odd in the pile of loose leaves that had been used to cover up the remains in haste.

Samantha jumped back, turned, and fled. Without thinking, she bolted back toward the path, wanting nothing else except to get back to her car and away from this place. She sprinted blindly ahead, broke free through the dangling foliage until she found the trail.

Her heart pounded so hard that she could feel her neck throbbing. She didn't know how far she had run when she slowed down to catch her breath. Sam heard another sound drifting in the breeze.

She stopped, confused. Giggles sounded from behind the trees. Was this a sick joke?

Furious, she figured out what was going on.

"Josh, I'm going to kill you."

Sam felt her neck tighten as she spat out the words.

"You've gone too far this time."

The laughter grew louder. Josh and Kevin stepped out from behind a huge tree standing ten feet away from her. A whistle hung strung around Josh's neck.

"Sorry, Sam. I couldn't resist, it was too easy."

Josh wiped the tears from his eyes with his shirt sleeve. He tumbled out from the foliage to stand closer to her, half bent with laughter.

Sam gave Josh a slight shove. "You bet you're sorry," she said.

"We didn't mean to scare you," Kevin said. "I'm sorry, too."

"Prank time is over, you idiots. You scared me to death. How can you two be so juvenile?"

Her face burned, how foolish she'd been for falling for a lame prank. Of course, there's nothing here in the woods making strange shrill sounds. It was Josh and Kevin, goofing on her. How could she have thought for a moment that it was a warning of some sort, from her ancestors, or that something deadly was going on in the woods? Her imagination was in overdrive. Thinking of the old ghost stories of the Brunswick Curse had gotten the better of her.

Her brow was moist with sweat after her trek from the woods.

"Anyone got a handkerchief handy?" she said.

"Sorry. No tissues in the pocket," Kevin said.

He stepped closer to her. Sam gave him a sideways glance, wondering why he was so afraid of this place.

"Josh, where'd you get the fake hand? It looked so real," she said.

"What do you mean fake hand?" Josh said.

Sam looked up and saw Kevin's face turn ashen, his mouth a straight line. He pushed up his glasses and blinked a few times like he did whenever he was nervous.

"Give me a break, fellows. Enough is enough. You know what I mean. The fake hand. The one you staged in the woods. Come on, give it up. We have work to do."

Her voice sounded harsh even to herself.

"Sorry Sam, but we don't know what you're talking about." Josh appeared to be serious. "Are you okay, Sam?"

Sam's blood drained from her face in a sudden rush. She felt weak and leaned on the staff. "No, I'm not okay. You mean you two blockheads didn't prank me with a fake dead hand?"

"Hell, no. Why would we do that?" Josh looked confused. "We only blew this special dog whistle. We couldn't hear it ourselves and thought you wouldn't either until you came running out of the woods."

Samantha's stomach flip-flopped. Had it been real? She swallowed hard. "I saw a dead body in the woods . . . I think."

"Sam, what are you talking about? What exactly did you see?"

Josh's voice was raised in surprise, his eyes bore down into hers, skeptical of her she could see.

"You must be mistaken. It's something on the ground that looked like a hand, it was a stick or something," Josh said.

"I don't think so," she said.

Kevin touched her sleeve.

"Don't worry, Sam. It's all a terrible mistake like Josh said." Kevin's voice sounded shaken.

"No. I don't think it's a mistake. I mean, it looked real. When I heard you two, I had hoped it was a gag, done in bad taste. But since it's not then it must be real. Follow me. I need to go back to be sure it's real before I call for help."

She didn't want to go back into the woods, but best to be certain before calling the authorities. The last thing she wanted was to be the victim of a horrible joke. If things remained between the three of them, then it wouldn't be so bad, but to be punked in front of officers—not her kind of fun.

"Come on, this way," Sam called over her shoulder.

They walked back into the forest. Sam had run so fast that she wasn't positive of the way she had come. She headed down a trail that showed broken vegetation, hoping it was the same way as her first trip. The path narrowed, and they were soon forced to walk single file.

"Are you sure this is the way?" Kevin asked.

"Absolutely. Got the scratches to prove it."

Prickly shrubs grew wild on the sides and formed a thicket of dense brier below. Vines climbed the pines and blocked most of the late morning sun, creating a dark, eerie atmosphere.

"This place gives me the creeps," Josh said.

"At least the fog has cleared," she said.

He stopped, stood still, and lifted his hand to his ear pretending he heard something in the woods. Kevin watched his every move.

"Kevin, quiet! Did you two hear that?" Josh said.

Kevin reacted as anticipated, his eyes bugged out with fear. Josh turned away and went deeper into the bramble, squirming between the brush until he disappeared from Sam's view.

"This way, hurry," Josh called out to them, his voice fading.

Kevin followed but then stopped and ogled back at Sam, his face looked scared as if he couldn't decide which way to turn next.

"Josh, where are you going?" Sam called. "I think it's in the other direction." Actually, she wasn't certain which way she had come from, but she wasn't convinced Josh made the better guide.

"Over here."

"These prickers are so thick. Ouch. If this is the wrong way," she called. "I'm going to kill you, Josh. I mean it, you're mine."

"Promises, promises."

Josh sounded a few yards in front of her. She followed his voice, looked over her shoulder, and confirmed Kevin was still following her.

The ground was covered with soft, slippery, pine needles. The dense woods began here, the trees knitted tightly together, and blocked the sun. Soft pine branches swatted her face with the springy new boughs still damp from the dew, she breathed in their scent.

They had to be a mile away from the original path by now. This spot was pristine, people didn't venture into the dense, woodsy area. Here the animals ruled the forest. There were fishers and bobcats, coyotes and even the occasional marten had been spotted and documented. Sam wouldn't mind crossing their path to be able to see one of them, knowing they'd scurry back to their hiding places more afraid of her than she was of them.

"Sam, over here."

Josh's voice sounded scratchy.

"Quick, Sam, check this out. I found it. Oh my God!"

Josh stood motionless in the center of a grove of pine saplings.

She edged closer, taking note of his expression. Grief, no shock. Josh's eyes looked glassy, on the verge of tears. He wasn't joking now.

Sam bent down on her knee and leaned forward to get a closer look. Yes, it was the same hand she had seen before, loosely covered with leaves and barely exposed.

"Exactly like I left it," she said aloud.

Samantha inspected the makeshift grave, calmer now with moral support by her side. The mound of leaves didn't smell. The only odor in the breeze was of the pines and last fall's wet leaves fermenting into the ground. Sam used the walking staff to prod and loosen the wet leaves around the body. She pushed enough debris away to reveal the pale pink of a sweater between the rotting leaves. She deduced the corpse was female. She noted a few blonde strands of hair smeared with dirt and mixed in with the leaves from underneath. Sam stood and stepped back.

"Let's go. Now. We have to get back and call the police. Whoever this is, she's definitely dead."

Her voice sounded commanding and far away to her own ears as if an impostor had replaced her. She looked up and saw her friends' faces turning white as ghosts. Kevin leaned over sideways, ready to vomit, but then straightened himself back up.

"Are you okay?" Her voice still sounded foreign.

Kevin nodded, then the three of them turned and headed back. Walking in silence, no one said more than a few words, the dreadful sight numbed them all. A person never thinks of how to react after witnessing a dead body. And she was dead, and Sam presumed most likely murdered.

Was that the reason she had broken down into tears earlier when she was alone in the woods? Sam must have sensed an ebb of sadness emanating from the dead body and her senses had implored her, screamed at her, that something was horribly wrong. Could her ancestors be reaching out to her, trying to tell her that a soul needed closure? Her mother had told her of these things, but that was so long ago, stories to a child. She didn't want to think about it, not now.

Instead, she kept moving, managing to keep her wits, reacting purely on autopilot. Sam marked the way with yellow plastic ribbons tied to the lower branches along the path so it would be easier to find the same spot again. Someone would have to guide the police back to the scene.

Kevin and Josh marched without any lame remarks, a miracle. They must have been shaken up by the sight of the dead body as much as she was. Thankfully, no one screamed or cried, they just walked.

The North East Kingdom didn't experience death often, only the elderly died, and for the most part from natural causes. On occasion an accident, like the one that had taken Sam's mother, but it was unusual. Their little corner of the world was a small community. Everyone who lived in Brunswick, Maidstone or Stratford was a nature lover. The people in these parts hunted during season, fished a lot as well, but never hurt people. Only the occasional fist fight happened when a party got out of hand with too much drinking and frivolity.

A local police force was non-existent. She wondered who she should call to begin the investigation for a death scene, knowing full well this was way over the county sheriff's expertise and he didn't have the staff to handle it. Besides, the Essex County sheriff was based out of Guildhall Vermont, not exactly close by. The nearest town was Stratford, and they transferred 911 calls to Lancaster, New Hampshire. She would call there, and ask for her friend, Grady. He'd know who to call. The state police would be the best choice to handle this situation. Since the body was closer to the New Hampshire border, that's the call she'd make, assuming they had jurisdiction over the area.

But calling in the New Hampshire State Troopers meant another problem. Samantha might cross paths with her old friend, Zachary Gerard. Sam knew he was in the Major Crime Division. She had sworn to herself not to think about him, let alone see him again. Her infatuation years ago had distracted her to the point of unhappiness, but it was over. She overcame her broken heart. For years they never ran into each other. He had his job and life, without an inkling of concern for her.

Unfortunately, it looked as if fate had chosen to appear and test her resolve. Samantha swallowed hard, promising herself that if Zach did get this assignment, she wouldn't make a fool of herself. Her deep affections had to remain hidden. She can't allow him to creep back into her heart, because if he did, then it would break. Nothing was worse than unrequited love.

7 - Troopers Arrive

S am didn't remember walking back through the woods but was glad her levelheadedness had kicked in. She marked the trail as they trekked back toward the parking area. Going straight to her Jeep, she fished out her phone from the glove box to call Grady in the Lancaster office. She tapped the numbers against the face of the phone that was smeared with her sweat, her shaking fingers slipped against the smooth glass surface. Cursing under her breath, she willed herself to stop trembling. This was an emergency, she had to stay calm. She wiped her forehead while explaining to Grady what they saw. She pressed her lips together, tried to listen and make sense of his words, but all she noticed was the taste of salt from her sweat.

Everything still drifted as if on autopilot. She answered the questions Grady asked, and he dialed the New Hampshire State Police while still on the phone with Sam, and together they had a conference call. Sam repeated her story, stating the facts as brief as possible like a robot.

She kept hearing her voice say, "Yes, a dead body. In the woods."

The conversation finished, Sam put away her phone. She became weak in her knees, ready to give in, as she walked back to her friends. She joined Josh and Kevin, and the three of them leaned against her Jeep's bumper while waiting for the police to arrive. None of them spoke. Josh and Kevin seemed just as disturbed as she was, maybe more, she thought.

Sam couldn't concentrate on anything. The image of the dead hand and the mottled pink sweater kept popping into her mind. It was wrong for death to happen in a place filled with so much life. She closed her eyes and took deep breaths, smelled the fresh spring air, and calmed herself.

The Troopers showed up approximately ten minutes later. Sam was looking at the ground but heard their arrival when the police vehicles' tires crunched over the stones littering the opposite side of the street in front of the old school house. Soon the troopers would be disturbing the quiet of the forest. Marching back and forth with a forensic team and equipment. She hated the idea of the foliage being torn up. Animals might even be pushed out of their spring dens and eating grounds. But it couldn't be helped. That poor girl, whoever she was, deserved to be identified and have a decent burial. She must have a family worried about her.

Sam gazed up at Josh and Kevin. They stood close by, looking down at her, their foreheads rippling with worry lines.

"Are you going to be okay?" Josh asked, his eyes intent on hers. "I'm here for you, Sam. You know that, right?"

She wondered if he meant okay dealing with the sight of a dead body, or concerned about the possibility of her meeting up with Zach again. Josh knew in depth all about her obsession for Zach. Josh had been around when she fell into depression, and he helped her to get over her broken heart. Josh was still there for her, the guy who cheered her up and sometimes irritated the hell out of her.

"No problem, I can handle this. I'm all grown up."

She smiled, hoping to let them know everything was all right. But deep down her gut churned, flipping topsy-turvy, making her sick. She wanted to vomit. Instead, she swallowed back her saliva, the acid burned the back of her throat.

Sam walked toward the incoming vehicles. The sunlight bounced off the chrome details, and she raised her hand to block the glare.

Two forest green cars with roofs painted copper-pink cruised to a stop. The lights were flashing like in the movies. The driver's door of the first car opened. She noticed the reflective emblem on the side panel. It had a sideways arrow that looked like a flipped V. In the center was a picture of 'The Old Man of the Mountain' a natural rock formation. It used to stand at Cannon Mountain but had collapsed over ten years ago, when Sam was only thirteen. It had seemed so sad back then, and seeing its' image on the car door panel stirred her heart.

Everything seemed miserable. Sam wished this was nothing more than a bitter dream that would be over with soon before the nightmare became a reality. The day had begun so peacefully, then a dead body shows up. Sam drew in a deep breath and thought of the poor girl. The day couldn't get any worse, or could it?

Zach stepped out of the first cruiser. She knew it would be him. He stood there tall and handsome, straightening his belt, an automatic check that his gun was situated just right. She heard the leather belt crease as it moved when his fingers fit everything into its comfortable place.

Zachary Gerard had been a Trooper for over five years. After college with a degree in Criminal Justice, Zach trained with the New Hampshire Police Academy in Concord. He worked his way into the Investigative Services Bureau and then was assigned to the Major Crime Unit. They handled all the homicide investigations of the state. Zach, who was a Detective Sergeant, responded to all calls for Troop F and was responsible for northern New Hampshire and the unincorporated rural areas, which included their hometown, Stratford. Of course, nothing happened there requiring his attentions. She hadn't seen him in years but knew of his achievements.

His mother bragged about Zach after every Sunday Mass, reminding fellow parishioners about what a great son she had raised and of how proud she was of all his accomplishments over the years. Samantha remembered back when they were in Grover High School, all Zach talked about was being accepted into the academy. Always the athlete, he had worked his body hard to get in shape and prepare himself. Now, he was living his dream.

She scanned him with a quick up and down, taking inventory of the man who was four years her senior and officially over the thirty-year mark. He still looked healthy and hadn't allowed himself to get soft over the years. Zach's body was firm, his muscled torso showed under his crisp uniform. The dark green shirt had gold buttons and taupe piping that matched his pants. The forest color complimented his eyes—hazel with green flecks. A kind soul, his nature had always been to care for others. He had been attentive to her, listened when she needed a sympathetic ear. She thought they had a connection, how could she have been so mistaken. His dreams of being a Trooper had been more important than her. Samantha felt her pulse quicken, her facial muscles tensed.

Well, she had dreams, too. She swallowed, suppressing her emotions, afraid of giving her vulnerability away. She focused on what she loved, the forests, and how they needed her protection as much as people needed Zach's. Animals were hunted and pushed from their natural habitats to near extinction. She had been so happy earlier in the morning to see the black heads of the loons and their black and white spotted bodies floating on the lake. Finally, their numbers were returning after listed as nearly extinct. She liked to think that in some small way her work for the study had helped recoup the loon population.

Sam held her head back, stepped forward, and met Zach with her arm outstretched. He accepted her hand, and they shook. His skin felt warm and smooth against hers, and a warm tingle vibrated through her body. She looked up and met his eyes and saw him gazing into hers. Does he remember me in a special way? A lump formed in her throat. His eyes reflected the sun and sparkled, he smiled for a split second, then his face returned to a serious expression, his mouth forming a straight line.

Zach had left without even so much as a goodbye. Devastated, his rejection had slammed her fragile teenage ego. Even though Zach had never said he loved her, still Sam had thought he cared for her deeply. They used to speak so freely, in sync, like they were of the same mindset. How blind and stupid she'd been. Now he stood in front of her and looked more handsome than she remembered. Tall and firm, his skin was tanned even though it was still only spring. His eyes bright, smart. Honest.

Sam breathed, her chest rising as the air filled her lungs, then she exhaled slowly. Determined, she would get through this situation. The only important thing to consider now was the poor young woman dead in the forest. She cleared her throat and tried to speak in a professional manner.

"Detective, thank you for coming so quickly. You remember Kevin and Josh? They both work with me."

Everyone nodded to everyone else. An awkward moment passed.

"Please, follow me. The body is this way."

Sam turned and led the way toward the path.

8 - The Scene

Sam instructed Kevin to drive back to the office and report the news to their boss, Mr. Livingston. Josh was assigned to wait for the Medical Examiner, then to escort the M.E. crew back to the spot where they found the body.

Samantha led Zach and his fellow officer, Thomas, through the haphazard trail she and her crew had forged earlier. She hoped she'd be able to find her way back to the body without getting lost.

No one spoke. Sam looked over her shoulder a few times and made sure they were still following. She wondered what they were thinking. Both officers wore their trooper hats, and the brim cast a shadow across their faces, shading their features. Their eyes were obscured and made it damn near impossible for her to read their expressions. She wondered if seeing the dead girl would bother them as much as it had her.

The body site was easier to find. The three of them made good progress following the yellow ribbons Samantha had tied to the random branches, plus the path had already been trampled down, and the sun was brighter. Mid-afternoon, siesta time. Sweat trickled down Sam's face, she wiped her brow with the back of her hand, while still trying to maintain a professional demeanor despite her melting body. She stopped.

"Here's the spot." Sam pointed. "She's right there. In the

center by those pine saplings."

Pretending the exertion from the walk hadn't bothered her, she paced around the area scanning the ground. In fact, she was exhausted. Her limbs were sore, her legs unstable like rubber. Even so, she inspected the scene perimeter for anything out of place. She didn't notice anything unusual in the immediate vicinity, no strange footprints, drag marks, or ATV tire treads which would be the only type of vehicle that could possibly maneuver these woods. Nor were there any littered bottles, boxes, wrappers or anything else that didn't belong in the forest.

Leaves still covered the girl's body. Sam watched as Zach thoughtfully moved closer to the mound and kneeled beside the body. He snapped on a glove retrieved from his pocket and brushed away more of the leaves. His eyes swelled, tears forming. Her own eyes blurred, she blinked. It wasn't any easier for him to see the corpse for the first time than it had been for her. Thomas stood close by, but he didn't look down at the body.

Sam watched Zach inspect the mound of leaves with precision, his eyes darting back and forth in a grid-like pattern. She found herself examining it, as well. There weren't many insects crawling over the heap, which seemed odd to Sam, especially since spring weather usually instigated extra bug activity. Samantha moved closer and bent for a better look. She pointed at the exposed area of the body's arm. Clearing her throat, she spoke softly.

"The body hasn't been here long, look, hardly any bug activity. That means—Oh, no." Sam covered her mouth, then finished her thought. "Whoever brought her body to this spot might have been nearby in the woods when I first arrived."

Sam felt her blood drain from her face as she recalled her movements and everything she had noticed in the forest, the strange sounds and creepy feeling she experienced before stumbling across the dead body. There had been an evil presence, Sam had sensed the danger. The killer could have been standing nearby—watching her—thank goodness she had run. In a blink of a second, the ghost stories about the Brunswick Curse and the deaths that had supposedly happened in the woods, passed in her thoughts. Things suddenly seemed eerily quiet.

"Do you think the killer is here? Now. In the woods, I mean," she asked.

Zach looked up and blinked, then looked down at the victim again.

"She may not have been killed, you know. It could be an unfortunate accident. Do you remember seeing anyone or anything out of the ordinary this morning?"

Zach didn't look at her when he spoke but continued his scrutiny of the leaves that scantily covered the dead girl.

"No, I didn't see anyone, except Josh and Kevin of course. But I had a creepy experience. It was like an awareness of something evil lingering."

She looked at his face; he wasn't buying it.

"Okay, I know it sounds wacky, but I felt as if something was off. Oh, and I'm positive, the body wasn't here for long. Take a closer look."

She pointed again at the exposed area of the dead girl's arm, the exposed skin, so pale and smooth, and had a clear quality revealing the state of the body. Zach's attention followed her hand.

"Look at the bare flesh. See? No signs of animal activity whatsoever. If she had been here for any length of time, the animals would have gotten at her. Nibbled at her at least," she said.

Zach turned his attention to her, a captivated audience.

"Add to that the fact that it's spring—the animals are out of hibernation and on a desperate search for food. She couldn't have been here long."

Zach and Thomas both nodded.

"Nasty," Thomas said. He had been standing behind Sam, but lost interest and turned away to resume his processing of the area.

Zach stood and stepped back then reached down and helped her up.

"Well, once the Doc takes a look at her, we'll have a better idea of when she died," Zach said. "Until then let's not get ahead of ourselves."

Sam nodded while biting her lip. She could take a hint, not her job. But still, there were so many troubling things about this scene.

"I just wonder, though, how did she get here? I mean, there's no drag marks or vehicle tread marks . . . It's odd."

She softened her voice, sensing she was getting too impassioned.

"She looks too young to have had a heart attack while walking here, by her lonesome."

"What makes you think she's young?" Zach asked.

"That's blonde hair, not gray. Besides, there's no evidence of anyone walking to this point. The trail we followed had initially been overridden with the wild ramble. My coworkers and I cut things back to pass just late this morning. I don't see any other paths. Do you? No broken or bent branches, no footprints in any other direction. Puzzling, don't you think? She was dumped here in the middle of nowhere on purpose. But how?"

Zach and Thomas nodded their agreement, and the supposition ended. Both men chose not to add to her commentary, and so she remained quiet, biting her lip until she tasted her own blood.

The Medical Examiner, a Doctor Howard, arrived with his entourage. His shirt and trousers were rumpled and hung off his limbs as if he were a giant clothes rack. Doc was older, maybe near retirement, but he worked as if this was his first assignment. He dropped his gear, ordered his associates to do the same, and pulled out an expensive camera from his bag. He snapped pictures of the area and the body. Next, he knelt on the ground for a closer inspection of the body and took a few more close ups. The doctor handed the camera to Thomas.

The doctor removed more leaves away from her frame and instructed Zach to brush everything away from her leg area as well. He retrieved the camera and took a couple more shots. She was face down, wearing a pair of faded jeans, and a pale pink sweater made of fluffy cashmere or a knock-off at least. They all gasped when the M.E. turned the body over. Her face looked up at them—cold, bloated, and dead.

Sam had to turn away. Her queasy stomach rolled as she heard a few more clicks of the camera.

"Small frame, frail in structure. It's a young woman in case the pink sweater didn't clue you in. Guess you never know for certain these days," Doctor Howard said. "No visible wounds or blunt trauma. I'll learn more after I examine her on my table."

Sam turned around and focused on the blonde hair. It fell just below her shoulder. She had curls—no. She had waves that gleamed in spots where streaks of sunlight filtered between the tree limbs and touched the golden stands. Even though she was dead, her hair seemed to bounce when the M.E. jerked her body up, and as he struggled to get her into the body bag, she almost seemed animated.

Sam wanted to look away, to get sick, but instead swallowed back the burning reflux and continued to watch the M.E. at work. He used a thermometer to take the body temperature, read it and recorded something into a pad of notes. She noticed the dead woman's hands had a few scratches, so perhaps there was a bit of animal activity after all, but it didn't resemble any animal marks she'd studied before.

One of the M.E.'s assistants placed plastic bags over her small hands, then snapped rubber bands to hold it in place and preserve the evidence. The two assistants zippered the bag closed.

"Are you okay?"

Sam heard the tender voice, looked up at Josh, and nodded. He stood beside her, switching his weight from one foot to another, his arms folded.

Doctor Howard stood and took one last inspection of the area. Then he motioned for his assistants to gather everything up and get ready to carry the body back to the coroner's vehicle. There was nothing else to be done, so they all packed up and headed back toward the trail. The men with the body bag followed in the rear, carrying the clumsy load on a nylon stretcher.

"How did she get here?" Doctor Howard asked aloud.

"We haven't a clue. Yet," Zach said. His voice sounded determined, ready to go to war.

Sam responded to the doctor's question.

"To my knowledge, no one has visited the Spring area yet this season. Everything seemed pristine this morning."

"Ah, yes. So then it must have been the Brunswick Curse that doomed the poor girl, no doubt."

Doctor Howard sounded sarcastic. He laughed at his feeble attempt of jest as if his comment had been terribly funny.

Sam smiled and nodded at his snarky remark, but she was a bit surprised that he'd find humor in these sad circumstances. Everyone had their coping mechanisms, she guessed.

9 - FOLKTALES

"Have you heard the story of how the curse began? No?" the doctor said. "Well, you're all in for a treat." He began the tale.

"Hundreds of years ago, the French and the English regiments fought in this area to stake a claim on the land. Most of the Abenaki people sided with the French back then. They took refuge in the missions and fought to protect them. But they had to change sides or flee to Canada once the British won control. Then, one day, long ago, the tribe found a wounded white man, a British officer, dying in the nearby woods. They healed him with the medicine powers from the Spring. The grateful soldier was amazed by the water's healing powers, and when he left, he told others about this place. Word of his experience mushroomed from settlement to settlement. Soon others came to taste the magic waters and hoped to be healed of ailments as well."

Doctor Howard slowed his pace a little and readjusted the bags he carried, then continued his story.

"So how does that make it a curse?" Josh called out.

"It doesn't," the doc replied over his shoulder. "Let me finish the story. So then, many others came to be healed, right. One day a traveling salesman came across the tribe. He was hauling a wooden wagon full of colored glass bottles, blue and green, and they rattled with every bump and root in the road. He intended to fill them with the spring water and to sell them in the towns as a cure. He would have made a fortune back then selling his snake oil. Well, the tribe didn't like this. They gathered around the man, shouted their objections, and blocked him from entering the trail to the Spring. They said he couldn't sell the spring water for personal gain, the spirits would get angry. They believed the powers in the water were magic, a gift from the healing lodge for all people to share, and not for any one man's profit."

Sam smiled. "My mother said the same thing to me when I was a kid."

The doc nodded.

"So, you must know the rest of the story. The tribe stuck together. The men and women locked arms and formed a solid line, and stopped the salesman. But the man was crazed with greed and argued for them to get out of his way. He pulled out his Brown Bess, pointed it at them, and threatened to kill them all."

The doctor added a few theatrical movements but never stopped his pace.

"Then the white man pointed the rifle at the leader, she was a Sorceress Princess of the Abenaki, and a healer."

"Like you, Doc Howard," Josh called out.

"Well, I guess in a way. I'm more of an after the event doctor. She wasn't a medical doctor but hands on, and she controlled the medicine lodge of the Abenaki. Anyway, according to the story, her brave husband and their young son stepped in front of the Princess to protect her from the man pointing the gun. Shots rang out, kapow, kapow, and echoed across the river. The two tribesmen, the husband and the son, dropped to the ground their bodies pierced with bullets."

The doctor swung his head. "As you can imagine, the Sorceress was more than angry. In her grief, she placed a curse on any person who would dare to use the sacred Spring water's magic to gain power or wealth. That's why in later years, when the hotels burned to a crisp, the locals claimed her curse was to blame. Some folks argued her spirit was a Skadegamutc or the ghost-witch, who comes back to haunt Brunswick Springs. According to Wabanaki tales I've heard, a Skadegamutc is an undead monster."

"You mean like a zombie?" Samantha asked. She had never heard this version of the tale before. The doctor nodded.

"Local lore says one of these creatures was created back then when the Abenaki Sorceress lost her husband and son. Now she's referred to as the female witch, and supposedly, she refuses to stay dead. She uses her evil magic and takes revenge. She comes to life at night to kill, eat, and throw curses at any unlucky human who comes across her. The Wabanaki lore says the only way to get rid of the ghost-witch is to burn her. People in town fear her shaman spirit is still haunting this place."

Samantha couldn't believe how ludicrous the doctor's tale sounded. Rumors of the Spring's curse already flew rampant in the area, they didn't need retelling, and it definitely shouldn't be associated with this incident.

"That's ridiculous," Sam said. "Just another horror story. Even more hurtful, it gives the people around here a reason to fear the local tribes and their beliefs."

The doctor stopped in his tracks and created a chain reaction. Samantha nearly bumped into him, she looked up and felt her face burning with the heat of the workout and the anger she tried hard to stifle.

"You're right," Doctor Howard said. "Superstition still remains rooted in people's hearts around here. I apologize. I'll try to remember to use respect, and I promise not to mention the lore in the coroner's report." He crossed his heart with his finger and smiled. Then he turned, walked away, and called over his shoulder. "We'll get to the bottom of things, don't you worry."

Enough with the ghost stories surrounding this sacred place, Sam was determined to learn what happened to the girl for real.

"It's a mystery for sure," Zach said.

"Yes, a mystery," she repeated under her breath.

Sam studied the ground the remainder of the hike back. She refused to let the crime done to this girl get swept under the rug by blaming the incident on an old curse. She'd make sense of things, one way or another, Sam would find justice for the dead girl, whoever she was. It felt as if it was her responsibility, for some unknown reason.

10 - GUARDIAN OF NATURE

The return trip proved to be a sweaty experience, their exertion made harder because of the unusually high temperatures, eighty or so, hot for the North East Kingdom, especially this time of year. Hell, any time of the year. The M.E. was finished telling his stories, and slacked back a bit, losing his stamina.

The group hiked out of the woods in single file, and now Sam led the way. Mosquitoes buzzed near her ear, she swatted them away but couldn't entirely escape from being bitten.

It was late afternoon, and the sun had heated up the earth to an uncomfortable humid temperature. She had drunk all her water from her canteen but never bothered to eat the granola bar in her pocket. It didn't matter, she certainly had no appetite.

The back of her T-shirt clung to her skin, and she hoped she didn't smell as bad as the men behind her. Before they headed back, she had gotten a whiff of one of the men who assisted the doctor while helping him pack the supply bag. The assistant smelled like garbage that had been sitting in the sun all day.

She recognized the scent. During her two years of Ranger training after college, she encountered the inexpungible smell while working trash detail, one never forgets. She never had a problem doing the required grunt work no matter how unpleasant because she had goals worth working toward.

Her two friends had no initiative; Josh and Kevin would remain part-timers in the summer, and unemployed every winter. She couldn't understand their lack of motivation. She tried to encourage them, but Josh was always hanging out with the tribe in Swanton, helping them for free. Noble of him but shouldn't he take care of himself first? Josh claimed that by connecting with the tribe, he was taking care of himself. They went around in circles every time they had that discussion.

And Kevin, who knew what he did when he went home to his mother? He, no doubt, was ordered around like her little slave. Sam hadn't seen his mother in years, but who could forget the way she yelled at Kevin when they were kids. Some people never change.

Samantha would never change, she saw herself as a guardian of nature, trying to keep the parks, lakes, and forests thriving, not only for today but for future generations. Working alongside environmentalists on projects that protected endangered wildlife was important and more needed to be done. She pledged to help whenever she could. Things often go unnoticed by most, so she worked extra hard to make up the difference.

Most people who visited the parks in the North East Kingdom were nature lovers and loners, who caused no trouble. This suited Sam because of all her duties as a Ranger, her people skills were at the bottom of the list. Still, a Ranger must always be prepared like a good scout. Any situation had to be dealt with by using a reasonable reaction. She'd been trained to work with law enforcement in sticky situations. But honestly, her assigned parks were the smallest and quietest in the state, she never had a major incident. That was until today. She never dreamed she'd stumble across a dead body.

The return hike seemed to go on forever. Sam heard grumbles behind her and saw the black zippered body bag slide off the stretcher. It had happened a few times as the men maneuvered the cadaver walking the rugged trail.

"No worries. We're back on the main trail. Walking will be easier now," she called back.

Finally, they reached the parking area. Sam crossed the street and headed straight to her Jeep. She owed her boss, Mr. Livingston, an update. Unsure of what Kevin had actually told him, she wanted the report to be thorough. She opened her door and leaned against the front seat of the Jeep, tapped the number, and waited. He answered after three rings. She delivered a brief summary, and they arranged to meet later at her office.

"Can I talk with you?"

Sam lifted her head and saw Zach walking toward her.

"Sure." She slid her phone into her pocket and avoided looking into Zach's eyes. It would have melted any strength she had left, or she might cry, right there on the spot.

"I'll need a statement from you and the two guys who were

here with you before." His voice sounded calm but authoritative.

"Yes, of course. I was heading back to my office. Why don't you stop by there to take statements? My coworkers are there already. I'll give you the address," she said.

"I know where your office is," Zach said. "I'll be there as soon as I finish with the medical examiner."

Sam watched with wide eyes as he turned and headed toward the other vehicles. How did he know where she worked? She gawked at his broad back and shoulders as he walked away from her. His masculinity evident, his back covered with sweat, causing his cotton shirt to cling to his body which emphasized his muscles even more. Sam shook her head, she didn't have to wonder why she was still so attracted to him. Think of something else, fast.

He had spoken to her very official like. He probably didn't remember their relationship years ago. She hadn't meant enough to him to cherish their moments together like she had. Silly girl, she chastised herself.

Sam drove back to the office, her mind combed through the things she witnessed. The poor girl—the dirty pink sweater—the strange sense of evil she had felt just before finding the corpse. That part she didn't understand, and it gave her the creeps.

She parked the Jeep in front of the office. It was a rustic cabin, made of old logs cut down years ago. It smelled of timber sealed in oil-based stains, one coat applied over another, repeated over many years. Sam often wondered how fast the place would go up in flames if unlucky enough to be struck by lightning. She turned to look at the other building sitting a hundred feet away, a shed they used as a workstation and storage for tools. It was built twenty years ago and filled to the brim with junk accumulated by the previous Rangers. She'd been working with her staff to haul away the overflow, getting rid of unneeded items. Two years of hauling away, and still not finished.

After Sam had finished college, passed the exam, and put in her two years of work training, she was assigned this Ranger position. She ran an efficient office and received praises for her efforts. There were no other advancements in sight unless she moved or until her boss, Mr. Livingston decided to retire. She was patient and could wait her turn.

She proved her patience with her pet peeve project of removing the junk. They had already sold a good amount of the stuff at a nearby auction house and donated the funds to the local Aquatic Nuisance Prevention Program. The remaining money was donated to purchase playground equipment for a school. In a small community like Maidstone, most of the folks had slim bank accounts, and funds for special projects was hard to come by.

The area was hard pressed for the extras that many people in the cities took for granted. Simple things like locking on to a good radio or television station.

Sam walked into the office, the screen door squeaked behind her as it closed, then slammed against the wooden door jamb. Josh and Kevin both looked up.

"Hey there, Kevin. How you doing?"

"I'm fine. Don't worry so much, Sam. I'm not helpless, you know."

Josh flagged a piece of paper in the air.

"We've been trying to write down a few things we remembered about the scene," he reported. "In case they need our statements."

"Good. They do. Zach will be here later to talk with us all."

"You mean to question us as if we were suspects," Kevin said.

Sam looked at him; he sounded put out and was crushing a piece of paper in his fist.

"No worries, Kev. All standard stuff, I'm told. Coffee?"

Kevin nudged his head toward the counter.

"Just made a fresh pot," Josh said.

"My savior." She poured herself a cup. Sam needed a pick me up and welcomed the coffee aroma. She took her steaming mug, walked to her desk, and booted up her computer.

"We've determined she's not a local person," Josh said. "There's no missing person's report in the area, and you know how fast that kind of thing travels."

Sam swallowed a sip.

"Let's leave that stuff to the Staties."

"In other words, leave it to Zach." Josh straightened up in his chair. "I Googled and found out that he's the only Major Crimes Trooper in the area. Too bad we can't request another trooper to take the case. But we're not significant enough to warrant a real police department, so we'll have to take what's available. I suppose we're lucky to have him."

"Since there's little crime in the area, we don't need a large, expensive police department. And Zach will most likely have the entire state's services behind him. Sharing knowledge between departments is a click away these days. Besides, people savor their freedom around here, they don't want a police force," she said.

"Still, Sam after everything that happened—"

"No worries, Josh. Everything is water under the bridge."

"Sure it is." Josh resumed writing.

He meant well, but there was so much Josh didn't understand, Sam thought. She had gotten over things years ago, well almost.

An hour later, Zach's vehicle pulled into the parking area.

"So, he's stopping by the office as he promised," Josh said.

"Of course, why wouldn't he want to question us?" She closed her computer files and met Zach at the door.

"Hello, Trooper Gerard. Please have a seat."

She waved her arm toward the only chair that wasn't behind a desk.

"Nice place you've got here," Zach said.

Kevin harrumphed, loud enough for everyone to hear.

"Can we please get on with it?" he snapped. "I need to go home before mother gets in a panic."

It had been a long day for Kevin, he had no patience left to tap. Samantha hoped he'd get through the interrogation without any argument. Kevin could be high maintenance at times.

"Okay, I'll start with you, Kevin, if that's okay?"

Zach glanced at Sam, and she nodded.

"Come on, Josh."

Sam walked over to his desk and put her arm in his, pulling him to his feet.

"You and I can step out and do some work until they're finished."

Sam nodded to Zach as they left the office.

"What's that all about?" Josh asked her when they got outside.

"Kevin's upset. Can't you tell? I think it's better if he talks with Zach alone, that's all."

"Oh is that all? I thought maybe you wanted to get away from Zach."

She gave him a light punch in the arm. Josh rubbed it with exaggeration.

"Come on, let's tidy up the shed a bit more."

Thirty minutes later Sam was sweating up a storm and feeling sticky all over.

"That's it! I've had it for today," she said.

Leaving the shed, they walked toward the office.

"I guess it's my turn," Josh said. He pointed toward the parking area.

Sam looked across the lot and saw Kevin piling into his old rusted up Chevy station wagon. He waved a weak goodbye as he passed them and drove away. Sam watched as he left, his lanky frame slumped behind the wheel. She couldn't see his eyes, his shades were snapped down in place, but she wondered if he was okay.

"You think he's all right," she said.

Josh's forehead wrinkled, his dark pupils looked like tiny pin dots, he squinted as the old car drove away.

"My guess is that he can't get the sight of the girl out of his thoughts."

"No, I suppose not. Death became real today," she said. "Come on, it's your turn."

Zach was on the phone when they walked in, he lifted a finger for them to wait.

"Yes, I want the search extended," he said. "If we're lucky a match will surface from the generic description. Someone must be missing the girl. Yes, these cases are always sad."

He hung up the phone and turned his attention to Josh. The two of them began to talk. Everything they said sounded like blah, blah, blah to her. She was exhausted.

Sam absently went to her desk, thinking of how she felt bad for Zach. They will eventually discover the dead girl's identity, and when they do, then he'd have to deliver the news to the family. That had to be a horrible task. He'll have to watch and be strong as the family breaks down and mourns the girl's death. Any parent who lost a child would break. It had to be the deepest of human tragedies and Zach would have to witness it all first-hand.

Samantha didn't envy his job in the least certainly not that part of it anyway. Even though Zach had always been a pillar of strength, everyone had limits. Sam crossed herself and quietly prayed for the victim, her family, and for Zach.

11 - The Victim's Identity

Sam had cleared an extra table for Zach to use as a temporary work space. She noticed his efficiency, his laptop already signed on and a portable printer that he had brought in from his car was connected and functioning in full swing. After retrieving a few papers, Zach questioned Josh in detail, had him write it down, then read his statement aloud.

She remained quiet and tried not to eavesdrop while Zach interviewed Josh. Sam was waiting for Mr. Livingston to arrive but it looked like he'd be a no show. She stayed busy writing up reports and creating a data chart for a project. She tried not to overhear, but couldn't help admiring Zach's technique, he got straight to the heart of things and built an easy rapport with Josh.

Zach casually asked about Josh's eye and received an exuberant story of his weekend brawl. Sam didn't want to know the details, so sunk herself back into her work, but she gave one last glance up. She caught Josh's expression, and it unsettled her. His eyebrows were raised high on his forehead, the way they looked when he told fibs. He'd never been a good liar, and she wondered why he wasn't forthcoming now. It didn't matter, the person they found was still dead, no matter what happened last weekend.

Was it an accident or murder? If there was even a remote

chance that there might be a killer out there . . . The thought of it made Sam uneasy.

Someone knocked on the door. Thomas and another hefty officer entered the cabin, and soon all the air seemed to be sucked from the room and the space shrunk by the seconds.

"There are no surveillance tapes to go over," Thomas said. "This area is full of nature lovers—not a single security camera anywhere in the vicinity. Sorry Zach, but there's nothing left to investigate at the moment."

Thomas turned to leave.

"We need forensic evidence. There's got to be something out there, and that's our priority. Without any leads, we'll never figure out how the girl ended up in the middle of the woods." Zach heaved his chest. "Okay, can you two go out there, search the area again, first thing in the morning?"

"Sure thing, Zach," the other large man said.

The men left, and the air circulated again. As soon as the door closed, Zach's phone rang, it was Doctor Howard, who apparently was acting as M.E. and coroner.

"Did the body arrive at the morgue okay?" Zach asked. He nodded to the coroner's reply. "Please, Doc, let me know right away if anything new pops up." He nodded. "Yes, I understand that the final results might take days. Keep me posted all the same, all right then, thanks."

No news. Sam had a gut feeling that this wasn't the run of the mill, and it unnerved her that they couldn't surmise or react until they found evidence. Meanwhile, if it was murder, then a killer was out there. The homes around these parts were remote, and if any trouble happened to a citizen, it might take days before it got noticed. On the flip side, if the locals were alerted to the possibility of a killer trolling the area, then there could be a panic, which would be bad for this small community. People behaved strangely and did bad things when scared.

Sam had to do something. Otherwise, she wouldn't be able to live with herself. An action plan evolved. She'd make inquiries at the neighbors' houses around Maidstone Lake, just as a precaution. She'd have Josh and Kevin help her touch base with the residents, starting first thing in the morning. As a cover, they'd ask if the resident's planned to participate in the yearly Green Up Day. That was a simple reason to knock on doors without alarming anyone needlessly, all the while checking to ensure everyone was who they should be.

Finally, Zach finished with Josh, who signed the document and was headed for home.

"Bye, Sam." Josh waved as he walked out.

"See you in the morning."

She looked out the window; it was dark already. Her boss was a no show, and it was too late to make any other calls. Time to call it quits. Sam heard the rustle of papers and noticed Zach bent over the table gathering the statements, ready to take his leave. In one swift movement, he scooped up his things, tucked everything under his arm, and was out the door. Sam got up to follow and stood in the doorway, watching as he buckled up.

"I'll stop by tomorrow and let you know what turns up," he said.

He was polite and professional.

"Hey, I thought you Troopers didn't use seat belts?"

He grinned at her remark.

"I like to stay safe." He rolled up his window and zoomed off.

Samantha waited for Mr. Livingston for another half hour, but he never showed. By nine o'clock she called it quits. She locked up and slogged to her Jeep wanting nothing more than to go home to her bed. She was physically and mentally exhausted and smelled like she had rolled around in a swamp. Even the cool evening breeze couldn't refresh her.

She drove down the dark highway and while crossing the bridge that connected Maidstone to her hometown of Stratford, she stopped the Jeep midway. The engine idled, her foot remained firmly on the brake. Looking out of the window, she watched the dark, angry waters below, flowing swiftly downstream. The churning rapids looked angry. She was angry, too.

Sam wanted answers. Something horrible had happened to the girl they found in the woods. Sam knew in her gut that it was a crime, not a tragic accident, and a good likelihood the victim was murdered. The important thing to ask right now was the who part of the questions. Until the person responsible was caught it meant trouble for everyone in the area. There was a killer out there, Sam felt it in her core.

After the old geezers in town hear about a body being found in the woods, all hell will break out. They'll spend their days sitting around the Riverside Market, drinking coffee, and spinning their tales. Crazy old stories that supposedly happened at the Springs would be rehashed, it happened over and over again. This incident will soon become the center of another ghost story. Would more stories keep the tourists away this season? Or bring them out for the gory details. Zach said that he'd keep her informed. She hoped that he'd meant it.

The next morning Zach called Sam with the news. The victim's name was Jessica Taylor, a nineteen-year-old college student who attended Dartmouth which was ninety miles away. That's well over an hour's drive from the Springs. The young woman had been reported missing by her family. She lived at home with her parents in the small college town of Hanover.

Zach said that her father ran a small bookstore on Main Street, and her mother was a nurse at the County Hospital. Zach had gone with the coroner to inform the family of her death and briefly interrogated the parents. He intended on returning to question them in more detail once they had a handle on their grief if that was even possible given the circumstances.

Later in the afternoon, Zach brought the report to Sam's office as promised and allowed her to read the family's statements. Sam offered Zach a cup of coffee, which he poured for himself, while she stared reading the transcripts.

The parents said Jessica had gone to the movies with some friends but never made it home. Her car was found locked and abandoned in a back parking lot. There were no signs of struggle, and no video available to see if anything unusual had happened. Her friends said they had all left the movies at the same time, but they parked on the main street and Jessica had parked in the back lot. There were no other leads concerning Jessica Taylor.

Both friends mentioned their sorrow for the dead girl's family in their statements. The paperwork seemed in order, but the sadness each person felt was evident in the chosen words.

"I'm heading for the coroner's office," Zach said. "He's meeting me there to go over the few details he knows so far, which isn't much, I'm afraid."

Zach finished his coffee and nodded to Sam as he left her office.

She hoped he would include her in his investigation, but then realized how silly that idea was, after all, he was with the Crime Unit, and she was a Forest Ranger. They both served the public, but that was where the similarities between their worlds ended.

Sam sunk herself back into her daily work, starting with her action plan. She walked along the shoreline and tapped on doors. She checked in with the neighbors who were around for the summer and if they intended to join the community Green Up Day efforts.

Perhaps her small part will help someone somehow.

12 - HENRY'S RED HAIR

Three days passed since finding the body and life at Maidstone Lake continued. Sam worked alongside Josh and Kevin, checking on the necessary maintenance around the place. The three of them remained vigilant, nonchalantly tapping on doors and checking in with the residents, a simple hello. Most of her time was spent logging her observations of the local wildlife; it was a requirement for the preservation survey she had volunteered to assist.

Rangers were encouraged to help conservation studies on wildlife, and this had been a major pull for Samantha to join. She often found it hard to mingle with people, but give her a chance to interact with nature, and she was in heaven. She put in another full day and then headed home.

Sam was famished and decided to stop at the Riverside to pick up dinner on her way home. Her Jeep crawled through the small township, Stratford seemed like a beehive of blather. Men sat on their porches or idled their trucks in a friend's driveway, gossiping and pointing at her as she rode by. Looking into her rear-view mirror was disturbing. The small community gushed over the recent news, it had become the local scandal. People enjoyed talking about other's troubles, making their mundane life seem better somehow, but this newest fascination sickened her to the core every time someone asked her about the dead girl.

The past couple of days, customers dropping by the Riverside Market & Tavern had added their unique twist to the tale, now blaming the curse for another death. *Bullshit.* Yesterday when Sam stopped by to pick up her take-out, Henry was more than happy to give her the newest revelations of the local crime story. None of it was true, she knew and told him so. Still, the locals took pleasure in retelling the details that they had heard from others. She understood their excitement— they thought they were downright, genuinely helpful.

It was the third day after the body was found, a Thursday, her payday, and her usual day to stop by and buy a few groceries for the week. But tonight she didn't have any energy left; she would only buy something to get her through the night.

Sam opened the door to the Riverside. The bells jingled and announced her entrance. Sam looked across the store. It was Henry's turn to work this evening. The place was empty despite it being the only decent place around to eat that was still open. Two teenagers, who had no place else to go, sat at a small table talking with each other while sipping soda and nibbling on a giant cookie that Henry had baked in-store. He was a good cook.

Sam remembered a time when that would've been her and Zach sitting there, telling stories and sharing secret desires. He had wanted desperately to be a trooper and lucky him, his dreams had come true. It had been years ago when they dated, but it still seemed like yesterday to her. Zach was a looker and surely had a lot of girlfriends over the years. Pop had told her back then that young men at his age liked all girls, but they never remembered any of them. *Guess Pop was right about that, at least.*

"Hi there Sam, what will you have tonight?"

She jumped.

"Sorry, didn't mean to startle you." Henry went around the counter and stood behind the deli case.

"Of course not, sorry I'm a bit punchy tonight, Henry." She scratched the tip of her nose. "Please give me one of those five dollar Nacho specials, and hold the hot sauce."

He nodded and turned to get her order together. He worked agilely despite that he was slightly overweight. She often wondered why Henry stayed living up here in the north where no one appreciated his cooking talents. It must be difficult for a person like Henry, unique to say the least.

"The food smells delicious," she said.

"Thanks," Henry replied without turning away from his work.

The flavors from the seasoning wafted through the air as he warmed the meat on the grill. She walked over to the cooler and grabbed a seltzer water.

"So anything new?" he asked

"Nothing that I know of, but I'm sure someone else must have had a new update for you today."

Henry laughed at this then whistled as he flipped her food with a spatula. By the time Sam walked back to the counter, Henry had her dinner wrapped up and ready. He bagged her meal and rang up her order.

"Don't forget to add my water,' she said.

He nodded, his eyes flicked up and down as if sizing her up. He added the soda water on the register quick and waited as she slid her card through the card reader. Sam looked up and noticed his hair for the first time. Usually, he wore it dyed pink and spiked up the middle, but today his hair appeared to be a darker reddish color, almost normal looking and cut with a contemporary style.

"New 'do?" she said.

Henry smiled but didn't respond. He stared past her, preoccupied, looking without seeing anything.

"What is it? Something on your mind, Henry?"

"Well, I hate to gossip," he said. His puppy face looked worried, the color of his cheeks matched his scarlet hair and sudden doomsday attitude.

"I don't have all day. Out with it." She rubbed the back of her neck, picturing her bed at home.

"I heard that Zach has a suspect. Someone said that they heard him say, that he wanted to run something by you. I was wondering if he met up with you—you know—told you something. Maybe you'd like to share?"

Sam smiled.

"So, you want the skinny on what's going on. Sorry to say, I haven't run into Zach for a couple of days. Should I bother asking who told you this?"

She wondered why Zach hadn't gotten in touch with her after he spoke with the coroner. Not that he was obliged to do so. And given his track record of taking off without a word, she shouldn't be surprised. She'd almost called him a few times to ask for news, but then thought it would've been awkward, and politically the wrong thing to do. The last thing Sam wanted was to look unprofessional. Worse, he might think that she wanted to talk with him. Of course, she did. Despite telling herself that she should avoid Zach, she looked forward to being with him again.

"It was no one special, don't worry about it," Henry said. "If you do get any news let me know though, I'd rather people know the truth. I mean, it's a shame and all, the whole thing is heartbreaking."

His drawn-in face gave Sam the impression that he had a different question going on in his head.

"The folks around here gossip a lot, but they have good intentions," Henry said.

"Spare me, okay. I understand, Henry," she said. "If talking about the incident eases their mind somehow, and helps them process the situation, well then who am I to judge them. But, no matter what people say, it still troubles me. How are you doing? Handling everything okay? You seem a little blue today despite your red 'do." She smiled.

"Couldn't be better. Thanks for asking,' he said. Henry slapped his hand on the counter. "Oh, I almost forgot. Your father stopped by. Asked me to have you stop by his place tonight."

Sam slumped against the counter. "I wish you'd forgotten," she replied.

He shook his head and wagged his finger in her direction.

"Be a good girl. See what he needs before you go home yourself, okay? Good."

"Was Pop drunk?" she asked.

Henry nodded.

"But I didn't serve him anything, promise."

He turned his attention to a customer who stepped up to the counter, another old crony here to buy a six-pack. Man what an exciting town.

She grabbed the bag and left the store, but somehow un-convinced that things were all right for the guy. Henry seemed more than bored with his life. He looked like something was on his mind. Was he sick and didn't want anyone to know? Henry lived his life different than most around these parts. As they say, he marched to a different tune, or was that a different drummer? No matter, being different could sometimes be lonely, Sam knew that first hand.

Well, it didn't matter right then, all that was important was figuring out how the girl got in the woods and discovering what actually happened to her. Sam wished she knew what the coroner had to report. Jessica Taylor deserved justice, and Sam worried it wasn't going to happen.

13 - POP'S HOUSE

Samantha pulled into her father's driveway, put her vehicle in park, but didn't turn off the engine right away. She didn't want to be there, especially tonight. She was exhausted. She sat still and stared at the garage door. It leaned inward as if someone had backed into it once or twice. There was a crack in the center panel, and exposure to the wet weather had already begun to rot the wood. Her Pop's old house was falling apart around him. She sighed. She had to talk with him sooner or later. The quicker she got out of the Jeep and did her daughterly duty the faster she'll be heading home to her own bed.

She anticipated his hounding her again about moving back home and taking care of him and the house. Save your money, blah blah. No matter what he said to her, she'd remain firm. Sam needed her own place—her privacy—her peace of mind.

All trust between them had flown out the window a long time ago. He refused to stop drinking, and each year it grew worse. For years she received calls from the Tavern, asking her to come pick him up and take him home. That had gone on for too long, and finally, she drew her lines. It was Pop's problem, not hers. The last time the bartender phoned her, she had told him with colorful language, to please not call her anymore. She couldn't handle it, and she refused to enable his drinking any longer.

It had been hard to say no, to sit back and do nothing. But no more challenging than it was for her to be working her way through college with all his drama going on. Caring for a man who didn't want to live was no task for a young woman starting her life. Ah, but it wasn't that easy to simply stop caring for him. Even now with her own place, she still shopped for him, did the laundry, even cleaned up his empties now and then.

Sam couldn't afford much on her own but the small studio apartment she rented saved her sanity. It was located over a working garage, nothing glamorous but it was her space. The business below hummed with noise during the day—men working on vehicles, banging and the revving of engines—but at night the place was quiet. She could relax and sleep, and no one was going to get her to give it up, especially not Pops.

She turned off the Jeep and walked toward the back porch. Her father stood by the open door, she noticed the screen was tattered at the bottom as if a foot had pushed it in. The hinge was bent, had been for a while. To open or close the door one had to pull up on the handle to get the frame in sync with the casing and then push or pull the door open.

"I was wondering if you were gonna come in or s-s-sit out there all night."

His words slurred; she put herself on high guard. Pop wasn't a tall or big man, but she'd been told that in his younger years he was strong as a bull. His hair was dark, the same color as hers. He used to care about nature but had lost interest years ago. Sam couldn't recall the last time they went fishing.

"Hi Ya, Pops. Sorry, I was listening to a song on the radio, waiting for it to end."

"You kids with the music." He hugged Sam, squeezed her so hard that her arms hurt. He let go, apologetically, as if he was ashamed of showing his affection. She couldn't help smelling the booze on him, and he hadn't showered in a while. Great.

"I recall you liked music once, a long time ago," she said.

"Ya. I guess so." His eyes looked beyond her as if he couldn't focus.

"Your errand boy sent me. What do you need, Pops? Besides a hot shower and supper. Want a nacno special? I just picked it up, nice and hot."

He waved his hand at that. "That junk food will kill you."

She laughed to herself. Was Pop joking, what did he think his drinking was doing to him?

"I'm kind of in a hurry, Pops. Henry said you wanted me to stop by. What do you need?"

Her father went inside and sat in his favorite chair, a well-worn striped recliner that had duct tape holding it together, keeping the stuffing in. He waited, but when she didn't sit down, he blurted what was on his mind.

"I've been a wondering, what's been keeping you so busy these days? I haven't seen you all week. Is it too much for your ole Pop to want to see his daughter? Things can't be that busy at the lake. Man, Maidstone is the quietest place on this gawd damn earth." He smiled, his head swayed off balance.

"You're making me seasick, Pop."

"What?" She waved her hand. "I like that quiet old lake," she said. "But as it turns out, things have been unusually busy for me. Haven't you heard the news? A body was found at

Brunswick Springs."

"What's that gotta do with you? You're working at the lake." His face wrinkled, his dark eyes cringed into two slits peering at her.

"I was working at the Springs that day, Pop. Me and my crew, we found the body."

Her father's face darkened, his eyes clouded over, and he looked angrier than she'd ever seen before. He stood up quick and startled her. Pop took a step closer, stared into her eyes, and just like that she was a small, fearful child again.

That fateful day rushed back, the day everything in her world had changed. It happened years ago when Sam was in high school, the day she had reached her boiling point, her curiosity about her mother's death had intensified to teenage fury. She had been working on a Civics project, using the library's microfiche machine to research old newspaper editions for an article she needed, when an idea popped into her head.

She scrolled through the screens with vigor, looking for the archived paper editions from 1994. The answers to her questions were at her fingertips. She feverishly looked at the screen, her pulse raced, her skin turned clammy as she manipulated the machine. Back and forth, she flipped the knob, but she hadn't found a single word printed about her mother's accident. Nothing was reported about a car crash. She returned home that afternoon defeated and stormed into the living room to confront Pop.

She had demanded the truth from him. Instead of answers, she received a harsh reprimand. Pop scolded her, raised his voice in heated anger, and then his hand came down with a hard slap that stung her face. Horrified, she had stood there stunned into silence. She hated Pop for not telling the truth. He had no right to lie to her.

After a few seconds had passed, she dared to look up to see her pop's face, to read his expression. She had expected him to look angry, the same way she felt, but was stunned to see that guilt had crept between the lines of his face turning him sour, the shameful emotion rested in his eyes.

Pop winced as if he had fallen with pain, the skin on his face twitched, then he turned abruptly away. He left the room, a whiff of his Old Spice cologne that she had given to him at Christmas ghosted the empty space.

She ran to the closed door, pressed her ear to the wood, and heard him crying on the other side. A lump formed in her throat and made it hard for her to breathe. She turned her back, leaned on the door, and let her body slide down to the floor. She sat there regretting that she had mentioned mother, but it had been too late, there was no going back. The heat from his hand mark had lingered on her face for days.

Now the memory of that incident brought a tear to her eye; she wiped it away with haste. Samantha could still imagine her face burning and remembered how the imprints from his fingers had stung, not only physically, but emotionally. After their confrontation that day, Pop took up to cuddling with a bottle of regret. She anguished over his acquired drinking habit every day since. Their relationship existed like a fragile glass wall from that day forward. Sam played the role of his keeper and tried to keep him from self-destruction by liquor. Even though she had forgiven him a million times over, he never could forgive himself for striking her.

Horrified by the flashback that took a millisecond for her to experience, but felt like a lifetime, Sam stood dazed, holding her hand to her cheek. Then Pop's raised voice brought her back to the present, and she looked into his eyes and saw his temper flaring.

"I'll tell you, one more time, and it's the last time I'd better have to say this to you. You're not to go there, ever. I mean it, Samantha. You . . . You . . . Disobedient girl."

Outraged, Sam's mouth flung open, gaping as she fumbled for the right words. She could feel the blood rush to her cheeks heating up her face. Fed up with being patient, she exploded.

"I'm not a child anymore. I'm a grown woman, Pop. I have a mind of my own. You can't tell me what to do."

He shrugged.

"No matter, you're not to go to that place." He jabbed his finger at her chest, his anger growing stronger with each poke. "No matter how old you are, you hear me, young lady. You . . . You don't understand."

"Of course I don't understand, Pop. You won't tell me anything. What happened? How did Mother get into an accident, why was it never reported? I'd like to know what happened to her. And why don't you want me to go to the Springs? Give me the reason."

Her voice sounded harsh, and no matter how much she tried to rein it in, she heard the desperation in her words as they boiled over.

"She insisted on staying, there at the Spring that night." He raised his voice. "Don't you understand, she chose the tribe. Leave it alone I said."

Her father raised his hand up as if to strike her, but he held back, his face deepened to crimson. He turned away and smashed his fist against the wall. His hand went through the drywall. Pieces of chalky cement board fell, making a clunky rain sound into the empty wall channel. A huge gaping hole remained at the spot. His knuckles were red, his hand bled, trickling down his forearm and then dripped onto the floor.

"Gawd dammit."

"What the hell, Pops." Samantha ran to the kitchen sink, grabbed a towel and turned on the faucet. She went back to her father, wrapped his hand with the wet towel drenched in cold tap water, and guided him back to his lounger chair. He looked up at her, his face changed. His anger was replaced with a whitewashed fragility.

"I told your mother not to go there and look what happened when she did. She went to the Springs that night. She cared more about the damn tribe than she did you or me. And look, look what happened." He sobbed, tears rolled down his cheek. "Here we are, all alone. Just you and me. How could she have done this to us? I told her they would get in trouble, but she wouldn't listen. How . . ." More tears welled in his eyes, his face twitched, his skin pinched strangely as something pulsated across his cheek.

Sam held onto his arms to steady him and felt the strength of his body fade away.

"Pop, what do you mean? What trouble?"

He tried to answer her, but his words were mumbled groans. His jaw hung down frozen in place, and guttural sounds gurgled from his mouth. "Arry . . . arry."

Was he trying to say, sorry?

"Don't worry Pops."

Sam wiped the drool that dripped from his open mouth with the towel.

"It's all right, Pop. I'll take care of you. You're not alone."

Samantha noticed sweat pill on his brow, and he gasped for air. The veins on his neck bulged. His open mouth panted and swallowed gulps of air, his tongue made a freaky clicking sound. Then she sensed his body going limp under her hands, and he fell back against the chair's cushion. She let go, and his body slid down on the left side armrest.

Samantha grabbed the phone and dialed the fire department.

"Quick, it's my pop. I think he's having a heart attack or something."

"We'll be right over with the ambulance, stay with him, Sam."

Joe hung up, and Samantha was all alone with Pop, waiting. She didn't know what to do, so she watched him, he seemed to drift further and further away. Scared, she shook his shoulders, trying to keep him roused until the medics arrived. Her pulse raced, her heart tightened like a vice. She heard the sirens, they were getting closer, but not fast enough. Seconds seemed like hours, as she held onto Pop's hand and mumbled prayers under her breath. Pop's eyes were closed now, no more mumbles and jerking, and she was afraid for him.

Someone banged on the door. She jumped up and ran to open it, hitting her foot on the kitchen table's leg. Cursing under her breath, she pushed opened the screen.

Joe entered the small house. His crew of two other people whose names she couldn't recall, followed him in with a gurney. They maneuvered it, bumping into the bookcase then the wall, and finally rolled it near to Pop's chair. They went right to work, tore open her father's shirt, and loosened his belt.

Sam stepped to the side to let them work. She watched. Her Pop lay flat on the stretcher now, they put an air mask over his face, and someone gave him a shot. Joe pushed on his chest.

"The paddles," Joe said.

They stepped back. Sam heard the thump and a zap. The scene whirled in her vision. Samantha withdrew from what was happening, befuddled between her shame, disgrace, and his sickness. She had been embarrassed of her father for years. Most days she was angry and afraid of him at the same time. There had been moments in her life when she had wished him dead, but of course, she hadn't meant it for more than a split second. She had been an angry young girl and thought that if only her mother had been there, how things would have been different.

It was Zach who finally reached her, he had been kind and gentle. They used to talk, and he helped Sam understand the sickness her father struggled with daily. Smart and so caring, Zach taught her to appreciate the good memories she shared with her father. Her reverie was interrupted.

"Sam, I'm sorry. Your father's life is on a thread. We're taking him to the ICU. The next few hours are critical," Joe said. "You might want to join him there, in case he doesn't make it."

Joe had tears at the corner of his eyes, Sam watched them as they ran down his pudgy face. She touched her cheek and wondered if she would cry, too. Then Joe hugged her hard, and for a moment she couldn't breathe. Then all her pent up anguish spilled out, and she cried like a baby. Tears flooded, she tried to stop but found herself swallowing gulps of air and tasting salty tears which got Joe's shirt soaking wet. Sam didn't know how long they stood there embraced, but Joe let her go and stepped away.

The team left, rolling her Pop out with them. The gurney was loaded into the back of the ambulance, and they drove away. Samantha was all alone in her father's house.

14 - MEMORIES

Samantha woke with a stiff neck. She had fallen asleep on her father's sofa. The night before she followed the ambulance to the hospital. He was admitted to ICU and would remain in critical care. Her Pop was in a coma after having a heart attack, and the doctors had no idea if he'd recover. There were other issues, like a bad liver from excessive drinking, not unexpected. Sam was of no use there, so she had come back to his house for much needed sleep.

Yawning, she stretched her long arms and legs, inadvertently knocking a lamp over. It fell on the carpet and didn't break. Thanking the Lord for small favors, she picked it up and placed it back on the outdated maple end table. It was scratched and scuffed and had her initials etched in the corner next to Zach's. She had done that one summer night long ago when she dreamed of falling in love with him. She had only been a teenager, puppy love. Pop, of course, hadn't approved of her dating.

Rubbing her fingers against her scalp, she tried to wake up. The night before had hit hard, especially since she had been exhausted, to begin with. She cried herself to sleep, and now her eyes were swollen and burned like sand had scratched against her cornea.

She looked around the room, inventorying the small house

where she had grown up. It was the only place that gave her a sense of belonging besides the great outdoors. She wondered if her father would pull through, or if he'd rather move on, and if so would he be reunited with his wife in heaven like they preached on Sundays.

Sam couldn't sit still. It was a Friday, a workday, and she wanted to get back to her job right away. She couldn't fix anything sitting around like a lump on a log, being remorseful all day in her Pop's house. He was being attended to, in the right place for all his needs, and there was nothing she could do for him. Life goes on; she had a job. She decided to pull herself together.

The next hour she spent showering, dressing, and rummaging through Pop's house aimlessly. She stopped a moment here and there, to pick up a picture and remember, grabbing for any memory. She needed happy thoughts to pull herself together. A photo of Pop and her on a fishing outing when she was eight. A homemade frame she had fabricated while in grade school sat next to it with a picture of Sam and the boys, Josh and Kevin. It was taken the day of a class trip; she vaguely remembered that it had been a ton of fun.

Another old photograph of her parents on the day they married. They were both smiling and looked so young, and happy. She wished she could have remembered more. As she held her mother's portrait to her heart, Sam said aloud in the empty room "I love you, Mom." After a moment she set the gold framed picture back on the mantle.

Being so upset the night before she had never eaten her nacho special. It still sat in the bag on the passenger's seat, smelling disgusting by now. Her moseying around her father's house revealed he didn't have any food. Sam backed the Jeep out of the driveway and drove to the market for supplies.

The small store only had a few people milling around, and she thanked God that she could shop in peace. Picking up a hand basket from the stack near the door, Sam headed for the produce display. The lettuce was fresh, so she chose the greenest and placed it in her basket. She grabbed a few tomatoes, too. At the cooler, she found hummus and pita bread.

While still browsing she got an uneasy notion that she was being watched. She walked down the aisle and reached for a few cans of tuna and black beans. Still a sense of being spied on, she grew weary. Her intuition intensified, her back burned from a searing stare. Straining her neck, she looked for someone menacing who might be responsible for this ugly sensation. She only spotted Mr. Simpson leaning against the counter and idly paging through the newspaper. He patiently waited for the next customer, which was in fact, her. No one else was in the store any longer.

A sudden urge to get the hell out of there seized Sam. She needed fresh air to clear her mind, so hurried to the checkout.

"Is that all you're getting today?" Mr. Simpson asked.

His mouth drooped like an upside down field goal post, his eyes looked like he had a different question going on in his head.

"Yes, that's it for now, I'm in a hurry. I'll have to come back later for more," Sam said.

He turned and rang up the produce and bagged the items watching as Sam slid her card and waited for approval.

"That there bank reader is slow in the mornings," he said.

"Is everything all right, Miss Tremblay?" he asked.

Sam jerked up, wondering why Mr. Simpson asked such a weird question. He had been one of her father's buddies, but years ago they had a falling out, words were said between them. The man never spoke harsh words against her father to her, but the troubles between the men had cut their friendship deep.

"I'm fine," she said. "Wondering what happened to that poor girl, I guess."

"Ayah. Sad thing happened there," Mr. Simpson replied.

He seemed preoccupied and turned around, stared out of the window. He wasn't looking at anything.

"Mr. Simpson, how are you doing? Is everything all right?" Sam asked, hoping her effort to be polite didn't sound as strained as she felt while saying it.

"Couldn't be better. Thanks for asking," he said. His bushy gray eyebrows shot up. "But I heard about your father. I'm sorry, Samantha. I hope he gets better real quick."

Sam looked down at the worn wood floor. *This was how it would be from now on.* People obliged to give her fake sympathies, even though they never cared for the man. That's what happens when people are on the edge of death.

"Thank you, Mr. Simpson. He's in good hands, I'm sure he'll pull through."

Mr. Simpson nodded, his eyes squinted.

"Um, I err . . . Well if you need any answers, you know where . . . I'll be here if you need me, Samantha."

His voice faded away, just like his stare.

Sam was a little spooked. She grabbed her bag and left the store, unconvinced that things were all right for the old man.

He seemed more haunted than he looked old. Something was off with him. A stabbing idea crossed her mind. What if he knew something that Pop didn't want her to know? Looking back at the window, she saw that he was no longer standing there.

Stop imagining things—instead, go to the office. That was the one place she should be right now, to keep herself preoccupied. She shouldn't spend time with thoughts about last night, or her Pop's last words spoken to her in anger. She prayed that he'd wake from the comma soon so that she could talk to him again, get things straight. Otherwise, she'd be alone and feeling guilty for the rest of her life.

The garage was busy with people dropping off cars to be repaired. A radio was playing pop rock music, creating a lively scene. *Too much life for the early hour.* Was she the only non-morning person? Sam carried her groceries up the side steps to her studio apartment above the garage. It was a small place but gave the impression of being spacious because of the high slanted ceiling with exposed beams. Dropping the bag of food on the beat-up counter, she pulled the veggies from the sack and placed them in the fridge, the hummus, too. Then she changed into fresh work clothes and left for the office, grabbing a breakfast bar on her way out. There would be plenty of work to keep her mind occupied.

15 - FIRST CLUE

Sam called the hospital first thing when she arrived at the office, but her father's status hadn't changed. A few more calls were dialed throughout the day between the work. She asked for updates, but Pop remained the same. The day passed without any hitches. Now with work over, Sam watched the sun set from the picnic table on the small beach. The warm orange colors washed across the sky and made the mountains stand out like dark peaks. It was quiet, not a soul around.

She had finished walking around the lake's shoreline road, all was quiet and safe. No boats on the water, no stray bicycles, and all the trash emptied. Sam got up and turned back toward the cabin, watching the shadows of the tree branches that were cast across the dirt road. They looked like long fingers, mirages, created by the fading light.

She reached the office and unlocked the door. The guys had gone home already, and she was the only one left within earshot. It was a relief that they hadn't mentioned her father all day, perhaps they hadn't heard, and that was all right with her. She was thankful for the peace and quiet. Insincere laments from anyone about her father's health weren't welcomed. Of course, most folks around Maidstone didn't know her father, at least not to her knowledge. He had been success-ful as a recluse for the past decade, ever since . . . The drinking began . . . What, twelve, thirteen years ago? She couldn't recall. Sam didn't want to think about her Pop's alcohol abuse. That was something she couldn't handle at the moment.

Sam made one more call to the nurse's station. Nurse Leslie gave the same report, no change in her father's condi-tion, but she was welcome to visit the ICU at any time.

Instead, she was compelled to do more research about Jes-sica Taylor and her family. It was like an itch, something she had to scratch. She needed to find answers, to learn what hap-pened to that poor girl. There must be a reason she was taken, killed, and then dumped in the middle of nowhere. And Sam was convinced it was murder, she had that awful sixth sense about it all. *But why the woods at Brunswick Springs?* The miss-ing piece to the puzzle was out there somewhere.

She switched on the overhead lights. All the computers had been shut down for the day. The office was void of noise except the drip of water hitting the stainless steel sink in the break area every eight seconds. That would be her white noise as she worked. She went to her desk and switched on the gooseneck lamp and desktop computer, and within seconds the screen brightened.

She sat in her usual, familiar chair, its seat permanently sunk in the middle and conformed to her butt. Sam signed on and surfed the web. Right off she hoped that something would turn up. She Googled the victim's name and discovered her Facebook account. Sam signed onto Facebook using an alias account she had created for a case study the year before. From that account, she tried to friend Jessica and used a back-door algorithm, which an anonymous hacker friend had shown her. Hacking into Jessica's account was easy because she didn't use any of the security available or it wasn't set up correctly.

Sam wasn't proud of her hacker skills and never shared her secret knowledge. Ashamed of using it because she knew it was illegal, not to mention unethical, but this occasion called for drastic measures, and if it helped find what happened to Jessica Taylor, it was worth the guilt trip.

Jessica had over 500 friends listed. Sam clicked to view the most active friends and those who had posted on her wall. Most were fellow students, kids she had known in high school, and family members. Then Sam checked the pages and groups that Jessica visited, and most of them were the *'have a great day'* type of pages and posts. Lots of rainbows, cats, and yoga pages crossed the screen. Jessica's comments were upbeat, and she didn't seem to have any problems. Her most serious post was over what purse to buy. Sam was intent on doing a thorough job, so she kept digging into every site listed on her page or wall.

At last, pay dirt! Within the hundreds of pages she liked, there was one bizarre page called *Real Horror Games*. The page had a gruesome icon in the image of a bloody knife that looked too real for her taste. It matched the disturbing banner's theme which conveyed their tilt on horror. The digital wallpaper was a bloody scene with people dying on the floor, mutilated in a crazy room with bright colors. The mural design resembled the style reserved for comic book characters so managed to pass the scrutiny for acceptability. It was a page for one of those crazy online games. Reading the posts, Sam determined that it didn't make sense for a girl like Jessica, who liked daisies and peace signs, to be visiting this page. It was so different from anything else in her stream.

Sam clicked on the link, and the web page opened. The website belonged to a business that offered game services, just as Sam had guessed. It also advertised live role-playing. Her interest was piqued.

A rush of adrenaline flowed through her veins. Sam knew in her gut that this place was important somehow. She kept looking for more, her imagination went wild with speculation, as she clicked through the various tabs and links. Had Jessica Taylor joined this group to participate in a real-life role-playing game? Had she done something dangerous? Or she could have been forced to do something against her will. Samantha's thoughts spiraled, dreaming up dangerous scenarios in her head.

She jumped when the phone rang.

"Tremblay," she answered, her stomach still doing flips.

"Samantha, this is Mr. Livingston."

"Hello, Sir."

"Sorry, it's taken me so long to touch base with you. Things have been problematic, dealing with a lot of the brass on this one. Things have been bouncing back and forth between Vermont to New Hampshire task forces. It seems the New Hampshire Crime Unit won, and they will be handling the murder. Our little corner of Vermont doesn't have the capacity."

Samantha gulped in surprise. *Did he say Murder?* Until that moment, she hadn't known for certain that it was murder. She'd guessed, of course, assumed, but no one had confirmed the fact. No one had shared the coroner's report with her. Nothing like that was stated in the local area paper, only the gossip whispered of murder.

"Sorry to hear it's ruled a murder, Sir," she responded.

"Yes, well, it's a bad business all around. The thing is—well, the Troopers have limited workforce at their disposal in that corner of the world. They asked if we could spare someone to help with the investigation. Besides, the state of Vermont would like to be represented in some form, and the tribe also would appreciate you being part of the process. You know that we Rangers often assist the police, not usually murder, but I hope you will be up to the task. Certainly, you're qualified, and you've done great research for us in the past. I hope you don't mind that I agreed that you could represent the Vermont side of the equation during the investigation. I'd like you to write up reports and drop an email to the Essex County Sheriff's Department at the end of each week until this mess is all behind us. Of course, if you agree . . ."

"Um, yes, Sir. Thank you, Sir."

"Samantha, I heard the news about your father. I'm sorry. If there's anything I can do to help—is he getting good care?"

"Yes sir, he's in Critical Care right now, there's nothing else to be done except wait for him to recover."

"If you don't want this extra assignment under the circumstances, I'd understand. I mean, I could pass it on to someone else, if you'd like."

"That won't be necessary. I'd welcome the distraction. Besides, since discovering the body, I haven't been able to think of anything else. I'd like to be of service, in any capacity. I want to see justice done."

"Good answer. Your dedication is duly noted. The officer in charge is Zachary Gerard. Expect a call from him."

"Excellent, Sir. Thank you."

"No, thank you, Tremblay. Good luck." The phone clicked off.

She replaced the receiver, thinking of the new assignment. If she was to be part of the investigation, why hadn't Zach gotten back with her? She wondered if he was avoiding her, or maybe he wasn't aware that he'd been stuck with her as a partner. Since she was officially on the case per her supervisor, Sam decided to check the people who ran the *Real Horror Games*. She wondered if it was too late in the evening to visit the business. She looked at the clock. No, it was just after six, there was still time. Should she call Zach and tell him about the place? Or would he laugh at her intuition and dismiss the lead?

Samantha wasn't going to take any chances, to heck with protocol. No law said that she couldn't go down and check the place out as a concerned citizen, or better, a potential client. It was still a free country after all.

Focused, she rose from her chair and turned off the monitor. Opening her desk drawer with a key, she lifted a small pistol that she kept locked away for emergencies. She checked if the safety was on, then tucked it into the back of her belt. Grabbing her jacket, she pushed her chair in and turned toward the door. Sam lifted her head and was startled to find someone standing right in front of her.

"Ah!" A small screech came out of her mouth, in a high pitch that was worse than unflattering. Sam almost wet herself, scared to death.

Zach stood there, like a wall. His body shook up and down until finally, his laughter escaped. At least he tried to hold it back, she thought.

"God! Don't do that!" she said. "You scared the bejeezus out of me."

"Do what?" he said between snickers. He controlled himself after a few seconds, forcing his lips tight together.

"Hilarious! Do you always sneak into other peoples' offices and scare them to death?"

"Sorry, I knocked, but you were so engrossed, you didn't hear me."

He continued to wear his distinctive smile, and his eyes sparkled with mischief. He looked more like the way she remembered him, without that stern look he had worn the other day at the Springs.

Another suppressed snicker escaped.

"Okay, have you had enough fun on my behalf?" She smirked, acknowledging it must have been funny. "Can I help you? Are you here for a reason?"

Zach lost the smile.

Sam realized her voice had sounded rude, and she felt bad about that. She had had so many things going on in her head, important things, like what she was going to say once she reached the Real Horror Games' storefront.

"Do you mind telling me where you think you're going with that pistol tucked into your belt?" he asked.

His eyes were small, drawn tight and his brows scrunched. Sam caught the determination laced in his voice. She felt trapped in the act, like the time the assistant principal saw her behind the building smoking a cigarette. Her rebel days.

"Okay, you've got me. I was going to get in my practice shooting."

"I don't believe you. You're fibbing. Tell me the truth, Sam."

She gulped hard and tried to think quick, but that was always her downside. Samantha could think of effective responses hours after a conversation, but she could never come up with a quick comeback, or snappy retort on the spot. Especially not something witty that sounded real.

"Okay, okay. I was heading out to investigate a place called *Real Horror Games*. Jessica Taylor visited the business's Facebook page, so I thought maybe there was something to it. It might be worth checking into," she said.

She stared at him, letting him know she was determined and hoped he would agree to track down her hunch. It was his case, after all.

"How did you come across this information?" he asked.

"Her Facebook page."

He didn't answer right away but instead thought over what she said. His eyes stared past her, as he deliberated. She knew he wasn't the type to use social media, might not have a clue about things like following pages.

"Okay, let's go check it out. I assume you have the address."

Sam handed him the piece of paper with the address scrawled. He nodded and headed for the door. Sam followed and locked up.

"We're taking my car, to make things more official," he said.

He led the way to the car. Sam sat gunshot. It seemed

strange for her to be seated in a car with him again, even stranger, being in a police car. He fired up the cruiser, and they drove towards Lancaster.

"Sam, I heard about your dad. Sorry."

She nodded but didn't reply, hoping to avoid an unwanted outburst of tears. There was nothing to cry about. Pop was sick. At the rate he drank, it was fated that something bad would happen to his health. And now she had to continue with her life until he woke from the coma. Someday, she would reflect on everything that passed between her and her father, those last few words before his heart attack. But not now.

"Where's your partner today?" she asked.

She tried not to put any emotion into her voice other than friendly. Zach looked over at her for a brief second, then shrugged.

"I have a new partner, haven't you heard. She's working the case with me right now," he said.

Sam nodded again.

"You don't mind, us working together?"

She swallowed her excess saliva, embarrassed by her question. *What the hell could he say?*

"I used to have a full-time partner," he said. "He passed away six months ago. I'm still upset over the loss. Guess I'll never get over it completely. But we go on, right?"

"I'm so sorry."

"It happens. He had cancer." The car was silent for a moment. "I miss him, but he would want me to go on, and do my job well."

He did a half smile, experiencing a flashback of a good

memory of his late partner, if just for a second. She remembered another reason she had admired Zach. He was loyal.

So why did he leave without saying a word to me? And over the years, he never reached out to explain. The painful thought crawled into her head and hurt—piercing her heart. They had made a pact, always to be friends, to always care. What had changed that?

She wasn't going to say anything. She needed to forget her juvenile thoughts. They were adults now; childhood promises didn't matter. She drew in a deep breath and let it out. Composed again, Sam got back to business. Like her boss said, they had a job to do.

16 - A Store In Lancaster

From Maidstone, they headed south on 102 and Zach turned onto the ramp for Route 3 and continued south. She looked out of the window and watched tree after tree, as they clipped along. She should be upset over her Pop, crying or something, but all she could manage was to distance herself from the world. It was as if she was looking through a kaleidoscope. The drive to Lancaster usually took Sam twenty-five minutes but Zach cruised, and they arrived at the small town in fifteen. He pulled off Main Street and stopped at a Mobil gas station.

"I need to fill the tank," he said.

He got out without waiting for a reply. Minutes later he was back behind the wheel, and Sam asked if he'd stop at Dunkin, pointing to the building next door. He smiled and pulled into the coffee shop's parking lot. They both got out and went inside. He ordered a large then stepped back.

"A small, please," Sam said. "No extra sugar, just a dash of cream."

Zach paid for the coffee. Sam grabbed her coffee and sat at a table waiting for him. She took off the lid and blew the steam away before taking a sip.

"Um, that hit the spot." She looked at him as he sat. "So, anything you want to tell me before we go into the place?"

"Na," he said. "I've got no idea what this place is about. Do you know what we should expect?" Zach smiled for a second, then it was back to business. "Tell me exactly what you know."

"According to the website, the store sells all the newest video games. They have a link to sign up for this role-playing game. When I clicked on it, the first thing it wanted was a credit card. Looks like it costs quite a bit, too, won't even list the pricing. Says it's all secure and anonymous." She shrugged. "I can go into it again and sign up if you'd like."

His eyes did that cringing together thing like he had a headache. "No, not yet. Let's see what we can find out at the store first. Look, I need help with this investigation, and I know your boss signed off on your time."

Sam nodded and watched Zach as he blew on his coffee and took a sip near the rim.

"Hot," he said. He wiped his lips with a napkin. "Here's the thing . . . Well, I want to remind you that it's still my investigation. I don't want you going off on your own doing something crazy without me to back you up."

He looked across the table and met her scrutiny. His eyes searched her face for a reaction. Sam noticed the green flecks in his eyes, they shimmered in the light streaming from the fixture above, and for a split second, she saw something familiar there. He was confident, but she also noticed that he hesitated. She sat quiet, holding onto her cup and waited for him to finish.

"Let me ask the questions when we go in there. I value your input, and want you there to observe in case I miss something, but not knowing what we're dealing with . . . Well, it's best I keep the lead on the questions."

Merely a spectator, Sam thought. She nodded in agreement. It was better than nothing, at least she'll know what's up. After deluding herself of her importance, her ego was now in check. She reminded herself it didn't matter who was in charge. They were there to solve a murder case. Intending to be the best eyes and ears, she'd notice everything possible about the people in the store, then he'd appreciate her effort. What were they up against? Could she prove to be a good investigator for the case?

A weird impression came over her, and for a second she thought that Zach knew more than he revealed. She had to gain his trust somehow so he'd start sharing more details otherwise she'd have no idea what to look for.

"Zach, later, when we finish this road trip, will you show me the autopsy report? I know she was murdered, and I want to help find the killer, but I can't make any plausible suggestions if I don't have the details."

"Agreed. It's still ongoing, and we're waiting for more results, but I'll share what we have so far. Finished?"

She nodded, and they went back to the car.

Lancaster was a bigger town that Stratford. Sam counted four churches as they drove down Main Street. Zach rolled to a stop and parallel parked in front of an old building, painted in a pumpkin color with gold trim and accentuated with copper details on the roof area. It was a beautiful old building, well maintained.

"The street is down there." He pointed as he put away his phone.

Zach got out of the car, and she followed him like a good

little Ranger. They walked past a couple of other old store-fronts then took a right.

A line of buildings filled the side street, older structures with large glass window panes from ceiling to floor, built during the Industrial Era that once provided the community with jobs at local mills, producing paper products. The industries have since left, and most of the remaining buildings housed new restaurants and stores, that attracted the younger crowd. They tried to cash in by creating Wi-Fi friendly cafes and lounges, to give the new digital generation what they wanted. Lured to the streets, young spenders accounted for the only viable industry left—tourism. Like most old towns in New England, business owners struggled to make ends meet. Any new customers were pampered, and any paying tenant was welcomed by landlords without too many questions, as well.

Real Horror Games was located a few buildings down from the main street and looked like a store for gamers with a niche. It advertised *'for adventure seekers only'* brazenly printed on a banner across a big front window. The store had the old front glass, large and ornate with yesteryear trim, but painted over with modern colored twists and designed in bright colors of blues and yellows. It was attractive for the crowd they sought—young nerds.

"Well this is quaint," Sam said. She hoped he caught the sarcasm in her voice.

Zach remained stone-faced.

The door to the shop had a bell that tinkled as they entered, with the yesteryear sound that matched the store's structure. The floor was old wood, that swayed and creaked underfoot, as they made their way to the counter positioned to the side.

The ceiling was high and still showcased the old tin panels, most of them painted over in glossy white but spotted with exposed chips of rust here and there. The walls clashed with the old world style, designed with vivid murals of colorful swirls splashed across the walls with modern scapes of game worlds and planets far away, abstract design, and cartoon characters with exaggerated features.

For a moment, Sam wished she had a figure as busty and curvy as the girl drawn on the wall, touting a gun in one hand and giving a superhero peace sign with the other. Then she thought better, Sam may not be a bosom beauty, but she was strong. She accepted her natural beauty and didn't feel the need to become another person's vision of pretty. Her primary goal was to keep her body strong, healthy, and her mind her own. She wondered if Zach still thought she was beautiful. It was a long time ago when he had flattered her with his gentle touch against her cheek as he whispered praises of her beauty. Ah, she thought, there's no reliving the past.

Zach leaned over the counter and tapped the young man's shoulder to get his attention. He wore a pair of noise reduction headphones and hadn't even noticed that they were there. This clerk was any thief's best friend. He turned with a start and took off the headgear when he saw Zach's trooper uniform. He was intimidating, wearing the dark green of a state trooper. Zach smiled, and the clerk seemed to ease his nervousness a bit.

"How can I help you, Sir?" the clerk asked. His dirty blond hair hung straight against his thin face, and he looked like the kind of kid that had gotten picked on in school. Not smart, not athletic, not any group except different. Sam had always stood up for kids like him. Everyone has a right to be themselves.

"I need a list of your clients. Everyone who bought games at your place." Zach's voice never wavered, a man on a mission.

"Sure, no problem," the clerk said with quickened words. "I'll run a sales report; it will only take a few minutes. Just give me the time frame you need."

"The past month," Zach said.

"That might take a bit longer." The young man turned around and keyed at a desktop computer. He watched the screen through a cutout section of the counter that was covered with glass. The monitor was nestled below and pivoted up to face the counter.

Sam knew that wasn't the report that they needed, but she'd been told not to say anything. Instead, she tapped Zach to get his attention. He turned and looked down at her, frowning. She couldn't tell if he was angry with her or wondering, what the hell she wanted. She murmured through her teeth, but he didn't understand.

He bent closer to her face. His cologne tickled her nose when she inhaled the agarwood scent. It sparked another memory of him, a warm thought of their first kiss. Sam smiled as she whispered in his ear.

"We only need a list of customers who participated in the real-life role-playing games. They might not be regular customers."

Zach's cheeks turned pink. He turned to the clerk, snapping his fingers to get his attention. The clerk looked up, his eyes opened wide, his mouth slanted to the side.

"You know, on second thought, what we actually need is

a list of all your role-playing gamers."

The clerk's face paled. He stammered.

"Sorry, Sir, but I can't give you that information."

He grabbed a stack of packaged game cards sitting nearby on the counter and shuffled them, then placed them neatly near the register. He continued to fidget with his hands, rubbing his fingers back and forth on the counter, then pulled his hair behind his ears.

The lines on Zach's face deepened as he watched the clerk's reaction, his eyes looked astute.

Sam watched Zach's penetrating expression and admired his scrutiny. No wonder she had never wanted to date anyone else, no one could fill his place in her heart. Sam had kept that a secret for years, but no more kidding herself. Sam was bound to live her life pining for a man she would never have, at least not in the way she wanted.

"Listen," Zach said. "This is a murder investigation. I need that information now."

Sam turned her attention back to the clerk, who swallowed hard. She watched his Adam's apple go up and down, his meek voice floundering.

"You need to talk to the owner about that, sir. I can't help you, man. If I could, I would, but I don't have that information. Besides . . . You see . . . The boss promises to keep everyone's anonymity. You know how it is. Besides, most of them don't even use their real names. The owner's the only one with that information, honest."

Zach cleared his throat. "Okay, then, tell me. How can I contact him? The owner, I mean."

The skinny young clerk scrawled the phone number and

address on a pad placed near the register. He tore off the sheet and handed it to Zach. Zach's face fired up as he read the note. He turned and left without another word, a trail of heated anger followed him.

"Thank you," Sam called back to the clerk as she left. She followed Zach out, and they headed back to the cruiser in silence.

17 - KEATON HAKES

As soon as Sam closed the passenger door, Zach took off. They traveled back the way they came, heading north toward the owner's residence. Zach remained silent as he drove. Sam saw the note on the front seat and picked it up. The name scrawled in blue ink was Keaton Hakes. Why was Zach so riled up, who was this guy? Did he know him?

Any association he kept to himself. Secrets—they always bothered Sam. Her father kept secrets. She closed her eyes and pictured her pop, lying sick in his hospital bed. She remembered his expression when he learned she had been at the Springs. He looked alarmed, scared. *Afraid enough to cause his heart attack.* She swallowed hard, hoping to keep her tears in check. Maybe there was a good reason for him to fear the place. She wondered if it had anything to do with the murder.

Needing a distraction, Sam turned on the radio and found a channel with good reception, playing classic rock. She looked up at Zach and hoped to instigate a conversation with him again.

"Sorry I nudged you back there," she said.

He nodded and glanced over at her. His face still looked stern despite the sideways grin. She noted his chin, so precise and determined.

"Don't worry. I appreciate the help. Now we might get answers."

He smiled, but his voice sounded upset. Whatever he knew, it troubled him, and he wasn't sharing any knowledge with her.

She'd be patient and wait until he was comfortable enough to share the intel. The cruiser made it to the address in a few minutes. The car crawled up the long, steep gravel driveway, flanked by trees. The hilltop opened up to a paved section of road. A large house stood at the top of the hill with an adjacent carport. Beyond it stood a large garage separate from the house with six bay doors.

The home was gigantic, a three story old Victorian, with fancy details and a tri-color paint job. In the world of houses, this was a classic beauty. Zach and Sam exited the car and stood on the pavement for a bit inspecting the surroundings. They stepped up to the porch. The thick oak front door had a center window light with etched scrolled details in the beveled glass. It opened before Zach could ring the bell.

"Please come in Sir, Miss."

The door squeaked when the housemaid opened the door wider and bowed her head for them to enter. She was wearing a little black maid's uniform adorned with an apron, a get up one would only see in late night old movies. Her face was timid and small, with shoulder length dark hair, and a petite figure. Her cheeks looked pale against the bright red lipstick slathered across her plump lips.

"Mr. Hakes is expecting you. Follow me, please."

They followed her through the grand marble-floored hall

to a great parlor on the left. The room contained antique furniture covered in many gold patterned satins and colored velvets. The furniture's arms and legs were crafted from highly polished fruit-woods. The gleaming waxed floors were adorned with scattered oriental carpets. Bright bouquets of exotic lilies and roses in crystal-cut vases sat on top of the tables. A rattling noise caught their attention, and they both turned to look across the vast room, as another door opened. The French glass doors spilled more light into the parlor as a man entered the room.

He wasn't tall nor short, but he carried himself as if he lived above others' rank. His hair was pale blond, his face baby smooth, his nose pugged a bit and supported a pair of invisible frame spectacles, hardly noticeable. He dressed in odd clothes as if he were attending a masquerade or in a costume for a production of a play set in the 1700's. His white breeches gathered at his knees with neat ties. His shirt was white and frilly, also with ties done up in bows and covered by a red vest decorated with gold embroidery designs or the edges. As he drew closer into the room, the light from the chandelier glimmered and bounced off his attire.

"Good day to you, officer. My employee called and said you'd be stopping by, so I was expecting you of course. What can I do for you? Please, do have a seat."

Keaton Hakes held out his hand, which Zach ignored. The man then waved his arm out gallantly, offering them a seat and nodding toward the sofa and chair arrangement. Zach remained standing in place. He flipped open a notebook, a pencil in hand, and began asking questions.

"Mr. Hakes, we need a complete list of all the role players

that have been using your services, as well as the descriptions of said games. We'll need their real names, and of course user names, as well. Time is of the essence, sir." Zach stared at the man without a blink, as if expecting an immediate response and helpfulness.

Keaton Hakes shook his head and spat a long excuse, using phrases of concern and protection of his clients' rights to their privacy.

"You understand, to gain their trust, I promise to keep everything private. It states it in the signed contract. It's the only way they can truly be anonymous."

Sweat formed on his forehead as he rambled on, stopping his rant only for a moment to wipe his brow with a lacy handkerchief. The man walked back and forth in front of them, his hands clasped behind his back. His pacing reminded Sam of the ducks that circle on a wheel, waiting for spectators to pay and shoot, during the summer carnival.

"So you see, I can't divulge that information. It would jeopardize my business and the customer's right to privacy."

Zach listened but scowled. Samantha admired the strength he showed. He allowed Mr. Hakes to ramble a bit, a technique often employed by law enforcement. Sam remembered learning this technique during her training classes; there was an entire section on how to work alongside law enforcement during an interrogation. Presumably, relevant information might leak through the nervous gibberish. The revelations learned could be used as leverage by the interrogator. Zach's patience ran out after a few minutes, and he interrupted Mr. Hakes.

"Enough of your excuses."

Zach shouted the words at Keaton Hakes then his expression relaxed a bit, and he regained his composure.

"Your argument doesn't apply in this situation, and you well know it. If you don't cooperate, you'll be charged with interference with an investigation. I have cuffs, and I'm more than willing to use them right now if need be."

"Don't be so hasty." Keaton Hakes scowled, his color changed from pale to vibrant red. He didn't seem the kind of man others often stood up to. He turned away for a moment then turned and faced them again.

"We need your cooperation, Mr. Hakes," Zach said. "These questions are regarding an open murder investigation. It'll look bad for you, and your business, if word gets out that you're unwilling to cooperate because of your phony excuses. We need the list, now."

Sam had never heard Zach speak so harshly, his voice edgy, even dangerous. Glares were exchanged between him and Keaton Hakes. Whatever history there was between them, Sam wasn't privy to it and wouldn't likely be unless Zach decided to trust her.

She had noticed something significant. Keaton Hakes' eyes popped open wide when Zach called it an open murder case. To her, it seemed like Keaton Hakes was genuinely surprised and in the dark about the crime, like them. The murder hadn't been mentioned in newspapers or TV reports— yet. It was only referred to as an unfortunate death, which most people interpreted as suicide or the Brunswick Curse if you were from the North East Kingdom.

Keaton Hakes went to the large desk on the far side of the

room, never averting his cold stare. He opened a drawer, hateful glares darted in Zach's direction. Keaton Hakes was an intense man if anything. He pulled papers out and leafed through them. After finding what he was searching for, the man held out a few sheets of white paper, flapping in the air.

"I believe this is what you want, and assume you will not harass my clients. I pride myself in doing business with discretion."

Zach crossed the room to the desk and grabbed the papers from Mr. Keaton's hand.

"Let's hope that's all you need to worry about," Zach said.

He turned and walked out without another word. Sam bowed her head toward Keaton Hakes, then followed Zach out, still behaving like a good little Ranger.

They descended the porch steps and Zach stormed back toward the cruiser, got in and slammed his door shut. Clearly, Zach had strong animosity toward Hakes and Sam wanted to know why.

When Sam got into the car, Zach turned the key and drove off.

"What the hell was that all about?" she asked.

He shook his head, then shrugged, but didn't answer her.

Bewildered, she wondered what was happening to Zach, she'd never known him to be combative or instigating a fight. Sam understood that he needed to find the killer, he was after all the kind of man with a deep belief in right, wrong, and justice. That was one of Zach's qualities that she held dear. Still, there was more to this situation. Zach knew something that he wasn't sharing with her. The not knowing was driving her crazy.

"Where are we headed now?" she asked. He kept driving. "Wait a minute, let's talk this thing through."

He turned to face her, stopped, pulled over to the curb, and then put the vehicle in park.

"What is it? You want to scold me like a child or something?"

His voice sounded cold. Sam didn't want him to be angry with her, but his demeanor was off the charts. She deserved to know why and didn't need his attitude, especially since they were supposed to be working together.

"Look, I don't mean to tell you what to do—"

"Well, that's good."

"But, I think you should fill me in. I want to help with the investigation. If you have a relationship with a suspect, then I think I need to know."

He blinked, refocused on the road, then nodded.

"That man is filth, and that's all I know. He's a suspect in many of the investigations that the Crime Unit has ongoing. For years we've been chasing after this guy, but never can find enough evidence to arrest the creep. He does bad things, Sam. Appalling things."

"What kind of crimes? Do you think he could be the murderer?"

"No, he's never been involved with murder, not yet anyway. He's linked to drugs and sex crimes."

"He's a sex offender?" Sam's stomach did a sudden flip, and for a moment she felt like losing whatever food remained in her.

"Not exactly," he said. "There's an underground organization. We think its base of operation is hidden somewhere to the east of the Lost Nation area, deeper even than Mt Cabot. We've been tracking the business but never find evidence as if they were on the move all the time. But the money is linked to him and his friends. We know he has legit businesses as well, for cover. But I never made the correlation between him with this Real Horror Game shop until you discovered it today. It makes me wonder if he could be using that business as part of his underground network. How deep can we get, though, the chances that this list is accurate is close to null." He pulled the sheet from his inner jacket pocket and threw it on the front seat between them.

Sam looked down at the list. "Oh, I see. Have you interviewed him before?"

"No, today was the first time I met the man face to face."

"We should check the list anyway. I'll do it as soon as you drop me back at my office."

Zach put the car back into drive and continued down the road. He turned and smiled at her. His expression had changed dramatically. Now that he had unburdened himself he seemed more like the Zachary Gerard she had always known.

"Before you dive into more research, I think you need dinner. I know a great BBQ joint in town. How about it? Dinner with me, my treat."

She nodded and turned to look out the window and hide her flustered face.

"When was the last time you ate?" he asked.

She shrugged.

"Have you eaten since your Pop was admitted to the hospital?"

"Yes, I think so. I guess I'm not sure. Things have been so chaotic lately."

"Well then, you're in for a treat."

The entire drive, Sam's stomach fluttered. Even though she knew this wasn't a date or anything, she couldn't help but be excited. They'd be together, eating dinner, like before. The more she thought about it, the more she wished she'd refused. If they kept things at a work level, then she'd be safe from herself.

He drove back into downtown Lancaster. They passed the churches on Main Street, crossed a bridge over a river, and parked across the street from a large brick building that was filled with town offices. Sam got out and locked around. The sun had already set. She checked her phone, eight in the evening. A sweet, zingy aroma floated in the air when a customer opened the door leaving the Irish Pub on the corner.

"Looks like we're just in time for dinner," she said.

"This is the best around. Finger licking good."

Zach smiled. Sam couldn't get over how handsome he looked. She wanted to freeze frame that moment and keep him in her mind's eye forever.

18 - Only Friends

They were both content after a messy BBQ dinner.

"Thanks, that was delicious." Sam wiped her mouth, getting all the sticky sauce off her face, then tossed the napkin onto the empty plate.

"Glad you enjoyed it." He signed the receipt and folded his copy into his pocket.

"So, ready to head back?" she asked.

"Sure, we'll go back to your place."

Samantha raised one eyebrow.

His face turned red, and he corrected himself.

"Your office, I mean." Zach grinned. "I could use your help researching these people. You seem to have a knack for surfing social media sites. I hope you don't mind my exploiting your talents?"

"It's called browsing social media because I don't have a social life," Sam said.

"I find that hard to believe." After a moment he added, "It might help the case. I know you're dying to solve it just like me."

"Yes. I want to help, and besides, I'd rather be busy right now. Keeps me from thinking of my father."

Zach nodded, helped her from her chair and guided her to the exit. His hand touched the small of her back, and a sizzling sensation ran up her spine. It was a delightful feeling, warm, and caring. She wished he would keep his hand there all night, possessive and wanting, but his hand dropped when they reached the door.

They drove back to her office in silence. Butterflies fluttered in her stomach and Sam was acutely aware of the close confines. His reappearance into her life resurrected feelings that she had pushed away into a far corner of her mind. Sam thought that her love for him had withered, but here she was still yearning for a man that would never be hers. The candle was lit, her secret illuminated so that anyone looking close enough would see her weakness.

The car's fan blew his aroma in her direction, whirling intrigue to her awaiting senses. She smelled his woodsy cologne, the scent mingled with his sweat. She still desired him despite herself.

Snapping herself back to reality, she noticed the speedometer on the lit up dashboard. Zach was speeding; it seemed that he couldn't get away from Lancaster fast enough. She turned away and looked out of the car window. The night was dark, the streets went by without being able to discern much, just the occasional street light giving shadowy hints of life after dark.

Lost in her thoughts, she began listing questions she had regarding Jessica's body and how she could have gotten there in the middle of nowhere. Sam imagined what the victim might have felt and thought, and the fear she must have experienced. The abrasions she noticed on the victim's hands might reveal forensic evidence and give them some answers, then again, it may pile on more questions.

The crime seemed senseless. No theft, rape, or apparent motive. It was heartbreaking, just like her Pop's anger, she thought. Why had he been so persistent for her to stay away from the Springs? Did the place have more to do with the girl's death than Zach, and she had initially considered?

When they reached the cabin there was no moon or visible stars to light the way, it was pitch black. Sam took extra effort and shuffled to the door. She unlocked the cabin and switched on the lights. A burst of energy like a second wind overtook her. Wasting no time, she went straight to the computer on her desk and began keying in the name at the top of the list. The people on Keaton Hakes' list seemed to have nothing in common with each other. Fifty percent of them were college kids, the same approximate age as the victim, Jessica. Others were business people and even a Senator.

A chair scraped against the floor, as Zach pulled it close to sit next to her. She had already looked up the first three names. He picked up the paper and read the next name. As the information filled the screen, he looked over her shoulder and read.

"Look," Zach said. "Mr. Simpson's name is listed next."

"Why do you suppose Simpson is listed?" Sam turned around and noticed that Zach was watching her. A little rattled, she made an attempt to finish her thoughts. "Why would an old guy like Simpson be participating in a role-playing game? Money? Would they pay people to be listed as a live game player for the publicity? I know he's not doing well financially, but that would seem like grasping at straws."

"Does he need the money?" Zach said. "Even if he did, I don't think that having a guy like Simpson attracts the young players that they most probably want as customers. Still, money. Money. Hmm. Most crimes are about money. Why does he need the money anyway? I mean what's going on with him?"

"I'm not sure. Earlier today I had a strange conversation with him. He heard about my Pop's heart attack, of course, and gave his best wishes for a speedy recovery. But he said something weird," she said.

"The old goat's kinda weird anyhow, no? What did he say that ruffled your feathers?

"He said sorry about your father and that if I had any questions, to come to him. Isn't that strange? I have no idea what he was talking about," Sam said. "What questions would I have that he could answer and not my Pop?"

"I'll check into things tomorrow. I'll stop by the market and nonchalantly ask Mr. Simpson a few questions," he said.

There was finality to his words, so Samantha moved on to the next name. Exasperated with the process, she had hoped they would find answers, but the list was less than desired. Spending another hour Googling names, she pulled up basic information, but none of the names listed revealed anything suspicious.

Zach gathered all the notes Sam had taken and filed them into his bag. He stretched his long arms and yawned, squinting as he covered his mouth with his fist. His facial features were distinctive, with a strong jaw, broad forehead, and a nose sculpted like a Roman statue. Zach was a handsome man; there was no denying that fact.

"Well, we had enough for today," he said.

Sam knew she needed to get her thoughts off of him and stay focused on the case. She reached down and turned off the computer. Looking up again, she noticed that Zach had been watching her again. A rush of warmth flooded her cheeks. Her embarrassment doubled, knowing that her flushed face revealed all her emotions too well. Her blazing face deepened as her humiliation made her flush even more.

He kept his eyes focused on her and smiled with a vexing grin. A mischievous sparkle returned to his eyes, the kind of look she remembered he used to give her years ago. She'd told herself so many times that she had imagined it, that she had been just a kid and there was no future for them. But here he was, looking at her with those hazel eyes again. It wasn't her imagination or infatuation—it was real.

She reminded herself about what happened years ago, and why this notion of them ever being together was foolish. Back then she had felt close to him, thought he had felt the same way. Then he blew her off and broke her heart. He left for school, never a word from him, no letter, nothing. Then that day, when she was in the school lunchroom and overheard another girl, an upper classmate, bragging that she and Zach had dated his senior year—that was Sam's ultimate embarrassment.

How could she have been so naïve? How could her instinct regarding Zach have been so off? She wished she had forgotten everything, but she hadn't. His affections had been important to her but ended in her humiliation. She inhaled.

Sam smiled back at Zach, but it was forced.

"Friends?" he said.

Friends? Is that how he wanted things to stand? He looked comfortable, with no tension showing on his face. The old Zach she had known was sitting there waiting for her answer.

"Yes, of course, friends."

He nodded as he got up from his chair, held onto its back, and leaned toward her. Heat poured off his body, Sam felt the warm air float between them. A flashback of warm kisses brought her to stand still, and for a split second, she thought he was going kiss her. Her heart pounded in her chest, surely he heard it.

Zach smiled, then turned and headed for the door.

"I'll see you tomorrow. I'll be here early with fresh eyes, and we can go over the autopsy results together," he said.

It took a moment for his words to reach her brain, the meaning hanging in the air somewhere. Catching her breath, Sam experienced a twinge of regret, realizing he was leaving. She nodded, got up, and followed him out. She locked the door, sensing his eyes watching her as she got into her Jeep. He was in his car already and followed her down to the dirt road. Samantha headed east back to Stratford. Zach headed south. She wondered where he was going.

Exhausted by the long day, she needed sleep. She would visit her father the next day, simple enough.

So many regrets haunted her, hating that the last words between them were harsh instead of loving. Her Pop was still unconscious last time she called for an update. They promised to call her with any changes, but she hadn't heard a word from them all day. *What if her Pop died? What would she do?*

No, she couldn't think of that, they both needed more time to clear the air and make amends. Sam wanted to tell her Pop that she loved him, no matter what had happened between them. She was convinced that he was in a coma because he needed time to heal his body. She imagined that when he woke up, he'd be like a new person, and healthier. He needed time to regain his strength, that's all. After being in the hospital, he might have an easier time of stopping his drinking. She sighed in relief just from the thought. There was something for her to hope for, a chance to face her Pop again and make things right.

Parking in front of her studio apartment, she looked up at the floor above the garage. It was dark except for the one flood light in the front. The side stairway steps seemed steeper than usual as she climbed to the top. Sam pulled out her key and unlocked the door; it creaked as it opened and alluded to an emptiness inside.

Never bothering to buy curtains for the windows, they were bare, and she saw the entire space illuminate when the lightning streaked across the sky and filled the panes with a flash. Then a crack of thunder rumbled the floor under her feet. It looked as if a storm was heading their way. Finally, they may get relief from the unusual heat.

She went straight to the bathroom, undressed leaving her clothes on the floor, and took a long refreshing shower. Sam toweled herself and slipped into a long nightshirt then crashed onto her bed.

Closing her eyes, she cursed herself for being a romantic jerk. Zach was a gentleman for not saying anything, but his very presence flustered her, he must have noticed. After tossing awhile, punching her pillow and getting it situated just right, she fell asleep.

The next thing Sam knew the alarm clock sounded its obnoxious buzzer.

19 - Grab An Early Coffee

Five in the morning. Sam fumbled in the dark, her hand finding the clock, she slammed down the button. Whoever invented the alarm clock must have had a warped sense of humor. The annoying noise disappeared, but she kept her head under the pillow a little longer until her ears stopped ringing. It was the most annoying clock in the world, and that's exactly why she had bought it. It did its job every time. It was the only model that managed to wake her up and soon developed into a love-hate kind of thing, which was necessary since Samantha had never been a morning person even though once awake she enjoyed to watch the sunrise.

Swinging her legs off the bed, her feet shuffled around on the floor until she found her slippers. She pulled her robe on, half twisted, then swaggered to the kitchen cupboard. Rummaging through the shelves, she grabbed the coffee and managed to make a pot that tasted good enough to drink. It was strong, and the aroma woke her more than the caffeine.

She gazed out of the window, the street was still dark, but the floodlight gleamed white patches on the wet pavement below. It was raining, she noticed the ripples in the puddles, and she wondered if the rain would last all day. She gripped the mug tight, the warmth from the hot coffee felt good against her hands. It was the cup she had made years ago in the ceramic class that she hated but took anyway to fill her nights.

Questions popped into her head about the names on Keaton Hakes' list, they nagged her mind with hounding concern. *Why was Mr. Simpson on the list?* He was an old man, a small storekeeper, how was he involved with role-playing games? And what exactly had he meant when he told her he was willing to answer her questions? What questions? Images of the victim popped into her head. Perhaps he could answer a few questions about the murder? Her curiosity was piqued.

Decision made, she'd stop by the market early this morning on the way to the office since it wasn't going to be a good day to view the sunrise anyway. Mr. Simpson was there in the morning to open up. Sam could pry information from him with normal conversation, of course. It would be a great lift if she discovered something relevant to the case, then she could give Zach the good news first thing this morning, hinging of course, on whether she got the right answers.

Rejuvenated with the prospect, she took a hot shower and dressed in record time. Sam pulled her long, dark, wet strands back into a ponytail then put on a watch cap she had bought online at blauer dot com, shoving her hair into the hat. It was wool and fleece-lined and blocked the wind from her ears, an appreciated attribute on cold early mornings. Grabbing her gear, she raced down the steps and threw her stuff onto the front seat of the Jeep. She rode to the Riverside Market for another cup of coffee to go, and she hoped to hear pertinent local gossip, as well.

She parked her Jeep across the street from the general store and regarded the entrance. The building needed paint, and the windows were still filled with old signage from a few decades back. The only signs taken down lately were the cigarette ads.

Three men were loitering on the cement steps under the dark green canopy which showed years of wear, torn edges and a few holes that let water drip through. Each day in the early morning hours the old timers gathered on the front steps to gossip: farmers, local tradesmen, and a couple of guys unemployed by the paper mills shut down decades ago. They were still whining. The local preacher and a few others joined the group from time to time. They discussed hunting, their gardens, the weather, and anything else that was local news — like Jessica Taylor's murder, that was the big news and would be for years to come.

Theories of the crime weaved into conversations. It might be a good idea to listen to the old geezers, someone might slip a valid piece of information that might help sort the mystery. So it's another cup of java this morning.

Sam didn't want to mess up anything for Zach, so she planned on being the concerned local Ranger, and neighbor. Besides, she needed another cup of coffee; it was going to be a long day.

Sam nodded to them as she walked by.

"Howdy," one of the men said. He lived down the street

from her, but she couldn't recall his name. He was an electrician by trade and had moved to their quiet town not long ago. New faces were news, but she had never heard his name mentioned, the other men referred to him only as the new electrician.

"Good morning Sam," another voice chorused. His voice was familiar. She had taken piano lessons from his wife, Mrs. Roberts.

"Good morning, gents," she said.

No one spoke, so she moved on and entered the store, rubbing her hands together to warm them. She hoped they'd resume their conversations so she could eavesdrop when leaving.

"Good morning Mr. Simpson. Looks like a beautiful day, if you like rain. How's the coffee today?" she said.

He was at the counter, as usual, ready for any paying customer. He folded up the paper and turned his attention to her.

"Coffee's robust and fresh like usual. Help yourself, Sam. Planning on getting the rest of your groceries now, because my produce man won't be here 'til this afternoon after he makes his stops in Lancaster," he said.

She filled her cup, added creamer, and then topped it with a lid. She answered him while she walked towards the register. "No, just the coffee right now. I have a lot of work to do today, so I need an early start. You know me, I need the caffeine boost to wake me up." She laughed.

The old man gave a faint smile. He looked even weaker than the other day.

"Don't you worry Mr. Simpson, I'll be back later. It definitely won't be until after the produce gets here, though."

She laughed a little, but he didn't seem to notice. His mind was elsewhere. He stared off someplace past her. She turned around to check, just in case, there was someone or something there. Nope.

"Are you all right, Mr. Simpson?" she asked.

He looked down and pulled at a loose thread of yarn on his old worn sweater. Sam noticed it was the same outfit he's been wearing for years, now it was part of him, like a skin layer instead of clothing. She couldn't imagine him without that clunky old sweater. It looked hand-made. Maybe his wife had knitted it? The blue color was faded and now looked grayer. It frayed with age, just like the man.

Something was wrong, she sensed it, but wasn't inclined to prod a reserved man like Mr. Simpson into talking. But today was different, they needed answers.

She glanced his way again. Frankly, he looked especially uncomfortable. Sam frowned. Even though there were always people milling around his store, he was obviously, still lonely. Sam tried to recall what his wife had looked like, but she had died so long ago that Sam couldn't remember the woman at all. What had happened to her? Another thing she wanted to look up when she got back to her desk.

"So the veggies are due this afternoon after the Lancaster route. What else do you get from there? Any other deliveries from the city?"

She ventured a stab at the subject and noticed that his eyes seemed to react, though she wasn't sure how to interpret his odd expression. Sam wondered if he dealt with Mr. Hakes and if he sold video products from *Real Horror* here in the store? She roamed her eyes over the shelves, looking for games on the racks.

"Sure, I get other stuff from the city. Not much, though," he offered. "Slow business these days."

He grabbed the paper from the counter, unfolded it and began reading.

"Hey, Mr. Simpson, I have a kid that I mentor. You know, the big sister program, and she's into those digital games. Do you by any chance sell any of them here?" she asked.

"Sure, I sell a few. Ayah. They're over there."

He pointed to the other side of the store. Sam walked over and looked at his inventory. She took her time, picking up a game and putting it back, like a real shopper browsing and comparing the goods. Sam felt his stare on her, watching her from the corner of his eye. She wondered why. Was it so crazy for a girl to look at electronic games? There were quite a few displayed; most were military type hero games, a few were monster games, truck and car racing games, and one called *Real Horror Games*. Bingo.

Sam stopped cold. Chills ran down her spine as if something sinister had breezed past her. She reread the words, *Real Horror Games*. The store seemed eerily quiet except for the thumping of her heart. Glancing outside, she noticed everyone who had been loitering on the steps were gone. It was just old Mr. Simpson there by the counter and herself, but for an inexplicable reason, the thought of being alone in the store with him scared the bejeezus out of her.

She heard him behind her, folding his newspaper, placing it on the counter, and then he walked toward her. The old wood floor creaked under his footfall as he stepped closer. She heard his left foot-dragging, sweeping against the wood's grain with his shoe. He had told her the story of how he was injured during military duty and lucky they had saved his foot. It swept across the dirty floor, *swish, swish*. No reason existed for Sam to fear this man, he was after all an old fixture in the town. She'd known him most of her life, but still, anxiety rippled through her body.

The bell hanging over the door jingled. Someone had entered the store. A breeze of relief filled her, and she turned. Sam saw Zach, stepping into the aisle. Her body relaxed.

"How's the coffee this morning Mr. Simpson?" he said.

Mr. Simpson went back to the counter, and Sam followed him with the game in her hands.

"Please ring me up. I'll take this game, and I'll pay for both coffees." She nodded at Zach, who was pouring his coffee into a reusable traveling cup.

"That'll be fifty-two."

He took her money and kept his eyes averted, looking down at the counter, staring at the game he had placed in a bag.

"Is something wrong?" she asked.

"No. No, of course not." He deliberately avoided looking at her; odd.

Sam and Zach both left, tipping their heads to Mr. Simpson as they exited the store.

"My, you're up early, Sam."

"I know. I couldn't sleep."

Zach chuckled. "You couldn't sleep? Is the Pope still Catholic?"

"Okay, so I set the alarm on purpose. Lately, I've been getting up early to watch the waterfowl on the lake. But today I want to get back to the office and dig into a few things right away. I have a weird feeling regarding old man Simpson."

Zach leaned against her Jeep, his ass resting on the fender. "This coffee hits the spot. It's cold this morning," he said.

The drizzling rain had stopped for the moment, but the mountain air was still damp. She drew in a deep breath and smelled the rain like her pop had taught her. An old memory from years ago flashed through her mind, of Pop and her, conspiring to stay warm one early morning.

It had been drizzling that morning, too. Pop had declared it a fishing day because the fish bite better with a slight rain. He had taught her to appreciate nature when she was younger, and they often hiked and fished together. He showed her all the signs nature revealed. He taught her that a red sky or rainbow in the early morning meant moisture was in the air, it was bound to rain. He talked about how the direction and strength of the wind, the way the breeze twisted and turned the leaves of the trees, foretold of storms yet to come.

Unfortunately, things changed, and too soon she became his designated driver instead of his daughter. He wasn't a perfect man or father, he drank too much, and she had always sensed his sadness about what could have been. She missed her father's attention and for years prayed he'd stop drinking. Especially on a damp day like today—good fishing weather. She'd have to call the hospital first thing to check up on him; today he might wake up.

Sam kicked a few stones, no time for daydreaming. Looking up, she stared at the road ahead. Everything was foggy. Quiet moments passed, and then she turned to get into her Jeep. Zach grabbed her arm and stopped her.

"His name was on the list, that's what's bugging you and me. So let's dig for more information. I'll follow you. I'll sign into the police database and see what's there that social media might have missed." He smiled.

She felt a rush of blood warm her face, as her anticipation and curiosity heightened. She nodded, got into her vehicle, and headed for the office. They both drove toward Maidstone Park Reserve.

20 - Curiosity Gets Answers

They reached Sam's office, the small cabin was situated not far from the beach area where she usually drank her morning coffee. She finished her first on the drive over, so she put on a fresh pot right away.

Samantha made her call to the hospital only to find that her father's health remained stable but unchanged. The news gave her some hope, her father hadn't gotten worse, so she put worrying about him aside and dove into the tasks at hand.

She looked up the public profiles of the people listed on Keaton's list via the web. Zach had followed her in and was using the table as a workstation. He searched the names on the list in the police database. It wasn't long until Zach stumbled across something interesting.

"Sal Simpson," Zach said. He pointed to his screen for her to look. "Check this out, the old man running the Riverside Market must have changed his name. The alias he's using isn't as old as he is, look, it's a phony. The man is definitely older than twenty-five."

"Are you sure?" She read the dates which proved the point; Sal Simpson had existed for only twenty-five years. Before that, the trail was null, no records of the man's existence.

Zach picked up the phone and called a co-worker from another department. "I need a favor."

After begging and a little back and forth, he scribbled down a case number on a notepad. Zach tapped the pencil on the pad while listening.

"Thank you. Now I owe you one."

He immediately placed another call.

"Who are you calling now?" Sam asked.

"Marshals' office." He smiled then decided to fill her in, "I know someone there who might give me a heads up if I'm nice."

His expression turned businesslike as he waited to be connected.

"Hi Barb, I need a favor. Can you to give me the name of the person regarding a case if I give you the case number?" He read the details to his friend then nodded as he listened to the response. "Please, Barb. You know I'm not asking without a good reason, for God's sake it's a murder investigation." More nodding. "Yes, I need a name, no details on your case or anything. It's an old case anyway. Any information is helpful, just to be able to eliminate or make sense of this guy regarding my case. It would be appreciated. It stays with me, promise." Zach nodded. "Yes, just a nudge in the right direction and then the next dinner is on me."

Zach's voice sounded nice. *Too nice.* His eyes smiled with a warm twinkle as he listened to the person on the other end of the line. She experienced a twinge of jealousy, then realized it was nothing more than a way to get what he wanted. Now he was privy to information that under normal circumstances would have been off base. Sam watched him scribble notes on the pad, but his words were impossible to decipher. She wondered if Zach had ever dated this helpful woman, he was flirting as if he knew her well, and certainly doing a great job of being *nice*. He turned to look at Sam.

As soon as he hung up, Zach announced, "Sal Simpson used to go by the name of Larry Grimes." His smile conveyed that he was proud of his ability to get information. "Larry Grimes was an accountant for the Boston crime mob. He managed the money and bookmaking."

"A bookie? Mr. Simpson. I would never have guessed."

"That's the point," he said. "Back in the 90's, he provided intelligence against old Boston bosses who went to court on RICO charges. He squealed on the major players, even a few of the bad guys after Salemme took over."

"Am I supposed to know who they are?"

"I guess not," he said. "But it was news back then and made history. They ended up indicting thirty plus crime family associates on numerous charges of racketeering, extortion, narcotics, gambling, and murder. Our old storekeeper was a witness for the prosecution."

"No wonder the old guy looks worried all the time," she said.

"So now we know why Mr. Simpson is here, in Stratford. He's hiding his true identity under the witness protection program. Twenty-five years is a long time to be away from yourself. I wonder if he still has any family," Zach said.

"Let's take a look and see what we can find."

Sam returned to her desk and surfed sites, looking for information or people related to Larry Grimes. She found his old address in Franklin, a small town twenty-two miles southwest of Boston. Then information from his old town surfaced with archival articles and photos. It was surprising—the amount of information out there—old pictures with him in them.

Larry Grimes was one of the pillars of the community back then, his name listed under the annual photograph of the town board, also noted as a volunteer for the local town History Club, and listed under the church's group. Apparently, he had been married with a family. Would they need to dig into his wife's and children's past, as well?

They spent the next hour gathering information on Mr. Simpson but his past ran into dead ends. The big question remained—did this have anything to do with the girl's murder? Sam's gut didn't trust him. Zach must have thought the same, because every time she looked up, he was searching the files for something on him. There were no connections no matter how deep they dug.

A couple of hours later the door opened, and Josh and Kevin staggered into the room, mid-conversation.

"It looks like it'll rain all day," Josh said.

They both took off their jackets and draped them over their desk chairs.

"Look, Zach's here again. Hi, Zach. Any news?" Kevin asked.

Kevin looked at Sam and back to Zach but didn't say another word, and no one offered an answer to his question.

"Morning," Josh said. He bowed his head and mumbled to

himself.

Sam nodded in his direction.

"I guess we'll be stuck in here all day," Josh said.

"I'll start working on the report you wanted, Sam." Kevin sat down and turned on his computer.

"You kiss ass," Josh said. He darted sneering looks at Kevin. "Someday you'll tip over all the shit you're full of."

"Play nice boys," Sam said.

Josh sat down and unfolded the newspaper he had brought with him. "Did you see this? Seems the murder investigation made front page news in the Lancaster paper."

"I didn't know you could read." Kevin blurted the words then covered his mouth as if they had slipped out on accident.

Josh kicked the leg of Kevin's chair.

"Okay, that's enough. Clearly, there's work to be done, rain or shine."

Sam couldn't take it, her nerves were already short without enough sleep, and these two clowns pushed her over the edge. She snapped the pencil she was holding. They both took notice of her.

Standing up for the first time in over an hour, she stretched while barking a few orders at them.

"I want you two to work in the shed. Sort as much salvage as possible. We're so close to the end. If the rain stops I want you to keep at the trail clearing as well."

They listened not daring to interrupt her.

"Sure, no problem," Josh said. "You two can be alone all day, for all I care."

His grumbles didn't bother her, it was their job, after all. Still, she usually worked with them, but it was for the best that they work on their own today. The park will be officially opened for the summer season soon, and they needed to have everything in order.

Josh and Kevin put their coats back on, then departed rather noisily and begrudgingly pursued the outdoor tasks.

Zach stepped over to her desk and pulled a chair up beside hers. His scent lingered in her nostrils, bringing her back to a time when she had been happy. She liked that feeling of happy and wished it could last awhile.

"Let's see if we can come up with a common denominator here. We need to figure out how Simpson, I mean Grimes, and Jessica are connected," Zach said.

She turned and opened her drawer and pulled out colored markers and a large pad. Flipping it open, she drew a line down the middle. Sam wrote their names, one at the top of each column.

"First, both names are on Keaton Hakes list." She wrote that down on top. "But we don't know why, so we need to ask the question during your next interview with Hakes," she said.

Zach tapped a pencil, then pushed back into his chair, folding his arms across his chest like he was ready to command a platoon.

"Yes, that's a good question. Does Jessica's father know Simpson? Or Grimes?" he said. "Hmm."

"So, we need to talk with the victim's parents again," she said.

"No. I need to speak with them." He pointed to his chest. "There's no need for you to come. Not that I don't appreciate your help, but for real, I have to do that part of it."

He got up and pushed back the chair. "Are we good?"

She nodded, and he left the office. Sam watched through the window near her desk as he drove off. Just then thunder roared, and a streak of lightning lit up the room for a split second. It seemed the storm was a substantial threat to the day's work and the outdoor activities would be halted. She turned around and went back to her work. She'd use the time to dig deeper.

It wasn't more than a minute later when the phone rang, followed by a loud crack above the cabin as if it was an omen. She flung her arm across the desk and picked up the receiver. It was Doc Howard. Hopefully, he had the autopsy results.

"Good morning Sam. Zach said to call him there. Thought you two would like an update on our victim, Jessica Taylor," he said.

"Yes, of course. Zach just stepped out but should be back later. I can give him a message to call you back when he returns."

"Well, I'm busy today. Let me tell you, and then Zach can pick up the file whenever he has time. She was positively murdered."

She gulped. It was real. Of course, she was killed. Mr. Livingston had already said so, and she had known that in her heart from the beginning, had felt it. But somehow with the official word from the coroner, it seemed more horrific.

"Okay, Doc. Tell me the details."

Sam focused on his words, holding back the tears she wanted to cry.

"First off, she died from drowning," the doctor said.

"She drowned? Are you positive?"

"Yes, and thank God, she didn't suffer much, she was drugged beforehand." He took a moment of silence.

"Drugged how?"

"I found tiny prick marks on her chest, which appears to be the entry point. I'm still waiting for tox screens, nothing ordinary came up on the standard tests performed, so a more detailed panel had to be done. Plus we're analyzing the water found in her lungs. There were no signs of struggle, no bruises or contusions on her body, other than the prick marks and a small bruise on the back of her neck. Probably from how the killer held her head under water. She hadn't suffered much; no evidence was present that suggested sexual abuse. No harm was done other than drowning her, but of course, that's tragic in itself," he said.

Sam interrupted him. "Doc, what did you learn from the marks on her hands?"

"Ah, yes. The marks were scratches, light abrasions, but caused postmortem."

It seemed a strange thing—to be scratched after being killed.

"Doc, the scratches didn't look like animals or anything of the like. Do you have any idea of how the victim got scratched? Any clue left on the skin?" she asked.

"You're good at this, Sam. I took some samples of the surface for trace, but it will be another day or so before they get back an analysis report. Plus we're waiting for the water analysis, but the lab is backed up right now. They said they were busy working on water samples from the Moore Reservoir. I guess that's more important, at least that's what I was told."

He sounded put off.

"Thanks, Doc. We'll just have to wait until the trout get their water's bill of health and the all clear. But in the meantime, do you have any guesses, of what caused the scrapes? Off the record, of course."

"Well, in my humble opinion it looks as if her hand rubbed against something hard and metallic, maybe a metal door, who knows. Perhaps when her body was moved," he said.

"Like a car door?" she said.

"No, I don't think that would have done it, there're no visible paint chips. But it's not my job to venture a guess. I'll leave that up to you two youngsters." He laughed. "So, you're a trout fisherman?"

"I catch and release, mostly. I used to go with my father. That particular reservoir has all kinds of trout: brook, rainbow and brown trout, as well as bass and northern pike."

"I didn't know that," he said.

"Yes, well I only know because I help keep track of that kind of thing. The Moore Reservoir is one of the largest hydro-electric facilities in New England, so its water is monitored carefully."

"Well, it's a relief to know that someone is watching, though it puts a cramp on our results. Oh well, we need more care for our environment, I guess. So pass the message along, will ya, and thanks, Sam. Goodbye for now."

The doctor hung up, and Sam sat back in her chair, thinking. If the victim was drowned, then where? The nearest water was Silver Lake, or she could have drowned in the river. Had the girl known she was going to die? Had she seen something she shouldn't have? No matter, at this point it was all speculation. They needed to go back and ask Keaton Hakes more questions. She swiveled her chair around toward the computer and keyed a search for more information about Keaton Hakes' past.

Curiosity gets the cat. No, that's not right, she thought. Curiosity gets answers. Samantha discovered that Keaton was an established business leader and had been in the Lancaster area for the last twenty-five years. Bells went off in her head. It was too much of a coincidence. Both Keaton and Sal Simpson appeared in the North East Kingdom area at the same time— twenty-five years ago. Maybe a connection? And Mr. Simpson sold games he purchased from Hakes' store. She wondered if Keaton Hakes was also an alias for another name. She tapped her pencil against the desk, wishing for Zach to come back and rack up another favor.

21 - RAINY DAYS

Kevin and Josh stormed through the door, soaking wet and dripping all over the old plank floor. Sam had forgotten they were outside in the inclement weather. They shook with laughter, pointing at each other and cracking up.

"Raining?" she said.

"You noticed. That's why they pay you the big bucks," Josh said.

"Okay, so I've been a little distracted."

The joviality between her friends stopped. Only the rain sounded as it hit against the roof with a soft drumming vibration.

"Distracted? More like obsessed. Sam, you're not a cop. Why don't you leave the detective work to Zach? You're becoming consumed. Maybe you should head to the hospital and be with your father?"

She leaned back in her chair, surprised by what Josh said. He was usually the first one to lend a hand, of course, all while provoking the people around him.

"What? Sit around the hospital and mope when I could be productive instead? You should help, too," she said.

Josh looked across the room, staring at her and something passed through his eyes that she didn't comprehend. He seemed upset, she must have overestimated his coping abilities. He wasn't handling this death well after all. He wasn't alone, many people have a hard time after viewing a dead body. Josh had put up a good front the other day, but perhaps he wasn't as strong as she had assumed.

"Josh, I'm sorry. I know this is a horrible situation and I'm trying to be sensitive. But yes, you're right, I want to find out who did this to that poor girl," she said.

Josh cleared his throat. "I understand that you do. We all want justice. How can we help?"

"I'm not sure, but I guess you should keep your ears open for anything offbeat. Listen to what the guys say in your ATV club."

She noticed his thick, unruly, hair, was bushed out from the humidity. It looked as if he hadn't had a haircut in a long time, unusual for him.

"What are you staring at?" He sounded terse.

"Nothing. Just thinking," she said.

The past few weeks Josh behaved differently. His eyes seemed darker than usual, steamier, and then there was the shiner he sported. Lately, his stance was like a boxer's, ready to punch someone at any given moment. She had never known him to have a flash of temper. Josh usually got back at people with his practical jokes, always the kidder. Everything was a joke, and nothing was off limits, *except for dead girls in the woods*. Samantha swallowed.

She picked up a pencil and doodled on the desk blotter. She drew jagged lines and wondered if this event had changed Josh. Sometimes, people have tempers that don't surface until provoked. Some people use passive aggressive behavior. She wondered, does he do that? Was Josh doing that now?

Josh had been angry just a moment ago. Might he still be upset over the dead girl, or it could be something else? She scratched lines across the paper, pushing the pencil down hard, then dropped it on the desk. *Get back on track; time was of the essence.* She needed to concentrate on the facts of the case and not spend her time listening to her intuition.

"So tell me, how does the shed look? Get much done?" she asked.

Kevin laughed. "Na, not much, the recycle pile is bigger, though. But other than that everything is the same as always."

"He means no more dead bodies popped up," Josh said. He was smiling, but it seemed that his joke wasn't intended to be funny.

A bolt of realization hit her. All this time she thought Josh was just kidding, all these years, maybe he was just a smart ass.

A creepy apprehension darted up her spine, and her body quivered involuntarily. Something seemed off, but she couldn't place anything specific that was wrong.

"Since we're stuck inside until this lightning storm gives up, let's work on filling out the progress reports for the University of Vermont study. We have to do them sooner or later," she said.

"I'll finish up on the garden border plants." Kevin sat at his desk, his hand shook as he manipulated the mouse.

"Sure, where did you leave off?" she asked.

"My last entry was in the Ns, next up Northern Blue Monkshood. I'm familiar with that one; my mother grows it at the house. It's very useful" Kevin grunted, then began working down the list of plants.

She watched as he stopped to rub his glasses with the tail of his shirt, then placed them back on his face, pushing them up the bridge of his nose until snug. She wondered if he had any original thoughts in his head, he always followed directions and suggestions, but never offered his own opinion. It was as if he hadn't a creative bone in his body, or was he too scared of his mother. Sam turned her attention back to her computer screen, and they all got busy.

An hour later Sam looked out the window and noticed the rain had let up a bit, now only a gentle drizzle. With the storm finished, the afternoon looked gray, wet, but tolerable.

Zach returned. She watched as he exited his vehicle and jogged to the porch. He carried an umbrella over his head and dribbled rain all over the floor when he entered the office and lowered the umbrella to close the ribs.

"Hello," he said smiling. "It's nasty out there today."

He shook himself.

"How about lunch, everyone? My treat."

Josh looked over at Kevin, who was smiling at Zach with hero worship. As soon as Kevin turned and acknowledged Josh's stare on him, Kevin's face jetted down, back to his work.

"Sorry Zach, but I'm waiting for a call," Josh said.

"I understand," Zach said. "Kevin, you up for lunch?"

"No thanks. I brought my lunch. My mother would kill me if I didn't eat it, today it's her special tuna surprise," Kevin said.

"Okay then, Sam it's you and me," Zach said.

She grabbed her jacket and headed for the door.

"Guys, are you sure you don't want to come? You deserve a break," she said.

"Thanks, but not today," Kevin said.

He turned in Josh's direction then dropped his head back down and pretended to be busy. Josh didn't bother to reply again, preoccupied with whatever he was reading on his phone.

Zach held the umbrella over her head as if Sam was something that might melt in the rain. The thought of his gallantry made her chuckle.

"What?" Zach asked.

"Nothing," she replied. "Just remembered a joke Josh told me. It's not worth sharing, honest."

Good cover, she thought as she slipped into the front seat and looked out the window. She noticed Josh, standing inside by the window, watching them, darting angry looks in her direction. She wondered why he hadn't come, then thought he might be upset because she was spending more time with Zach. Here she was giggling like a smitten school girl. Sam had burdened Josh years ago with her secret heartbreak; perhaps he thought she was caving to the enemy. No, she refused to think of anyone as an enemy, except, of course, the killer.

Zach and Sam drove to a town nearby that had a little diner off the highway. They ordered a bowl of chili and coffee.

"Oh, by the way, Doc Howard called for you when you were out and said you could pick up his report. The girl was undeniably killed—drowned."

"Really, drowned? How could that be?" Zach said.

"Maybe the nearby lake?" Sam offered. "Or by the river? No suffering or abuse was apparent, thankfully. There were odd prick marks or needle marks on her chest so she might have been drugged before being drowned. And there was a bruise on the back of her neck, perhaps she was forced face down when submerged," she said.

Zach shook his head at the awful news but didn't act surprised.

"Strange for sure. Once they finish the tests, we might get a clue about what the marks actually mean. Was there anything else?"

"Well, they don't know what substance was used to drug her yet. Doc's waiting for lab results to determine if the scratches on her hands meant anything, too. "

He nodded.

"And you? Any progress with her parents?" she asked.

"Yes and no. I knew something was off, but I still can't understand why. They're good parents, and they're so distraught. I couldn't push them too much, you know. They never heard of *Real Horror Games* or anything about live role-playing. As a matter of fact, they asked me questions about it. They did say that Jessica hated the woods, and would never have gone into any forest alone. They want answers. The whole ordeal is kind of bizarre for them right now. Understandable. Unfortunately, they didn't offer any new insights," Zach said.

She was stirring her chili, trying to get it to cool.

"You know Zach, girls don't always tell their folks personal stuff. I never told my Pop what was going on. You know that first hand. You were my confidant."

She stopped herself from saying more, her face heated up, and she hoped that she hadn't blushed too much to give away her vulnerability. Sam looked down at her food as she continued her line of thought, stirring while talking.

"Of course, my Pop was drunk all the time. But my point is that Jessica probably behaved the same way as most college girls do. I'm confident her parents didn't know everything. We need to find out who she confided in."

Sam looked up and noticed Zach slicking his hair back, still wet from the rain. He wasn't smiling, but his expression still amplified a positive outlook laced with confidence, kindness emanated from within him. She couldn't help but smile herself.

"Of course, that makes perfect sense. Jessica's best friend was a Miss Katie Andrews. We need to speak with her and with Keaton Hakes again. I'm ready for him this time," he said.

"Sounds like you know him more than you let on," she said.

Zach shot her a piercing glance. Surprise, she had hit a nerve.

"Yeah, you're right. We crossed paths once before, but I didn't think it was important to tell you, it was a long time ago. Hakes was involved in the traffic of questionable product transported on the highway, on its way down to Connecticut."

He shifted his weight and leaned forward, finishing his thoughts with a lowered voice.

"There were drugs in one of the trucks along with his video games. Of course, I didn't know about *Real Horror Games* back then, so never made that connection. The hitch was that Hakes had used a contractor, so he was cleared of any wrong-doing. The DEA pinned the blame on one of the contract work-ers for all of it. Keaton Hakes got a slap on the hand and was told to be more careful who he did business with. I guess I'm a little pissed off about that and I suppose I let it show the other day. I'm sorry. That was totally unprofessional of me."

He shrugged, and she didn't say anything else. She'd let the issue die. Sam knew Zach better than she had thought and was glad they were starting to talk with each other more nat-urally again. He had been her best friend years ago when she first realized that Pop was lost to her, because of the booze.

Zach had been there for her when things got confusing, and he helped her see the truth—that she had no control over her Pop's sickness. The concept freed her from guilt, at least for a while. And then Zach became her shining star, until the day he was gone.

Part of Sam was happy to have him back in her life, even if briefly. She knew that after the murder case was solved, he'd be gone again.

"After we finish lunch let's drive to the victim's friend's house first. Katie Andrews still lives with her parents," Zach said. He took a big spoonful, then wiped his lips with his napkin.

"Okay, boss. I'm ready to go when you are."

22 - What Is Friendship

Hanover was a small college town, snuggled between the Connecticut River on its western border. To the east, the town was skirted by the thick forest along Moose Mountain Road. The victim had been a college student there, one of many in its long history.

They arrived at Katie Andrew's parent's house early in the afternoon. They lived in a middle-class neighborhood down the street from the local high school. The young woman was at home, according to her mother, Katie was too traumatized to return to school. Her mother escorted them to the living room.

Zach sat in a pub style chair situated across from where Katie was sitting, and Sam took the seat beside her on the blue plaid sofa. Katie's pale hands were folded on her lap, her black nail polish chipped. She tilted her head down, her dyed purple hair fell forward and covered her face while she stared at the floor. They sat a moment, Zach was giving her time to get her bearings. Katie lifted her face; Sam noticed her severe acne. Katie pressed her lips together and glanced up at Zach when he asked her the first question.

"I have your statement from earlier," Zach said. "You told me you didn't see Jessica leave, that you and your other friend parked in a different area. Has any new detail come to light, now that you've had time to absorb what's happened? Maybe you noticed something? Anything else that happened that night could be relevant."

Katie picked lint off of her dark sweater, shaking her head but keeping her head down.

"Sorry, but no. I can't recall any other car or truck around or anything else that stuck out that night."

Katie smiled but her eyes still looking down.

"We met at the Nugget that night, that's the local movie theater."

She looked up as she continued, her voice steady but soft.

"There could have been other cars, I just can't remember anything out of the ordinary."

Her voice sounded pleasant and conversational. Too calm for a girl who just lost her best friend? *Were they best friends?* Sam wanted to ask but didn't want to interfere with Zach's interrogation. So she watched Katie's body language as she answered Zach's questions.

Katie seemed intelligent. She chose her words carefully and answered directly, but she wrung her hands a lot and scratched her arms as if uncomfortable in her skin. The fidgeting could have easily been her way of dealing with nervousness. The grins may be the result of her nerves, too. Sam knew people acted in odd ways under stress, but she was getting a sense that something was off.

"How did you know Jessica? School?" he asked.

"No. We worked together, on a project at the Howe Library. We helped with the online stuff for them. Plus, I worked at the Senior Center part time, and she volunteered there. You know, now and then when she wasn't busy at school."

"Had you ever been in classes together?" Zach asked.

"No, I don't attend Dartmouth."

Her voice turned edgy like she would break into a nervous, uncontrollable laugh at any moment.

"I couldn't afford it. I go to a smaller local junior college. But I knew her in grade school, but that was ages ago."

Katie drew in a sudden breath and folded her hands. Perhaps she was tormented by her friend's death. Sam was sad for her. It was evident that something was wrong with this girl, there was an underlying tragedy that seemed to surround Katie. Sam sensed the vibe and was waiting for Katie Andrew to break down and cry buckets, losing the calm facade she was deliberately maintaining.

After a few more questions which supplied no new leads, Zach announced that the interview was ended. Katie never shed a tear.

Sam reached over and touched the girl's hand. Katie winced. Sam responded on instinct by taking hold of the girl and hugging her close, snuggling Katie in her arms. Sam felt Katie tremble, something definitely disturbed her but was unsure if it was because of Jessica's murder. In fact, Sam thought most likely not, something else was going on with Katie Andrews. She was a terrified girl.

Sam whispered in Katie's ear.

"Do you know anything about the role-playing games?"

Katie nodded, her head rubbed against Sam's shirt.

"Can you tell me more, sweetheart?"

Katie didn't look up. Her voice was soft, barely audible.

"It's played, you know, in the woods."

"Oh, I see. Tell me more," Sam said.

She stroked the girl's hair back, away from her face. Her eyes peeked up for a quick look then looked away again, but she remained content in Sam's arms.

"Everyone wears a costume and take on a secret identity. I played once, last year. It was fun. Please don't tell my mother."

"I won't." Sam soothed the girl, combing through her purple hair with her fingers. "Tell me more."

"A boy I met once, when I was hanging around town, asked me to join because they were short a player. I had nothing to do, so I went. But nothing bad happened. I don't even know his name, just that he was really cute." Katie jerked in Sam's arms. "Jessica asked me questions, you know, how to join the game."

"When did she ask?" Sam said.

"A few weeks ago. But I told Jessica I didn't even know the name of the game. I didn't even know the cute guy's name. I wish I did. And that was it. Promise."

Katie raised her head and looked up at Sam. Her eyes were a warm brown, and glistened with tears ready to spill.

"Honest, that's all I know."

Katie's lips quivered, then she leaned into Sam's shoulder again. This time Katie shed her tears, gulping air between sobs.

At least now they knew the game was likely connected, that was something. But no names, the trail was still cold.

"Look," Sam said. "If you think of anything else, call me. Even if you just want to talk for a bit. I'll answer any time, day or night, if you need someone to listen."

Sam let go of the young woman, pulled out a card from her pocket, and handed it to her. Katie nodded and took the card. She looked up, her face was streaked with lines of running mascara. Sam pulled out a tissue and handed her that, too. Katie took it and wiped her face.

"Thank you," Katie said.

Sam grabbed Katie's hands and shook them assuredly.

"Any time, I mean it," Sam said.

Katie nodded, and Sam stood. Katie escorted them back to the front door. Zach and Sam left the house and walked back toward the car. Her cell rang.

"Tremblay."

The voice on the other end of the line spoke in an urgent tone.

"Miss Tremblay, this is Leslie, the nurse assigned to your father today . . ."

Sam's face paled as she listened to the nurse. Feeling weak in the knees, she sat down on the wet curb, never registering the soggy ground. Her cotton slacks were saturated. Sam listened to the rest of the message mesmerized then pocketed her phone. Her vision blurred and a deep panic gripped her from inside, squeezing her heart until her fear tightened her chest and throat.

"I have to get back quick. My Pop. He's not doing well."

Her voice sounded foreign to her ears as if she heard herself from under water. She pushed herself up but slipped on the muddy grass. Zach leaned over and helped her stand, escorted her to the car, buckled her in and closed the door. He got into the driver's seat, handed her a cloth to wipe her hands, then took off in a flash. The siren and lights blared as they exited the small town. She looked out the window and saw the faces of people as they strolled the street, puzzled looks on their faces as the car whizzed by. When they reached the highway, Zach turned off the noise, but they sailed the remainder of the way with the lights still flashing.

Samantha looked straight ahead at the road; she wanted to speak, to say thank you to Zach, but not a word escaped her lips. Her Pop had woken up. He had another attack, the doctors weren't certain how long he could hang on or if he could survive, and he was asking for her. Why hadn't she stayed with him?

He had woken up from his coma, and she wasn't there for him. Sam closed her eyes, cringing at the thought. Nothing else mattered but seeing him again—seeing his old cynical face melt when he saw her—and for him to smile at her at least one more time.

She turned toward Zach and stared at him, memorizing his profile and the stern set of his mouth as he concentrated on getting her there in time. She turned away again. A tear dribbled down her cheek, then another. She tasted the saltiness then wiped them away with a quick swipe of her fingers and took a deep breath. *I'm on my way, Pop.*

23 - HOSPITAL

Zach dropped Samantha off at the entrance of the hospital. She navigated the white hallways illuminated with humming fluorescent lights and found her way to the ICU. A nurse dressed in blue scrubs and wearing big round dark framed glasses reached out and held Sam's hand.

"I'm Nurse Leslie. Let me bring you to him," she said.

Sam nodded and dutifully followed the woman who led her to Pop's bedside. Equipment was connected to him, his eyes were closed.

Sam stood close by his side and studied his face. She gently stroked his wrinkled cheek. His eyelids fluttered, and for a brief moment, he grinned. His face relaxed, his body fell limp, as if he had been holding his breath and finally let out the pent up air.

"I'm here, Pop."

Her father blinked his eyes, then opened them. They were moist in the corners as if he'd been crying.

"Don't worry, Pop. I'll stay right here with you. Sorry I wasn't here when you first woke up."

He blinked his eyes again, and Samantha was hopeful that he understood.

"He can hear you but might not be able to speak just yet." The nurse spoke softly. "Talk to him."

Sam nodded. "I love you, Pop."

She was hopeful that everything would get better. Yes, her father had abused his body, but now things would be different. She'd help him get back his strength, do whatever it took. He was alive; it wasn't too late.

The equipment's alarm beeped loudly.

Sam jumped then looked up at the screens and found that one seemed to be going flat in a straight line. Pop's heart stopped.

Without warning, a nurse shoved her aside and went to her father's side. Another nurse joined her and pulled the curtain shut while calling to Sam from over her shoulder.

"Please, wait in the hallway."

Samantha went to the hall and moved aside as a male nurse sped by with a crash cart. That's when everything went blurry. She leaned against the wall and slowly slid down until she was seated on the floor. Sam stayed there for what seemed like an eternity, her mind blank, not knowing what to do. She couldn't see beyond the white drawn curtain so settled on concentrating on the specks in the floor. Gold and silver flecks embedded into the resin white tiles.

A familiar voice startled her, but it took a moment for her to look up.

"Sam, are you okay?" Zach pulled her to her feet.

"My Pop."

A metal tray fell to the floor in her father's room and made a clatter that woke her to alertness.

"Do you think they can bring him back?" she asked.

"Sure, they do this stuff all the time." Just as Zach finished his sentence, the curtain opened, and the nurses gathered all the equipment and wheeled it away. The nurse with the big dark glasses came to her.

"I'm so sorry, dear. Your father didn't make it." The nurse looked up at Zach, and he nodded.

It took a few seconds for the words to penetrate, Samantha wanted so much to ignore them and make them unreal. She peered into the room and saw her Pop lying there on the bed, helpless with all the tubes pulled out of him. He wasn't breathing, wasn't moving, and Sam could see his color had quickly drained to a pale gray-white. She stepped into the room. A cold shiver gave her goose bumps as she walked to his side. Sam picked up his hand, his palms were cold, no heartbeat at his wrist. She stood for a bit holding Pop's hand, wishing she had had a chance to say more to him, to apologize for being an obstinate child.

If she had never dwelt on mother's accident, he never would have slapped her, and he never would have started drinking. It had been all her fault, and now he's dead, and she hadn't even said, *I'm sorry Pop.*

Sam, in deep thought, lost any sense of time, until the warmth of Zach's arm around her penetrated her reverie. She looked up, saw his face and read the sorrow, and there was something else, another emotion she didn't recognize.

"It'll be all right," Zach said.

"Thanks for being here." Sam turned and walked away from her father's death bed. With Pop gone, Samantha was all alone.

Sam woke up cranky. She hadn't gotten much sleep the night before, fading in and out of wakefulness, chasing thoughts of regret for not being a better daughter over the years. The tears shed during the night swelled her eyes, and she was forced to place cold compresses on them before attempting to drive to the church where Samantha met with the parish priest and made the funeral arrangements.

The priest had given the last Rites to her father in the hospital and told Samantha that years ago, her father had planned what he wanted for his service. The process was easy enough to finish, Pop wanted a quick vigil in the front of the Church immediately before the Liturgy Mass; he hated the long drawn out funeral parlor ritual. He had always said the smell of candles and the pink velvet chairs made him ill. Sam grinned at the thought. Pop wanted a simple song, *Sing with All the Saints in Glory Hymn* to be performed by the regular organist, nothing fancy. He had chosen the prayers, and she read them over.

Sam knew her father loved others in his heart; it was only himself he seemed to be at odds with. Pop was to be laid to rest next to mother in the family plot, and the Rite of Committal completed with just a brief prayer.

Samantha sat in the back room of the church on a wooden folding chair, the room felt warm and smelled of candle wax and old incense. She dialed the office and asked her co-workers if they'd be pallbearers, then she called a few other men from the town who used to fish with her father, and asked them to help. Everyone was apologetic on the phone.

By the time the loose ends were dealt with Sam felt feeble. She stood, the old oak floorboards creaked under her weight as she left, Sam was just as achy. The service would be the next day, no reason to prolong the process. Somehow she would have to drag herself home for dinner and to get some sleep. She grabbed her things and left, walked down the street from the church to catch a bite to eat at the Riverside.

A bell chimed when she entered the store. She hoped Henry was working today, but it was Mr. Simpson behind the counter sporting the same old sweater and reading his newspaper as usual. He looked up then returned to his reading. Sam darted for the cooler to search for a pre-made salad and chose a spinach with walnut and snagged a tuna sandwich, too. She added a fizzy water from the cooler and headed for the counter, hopeful the old man would respect her loss and stay quiet instead of speaking in cryptic messages like the other day.

Since learning of his old connections with the mob, Sam lost respect for Mr. Simpson. She always had a funny feeling when around him and thought perhaps she was a good judge of character. Drawing in a deep breath, Sam wondered, for a split second, the opposite thought. Perhaps she had no real sense at all. No matter how much she wanted to pat herself on the back, Sam knew in her heart she was a difficult person and had been a horrible daughter. Her mother would have been disappointed in Sam and the way she avoided Pop in the end when he needed her the most.

"Is that all you'll be eating for dinner? Interested in something warm instead? You know, Henry made a pot of soup.

Want some soup for the soul?" Mr. Simpson uttered softly, and the smile spread across his face looked out of place.

"No, thank you. I'm not sure I can even manage this much."

Sam paid for the food and turned to leave. She eyed the round security mirror hanging from the ceiling and thought she caught a glimpse of Mr. Simpson raising his hand to catch her up like he wanted her to stop so he could say something. Sam took off before he had a chance to speak. She wouldn't allow him to keep her there a moment longer. The last thing she wanted was to converse with him.

Her phone rang, she looked at its face, it was Zach. After he had dropped her off last night she didn't want to talk with him, or anyone. She had closed her door abruptly on him, not even muttering a thank you. She felt sorry for that. Later in the evening, Josh dropped off her Jeep, but Sam didn't invite him in either. She was on her own and would need to get used to the solitude without Pop to fall back on. *Who was she kidding?* Samantha Tremblay never liked leaning on anyone, and most likely pushed people away all the time.

It didn't take a crisis for her to get into a moody solitude. She knew that about herself but had never asked the question why and never tried to change. Perhaps it had more to do with the empty place inside of her after losing her mother when she was a little girl, barely four. *Or was that her crutch?*

She had become comfortable with that ache after losing her mother, it had become a familiar friend. Now she had no family, no mother or father, not even a grandparent, aunt, or cousin. People say we're all connected somehow, we only have to look into our family history.

Sam wondered if it was too late to trace her heritage. She wouldn't even know where to begin because there was no one left to ask. Samantha never felt so alone.

24 - GRAVESIDE

Samantha pulled her hair back in a ponytail, getting through the morning ritual unwittingly. She managed to down a cup of black coffee. Sam found an appropriate black dress in the back of her closet and a black sweater to drape over her slender shoulders since it was still cool enough to see your breath in the early hours. She understood now why people wore black after death. She felt dark, smothering in her deepest secrets, alone.

The funeral Mass was an early morning service. She parked across the street from The Sacred Heart Catholic Church, a white building with two steeples, one higher than the other, invoking a modest country charm. The service went quickly, the priest going through the motions like he was playing out a familiar rerun.

A small group of people showed up, and even fewer shared Communion with her. The men carried the casket to the hearse, and everyone followed it, by car, to Baldwin Cemetery, up on the hill. The coffin was placed near the spot where her mother had been buried. The small group listened to the last prayer her father had chosen.

The Reverend was a large man, gray hair and ruddy faced. He wore his dark cassock and had a white stole with doves embroidered into the cloth strung around his neck. He performed the burial prayer, ending with a sign of the cross motioned into the air.

They all responded, "Amen." Then everyone returned to the cars, but Samantha lingered at the grave site.

The air remained damp, the sky was dreary and threatened to rain. Samantha made the sign of the cross in front of her mother's ebony marble gravestone, then read the inscription while touching her finger lightly over the etched letters. She felt the groves, each one sending waves of remorse to her heart. The words slipped from her lips in whispers *Loving wife and mother who died too soon.*

"Your mother was a lovely woman."

The voice startled her. Mr. Simpson stood behind her. Sam nodded but wasn't in the mood to chat with the man.

"I meant what I said the other day. If you have questions, just ask me."

Sam turned, her scrutiny met his. He had tears in his eyes and the face that had always looked sorrowful now looked even more so.

"I'm not sure what you're implying," she said.

Mr. Simpson shifted his weight from one foot to another. Was the old man ill? Had he known her mother, and what exactly did he want to say to her? The best course of action was to ask and be done with it.

"You knew my mother?"

He winced at that and nodded once.

Hmm. A sense of curiosity came over Sam.

"Okay, Mr. Simpson, tell me, exactly, what questions do you think I need to ask you?"

Mud was smeared his boot. He'd been kicking the dirt piled to the side, part of the upturned ground for Pop's grave. The old man's brow wrinkled, his overgrown gray eyebrows shot up in the air.

"Well, first off, your father told me you asked lots of questions about your mother's death. Of course, you know firsthand how he refused to speak of it. I didn't happen to agree with him on that subject. We argued about it years ago. Then we avoided each other until we stopped speaking entirely. I still think you have the right to know about things that you feel strongly about. I thought you might like answers, especially now with your father gone."

Alarms went off in her head. Of course, she wanted answers to questions Pop refused to hear. But what could this mossback tell her that her father wouldn't? Sam didn't trust Mr. Simpson. However, right now more than anything else, she wanted to hear what the old geezer had to say.

"Okay, here's question number one. Did my mother die in a car accident?"

The man nodded. "Yes, of course."

"Why wasn't it listed in any of the papers?"

Mr. Simpson scratched his head.

"It wasn't? Oh, that could have been for a number of reasons. Why the Chronicle wasn't even around back then, and the Northwoods rag sometimes missed a week here and there. And I seem to recall there had been a change of editor right about then. Yes, that's right. The old-timer who ran it had passed away, and the paper hired the new guy. No big conspiracy there. Everyone around here knew about the accident; it was a tragedy, a crying shame. Your poor mother, and that young man, they both died in the car."

"Young man, what young man?"

"Oh, this young fella. He was hanging around Brunswick Springs, acting as caretaker, trying to help with the land deal and all. Things were hyped up back then, lots of opinions flying around about who's in charge and who's eligible to be a tribe member. None of it was my business. I don't belong to any tribe, and I'm not originally from around these parts."

"Yes, I know." Sam heard the tinge of antagonism in her voice. She worried her tone might offend the old guy enough to shut him up, but turned out he wasn't the sensitive type.

"A group from the Swanton tribe wanted to buy the Springs, you know, and they needed funds for the down payment. I even helped, believe it or not. I was sorry for them all. Anyway, things all worked out."

"I know all that, but what does it have to do with my mother?"

"The young man, I think his name was Joseph. Well, he was coming around. Your mother, bless her soul, helped organize a few small informational gatherings and asked for donations to fund the cause. She wanted the Abenaki to have their land rights so they could protect it all."

"Yes, my mother was Abenaki you know, so protecting the place was dear to her heart," Sam said.

"If you ask my opinion, your mother was a little bit influenced by Francis," he said.

Sam's fists balled up, she could feel the anger rising to her face.

"Francis was a bit radical as I recall from what I've read. Are you suggesting my mother was a nut activist?"

"No, of course not." The old man shook his head and stepped back from the graveside, but continued his story. "Your mother was passionate about the cause, and she wanted to attain the rights peacefully. And you know, there was a big celebration the night she died."

Sam shook her head, surprised by this statement. She had never heard mention of a party that evening.

"They managed to get the land at Brunswick Springs, and everyone was happy. Lots of people were at the party to celebrate. Even the townies were invited, and a handful of us showed up, even the folks who had secretly been against it all. It was a beautiful night. They lit a campfire, right down there by the steps to the Springs, and we were all standing around, singing. It was a fun time. Then all of a sudden a fight broke out. Your father got angry with that Joseph guy. The kid threw a punch at your old man. Then your pop stormed off like a bat out of hell and left your mother behind. Later, when your father didn't return, that young man offered to take your mother home."

Mr. Simpson whimpered, pulled out a handkerchief and wiped his nose.

"Then the accident happened. Supposedly, the brake line was broken, and Joseph lost control at a turn in the road. The car landed down the embankment at the edge of the river. Your poor mother, she drowned. They both drowned. It was a sad time."

Her heartbeat throbbed, pulsing against the skin of her neck.

"Was it murder?" Sam asked.

"No, of course not. There wasn't any proof the line was cut

on purpose. It was an old jalopy is all. But don't you see, your father still felt guilty cause he left her there. She would have arrived safely home if he had waited for her. Your father blamed himself, at least that's how it looked from my view."

Samantha gasped. "Poor Pop."

"I tried to comfort him, honest I did."

Mr. Simpson looked down at his dirty boots. Sam had never seen a more dejected stance. She felt sorry for the down-hearted man, he had no one who cared about him with his wife dead and no genuine friends.

"The more I tried, the more he pushed me away. At the time I was new around here, still considered an outsider. Your dad was kind to me when I first came to town, and I thought we were friends of sorts. No one else trusted me. I guess not even your father. Oh well, I thought you ought to know, Samantha. The truth I mean. I know your father was too jittery about the whole ordeal to speak the truth of the matter."

Mr. Simpson turned and walked away, slow and deliberate.

Sam raised her arm as if to ask another question, or say something to comfort him, then decided to let the old man go. She had absorbed enough information for the day and had nothing to give. Besides, what did it matter, both her parents were dead now.

Was Pop to blame? No, she couldn't go there, and if anything, she felt bad he had taken on all the guilt. She had accused him of keeping things from her, but now she understood. Some things are best left unspoken. Knowing what happened to her mother hadn't changed a thing. But for her pop, thinking of that night and blaming himself, only smothered him with regret to the point where he couldn't live with himself.

Sam leaned against the tombstone, burst into tears, and cried for both her parents.

25 - ANOTHER MURDER

It was early Tuesday morning. Samantha returned to work, trying to appear under control, and ready to move ahead. The coffee pot was empty, so she made a fresh pot and waited for the steam to finish brewing the grounds. After the last of the huffing noises, Sam filled her mug and sat down at her desk. She wanted to delve back into the case and catch the son of a bitch who killed Jessica.

Samantha mulled over the evidence that filled the files someone had left on her desk. The medical report was there. Sam flipped it open, saw the bloated face of Jessica, and quickly closed it again. Had her mother's face been as swollen and distorted? Did Pop have to identify her? Yes, of course, he had. Sam breathed deep and opened the folder again.

Josh and Kevin walked into the office. Today they were wearing clunky boots, making more noise than usual as they headed for the counter to pour themselves coffee.

"How you doing?" Josh asked.

"I'm fine. I know that my pop was on borrowed time. I want to stay busy, you know, get back to work and try not to dwell on the things I can't change. A wise friend once told me that."

She smiled at Josh, and he grinned back with a nod.

"Glad you were paying attention. Okay then, I'm off. I'll

see you after rounds." Josh walked out.

Kevin sipped his coffee, leaning against the counter.

"How are you doing, Kevin?"

He gave her one of those fake smiles and Sam immediately knew he was troubled by something.

"Problems at home?" she asked.

He nodded. "I'd rather not talk about it, Sam."

"Okay." Sam picked up the next file and began to read. She shot him a look each time she turned a page. He stood there staring into space.

"Okay, Kevin, spill. What happened? Did your mother cause a commotion at home again?"

"Yes, she did. Nothing new there. But this time I left the house and took a ride down the road to the ATV club. You know, the place Josh hangs out. Well, he wasn't there. It seems they had another one of those outings, and I missed the boat. More accurately, I wasn't invited." Kevin scowled, his eyes two thin streaks.

"I'm sorry that happened, Kevin. I didn't know you joined the group. Good for you," she said.

Kevin scraped the toe of his boot against the wood floor; an annoying scratching sound made Sam shiver.

"Actually, I haven't joined yet." He gave a quick glance at Sam then looked at the floor again. "I've been mulling it over. Those excursions they go on sound like fun. But they go so deep into the woods, places I've never been before."

"What excursions? Where does the club go?"

Kevin's chest rose and fell, and he tightened his lips together.

"Well, the ATV club rides together in the woods. You know

that. But lately, I heard some of them talking. There's another exclusive game they play on the deeper trails Not the regular trails, these go far back into the woods, where no one can find them. They go there and meet up with other people and play the game." He huffed. "I wanted to go, too. Josh told me no. Said I didn't have enough experience. Like I haven't been riding my ATV all my life."

Sam watched Kevin's face turn red; his hands crimped tight making a fist, ready to punch someone.

"Kev, don't get upset. You know how Josh is, he likes to be the expert all the time. He needs to always have the upper hand."

Kevin nodded and seemed to calm down a bit.

"I know, you're right. It doesn't matter anyway. It's not like Josh is the only one I can ride with."

"That's right. Maybe someday you can teach me how to ride one of those vehicles."

Kevin's face perked up.

"That would be wonderful. Thanks, Sam. Well, I'd better start working." Kevin nodded and walked out to catch up with Josh.

Another crisis fixed, she thought.

After lunch, Zach stopped by the office to check in. "How are you doing?" he asked.

"I'm fine. And I'm ready to dig into the case. Let's figure

out the connection between Mr. Simpson and Mr. Hakes."

Zach shook his head. "Sam, I called another office south of Coos County and asked for backup. They ran the two names, and there's no connection. By no connection I mean, they asked the Marshals' Department, and they confirmed the men weren't associated. It's a coincidence that they ended up so close to each other while in their protection relocation. As a matter of fact, they believe Simpson's case is so old, that there's no threat against him any longer. The crime families Mr. Simpson knew are obsolete. Replaced by bigger, and worse criminals, I guess. If they even cared about his testimony, he would have been toast already."

"Good to know," Sam said.

Zach moved closer, pulled up a chair, and sat. He spoke softer.

"Yesterday I also talked to another county department. They called me, seems they are interested in this area, over here."

He unfolded a map, reached across the desk, and pointed to the spot.

"They're planning a stakeout in the woods, right there. I thought you and I might want to join the venture. If my suspicions are correct, whatever is going on in there might trace back to the role-playing game. It might reveal a connection or suggest a possible motive."

"Listen to what you're saying, Zach. We still don't have concrete evidence to suggest the games and Keaton Hakes are involved at all, nor do we have a reason to go searching the woods anywhere other than the Springs. You're pointing to New Hampshire."

Zach's phone rang. He answered, his eyes blinked as he listened. Then his pupils dilated and fixated straight ahead at a random object across the room. His concentration was intense, he closed his eyes for a split moment.

"We'll be there as quick as possible, thanks for calling."

"Well?" she said.

"They found another body. In the woods."

"At Brunswick Springs?"

"No," he pointed to the map again. "East of Lancaster, somewhere in the forest between Mount Cabot and The Horn, but it might be the same killer. How often do we have bodies found in the woods? Seems possible that it's connected after all."

Zach's mouth drew in, he looked stern, as if he carried the weight of the world. "Another death in the woods."

His words hit her, it could be connected. Was it same MO? That would mean another young woman dead. Her stomach became queasy, and for a moment Sam thought she might puke. She stood silently as the concept of another murder sunk into her mind. Her hands shook as she grabbed her jacket from the back of the chair. They both headed for the door without another word.

They drove toward the area just west of White Mountain National Forest, taking less than thirty minutes. Zach flew down the highway but slowed once they reached the smaller

Routes that meandered alongside the rolling hills.

Zach slowed to navigate the rural outskirts of Lancaster, better known as Lost Nation, taking care and watching out for animals that might jump into the road, a bear or dear family in route to eat the reborn grass of the fresh fields.

The colors of spring popped everywhere with so many vivid shades of green it was impossible to count. Spring pastels dotted the roadside, yellows, purples, and other arbitrary colors washed across the foothills and fields in between weather beaten red barns. The apple orchards were budding, the light pink blossoms looked almost like a white cloud as they traveled past the local farmer's organic crop of fruit.

The many gray arms of trees still in the early stages of spring mingled with the greener spruce in the heavier wooded areas. They followed Herman Savage Road until it ended.

There were other vehicles parked on the side of the road, Zach parked behind them. They got out of his trooper car and examined the map Zach unfolded on the vehicle's hood. After getting their bearings, they entered the wooded area and followed Whipple Brook.

Sam noticed the freshness in the air, earlier it had rained here, and now everything smelled earthy. Spring was often chilly up north, but this year New Hampshire was sharing a warmer trend in temperatures, and the rain hadn't lingered in puddles or on the leaves of the new vegetation, but instead, the moisture evaporated quickly making the breathable air muggy.

The forest was thick; the birds chirped all around. Sam listened and picked out the call of Fox Sparrows, twittering high notes, rising higher and then leveling back to a chirp, calling to each other. She stopped a moment and heard the scratching noise they made as their sturdy legs kicked away the leaves to find insects and fallen seeds on the ground to eat. Using the small pair of binoculars she always had tucked into her pack, Sam peered into the thicket.

Deeper into the forest near the stream's zigzagging edge, she spotted the round little bodies popping around on the ground, their bright reddish tail feathers giving them away, their faces more of a gray color and the beaks were a pale yellow. Samantha wished she had brought her log book along with her field glasses so she could document the birds' activity in case another ecology group was tracking the movement of fox sparrows in New Hampshire.

"What is it? Why did you stop?"

Samantha broke from her bird watching and realized Zach asked a question.

"Sorry. Birds." She pointed.

Zach smiled, turned and led them further into the woods, she followed his lead.

In approximately twenty minutes they found the others. Yellow tape outlined an area guarded by an officer who didn't wear a uniform but had a badge displayed on his chest. The sun caught the badge and a glint of silver reflected in Sam's vision for a split second.

Zach went to him, and they shook hands, then he ducked under the tape. Sam followed his lead; no one challenged her presence.

A person was kneeling close to the body, apparently the Medical Examiner. A husky woman in her late thirties, dusty brown hair and wearing a white suit and blue gloves.

Zach and Sam stopped and waited until the woman stood and gave instructions to the others around her, pointing her finger as she explained what she wanted to be done. Zach approached her and held out his hand.

"Hello, Doc."

"My goodness, they called you in for backup? I would have thought you have enough on your plate right now." Her voice was friendly and didn't seem frazzled by the dead woman's body on the ground in front of her.

Sam leaned and rested her hands on her knees as she tried to get a better look. Right off, she noticed the woman who was killed also had blonde hair like their victim. Also, she laid flat on the ground, face down. Sam lifted her head and turned her attentions to the conversation.

"Okay, boys. Let's turn her over," the doctor in charge said.

Sam stood behind Zach but still had a good viewpoint of the body. After they had counted to three, they turned the corpse. The face stared back at Sam. The dead woman's face was bloated, just like Jessica's had been when she found her.

A thick knot stuck in Sam's throat, and for a second she couldn't breathe. Heat rose to her face until she was burning hot. She closed her eyes for a second and counted to three. Then she opened her eyes and took a deep swallow of air, the scent of death and moldy leaves lingered in her nostrils, so she blew out and coughed.

Zach turned around. "Are you all right?"

She nodded. Zach turned his attention back to the body, and Sam heard him speaking with the doctor.

"Looks like the same MO," Zach said.

"I pray we don't have the beginnings of a serial killer in the area," the doctor said.

She heard gasps from the others standing around the scene, then soft private conversations were mumbled amongst themselves. Sam felt odd like she didn't belong there. She had no idea what she should do, or if there was anything at all, she could contribute. She folded her hands behind her back and listened to them talk while she waited.

She wondered who would be in charge of this investigation. This crime scene wasn't in Zach's area of control. She noticed another man walking toward them, approaching from across the other line of tape. He wore the blue booties over his boots which made his feet look gigantic.

Zach met up with him, and they shook hands. Sam distinctly heard the man say to him, "It's the same, isn't it?"

"Yes, definitely," Zach said. "So how do we work this? Share information?"

"Yes, of course." The man glared at Sam, she was standing there as if standing guard. His blue eyes did the quick up and down and calculated a rash judgment of her. His mouth remained a flat line, nonjudgmental, but his glaring eyes challenged her.

"Oh, I'm sorry," Zach said. "This is Ranger Sam Tremblay. Sam, this is Detective Richards."

"Nice to meet you," the man said as he bowed his blond head.

"Likewise," she said.

He was tall, the same height as Zach, but he didn't have the muscle strength of Zach. His hair was cropped short, like the military wear, and his clothes were basic jeans and a dark green varsity sweat-shirt he must have purloined from a buddy who had attended Notre Dame. His badge was hanging on a silver chain lanyard draping around his neck.

"Sam is working the case with me," Zach said.

Detective Richards brows rose, and his head tilted back a smidgen, but he quickly recovered from his surprise. "I didn't know the Rangers were now involved in law enforcement, let alone a murder case."

"This is a unique situation," Zach said. "Our victim was found at Brunswick Springs, part of the North East Kingdom. It's so remote up there, so we got the call. It's a state cooperation thing going on. So far, Sam has proved to be instrumental in the case."

Zach smiled and glanced her way.

"I bet she has," Detective Richards said.

He turned and walked toward the doctor. Zach followed.

Sam didn't appreciate the tone of voice and innuendo that Detective Richards implied, so she decided to stay put and listen from afar. She would get any details she missed from Zach later. Sam watched and didn't like Detective Richards' attitude.

26 - ODDBALL

Zach dropped Sam off and said he'd touch base with her the next morning. He was heading back to the New Hampshire offices, then the forensic lab, to see if he could push things along, maybe learn something insightful from the new evidence. They had already reasoned it was likely the same killer in both cases, but physical evidence was needed for proof. The new crime scene may have trace evidence to help identity the killer.

Sam watched Zach drive off. Her thoughts went to the new victim. Seeing the poor woman lying dead on the ground had shaken Sam up, and proved if she had doubt, how fragile life was, never to be returned once taken. All day she had managed to forget Pop for a while, until now. She stood in the parking area staring off at the road, watching while the stirred dust settled back to the ground, and knew she had to get her thoughts sorted.

"Sam, there you are. I was wondering what happened to you," Kevin said.

He walked toward her, smiling, but there was something wrong with him, she sensed it.

"Well, I'm here now. How are things? What's going on?"

Kevin oddly shrugged his right shoulder.

"Did you hurt your shoulder?"

"Naw, I'm fine. And nothing's going on, we've done all the daily chores. I've been chatting with the neighbors around here. Thankfully, no one has seen anything out of the ordinary. Everyone seems pretty content around here. A few more summer arrivals are unpacking, and someone called in to rent the pavilion for a weekend at the end of June. Plus they want an extra lean-to for the group. I penciled it all into the ledger. I think it's for a wedding."

Kevin smiled again, but this time he added a little laugh.

"Someday you'll get married up there," she said.

"Naw, I don't think that'll happen. My mother says no one will want me. I'm an oddball."

His words struck Sam to the core, what a horrible thing to say to anyone. She turned and faced him. Kevin wore a strange expression on his face, but she couldn't begin to guess his thoughts. She stepped closer and put her arm around him.

"She's wrong, Kevin. I have no idea why your mother would have said such a nasty thing to you, but she's wrong. You'll make a great husband someday."

His head was down, and his feet kicked the dirt on the road. Kevin didn't say anything, just pulled away and went to his old station wagon.

"He's leaving, I take it," Josh said.

He had come up behind her and Sam jerked at the sound of his voice.

"A little jumpy are we?" he said.

"Yes, I most definitely am. They found another body," Sam said.

"Where? When? No wonder you've been gone all day. Up at the Springs?"

Samantha gazed up and smiled at Josh.

"No, not there, thank goodness. That's the one and only good thing. Another woman's body was found in the forest near Lost Nation," she said.

"In New Hampshire? Good. You won't have to go there, nice break for you. Those woods are pretty dense, makes sense. Hell, anyone could drop a body in there, and no one would be the wiser for months, possibly even years. Did you get the details from Zach? How was the body found? Had she been there long?"

Josh was filled with questions, and the last thing Sam wanted was to answer them, but she felt obliged. Besides, talking things over might help discover something. Anything to help the investigation was welcomed at this point.

"I went there with Zach. I saw the body, she was just like the first victim we found. Blonde hair, left face down in the middle of nowhere, only a few scant leaves covering her remains. It was terrible," she said.

"I'm so sorry, Sam. Why the hell did Zach take you there?"

She heard the anger in his voice, his mouth was drawn up tight, and his arms stiff to his sides.

"Stop worrying so much, Josh. Take a breather. I wanted to go. I wanted to see if we could learn anything from the second body. We have to find who killed Jessica. And unfortunately, it seems like it's the same killer. We have to find this guy before he strikes again."

Josh nodded. "Sam, I understand. But this could get dangerous. I'm concerned."

She smiled at his sentiment and slipped her arm into his and pulled him along toward the office.

"Come on, let's get some coffee and talk this over. I need to look at what we have so far with fresh eyes."

Settled at her desk, she spread the fact sheets across the top, stood, and contemplated them in one swoop. Looking down, she sipped her coffee while sorting things in her head.

"Josh, do you know about the ATV games out in the woods?"

Josh jerked up his head. "Yes, but why do you want to know?"

"Well, we think it might be connected somehow."

"It's not," he said. "My group goes on those scavenger games. It's all about mixing up the fun but nothing dangerous or anything."

Sam turned away a moment and looked out the window. She saw his reflection in the glass. Josh was fidgeting at his desk like a nervous animal, causing Sam doubts. *No, Josh was her friend. He told her the truth.* If he said the group can't be involved in anything sinister, he meant it.

"Josh, tell me, do you know anything about *Real Horror Game*? It's a store down in Lancaster."

"I know what it is," he said. "Everyone goes there for the newest gaming supplies. And yes, I know about the *Real Horror Games* in the woods. It's all fun like I told you. We dress up in costumes and do role-playing while going from clue to clue on our ATVs. It's all fun, Sam, honest," Josh said.

"Do you play in the White Mountains?" she asked.

Samantha watched her friend's reflection and saw him rise from his chair. He grabbed his jacket from the back of his chair. She turned around.

"Where are you going?" she asked.

"Sorry, I just noticed what time it is," he said as he glanced at his phone. "I have to be somewhere, and I promised I wouldn't be late this time."

She wanted to ask him where he was heading but got a distinct impression that he wouldn't have answered.

"Okay. I'll see you tomorrow then." Sam watched Josh leave and remained staring out the window long after he drove off.

Thoughts of the two dead bodies consumed her mind; she kept seeing the pink sweaters and the distorted, pale, swollen faces. They hadn't even looked human, the poor girls. All their beautiful features morphed into a dead, bloated grimace.

Her stomach tossed like a wave, and she dry heaved for a moment. Wiping her mouth, she also tried to wipe away the look of their faces from her thoughts.

She slid open her desk drawer and pulled out a photo-graph of her mother. Mother had drowned too. *Had her beautiful mother's face been all bloated?* Tears gushed out, Samantha sat in her chair and dropped her head into her hands, wishing she could hide from the ugly truths in front of her. The girls were dead, in the woods. Her mother had died, in the woods. And Pop had warned her to never go into the woods.

Tears raced down her face. She wiped her nose and mouth with the back of her hand. Looking aimlessly across her desk, she grabbed a tissue from the box and mopped up more of her face. The more she told herself to stop crying, the more she cried. Her body shuddered in spasms as hopelessness overcame her; she was weak and tired.

27 - HANGOVER

Somehow she had managed to get home. Sam didn't remember the drive, or taking her clothes off, or drinking all the bottles of wine spread across the floor.

She was lying on her stomach, looking through the open curtain that separated the bedroom from the living area. The mattress comforted her with its softness molding around her body, and she didn't want to move. Sam watched the sunlight stream through the windows and across the living room. She tried counting the bottles strewn across the floor but stopped at three because her head ached. She had missed the sunrise, yet again.

An urgent need to pee and a strong desire for coffee motivated her to move, despite being afraid to raise her head. Today she'd have a massive headache not only because of the wine she drank the night before but also from the crying party.

Sam moved slowly and managed her way to the bathroom. Once relieved, she meandered into the kitchenette and made the coffee, careful not to make noise. While waiting for it to brew, she drank a glass of water. Amazingly, the water made her feel much better. She took a couple of aspirin, got dressed, and poured a coffee to go. *Enough of this pity shit*. She wanted to get to the office.

Samantha had a nagging sense that something obvious was staring her in the face, and somehow she had neglected to see it. The answer was at the tip of her tongue. She hoped that if she sat at her desk and took one more look, the information they needed would congeal into the one clue that would lead them to the killer.

Kevin's car was already in the parking area. Josh's car was nowhere to be seen. Sam opened the door to the office and smelled the fresh brew. Already she needed another cup.

"Hi there, Sam. I just made a fresh pot," Kevin said.

"Thank you, you're a hero today."

He looked at her odd. "What's wrong?" he said.

"Too much feeling sorry for myself last night, I guess. I'm a little sore, too. I walked deep into the woods yesterday, and this morning I woke with a sore leg muscle."

Kevin smiled and opened his desk drawer.

"I've got just the thing. Sit down and pull your pant leg up," Kevin ordered.

"Why? What's that?" she said.

"This here is my mother's special ointment. She makes it with the flowers and herbs we grow around the house. She's been using it for years, swears by it. I tried it myself a few times after Josh punched me in the shoulder too hard," Kevin said.

Sam sat down and pulled up her right pant leg.

"Only on this side," she said. "Aches like a son-of-a-bitch."

Kevin gaffed and unscrewed the lid on a glass jar. He passed it under Sam's nose.

"Oh, it smells like roses," Sam said. "What's in it?"

"I told you, it's mother's secret." Kevin smiled. "I can tell you just a bit, she uses a base of mineral oil and rose water to soften the stuff and makes it smell real nice, too. One of the active ingredients smells a bit sour when it's by itself. It stinks even more when it's dried, but you'd never know it after it's all mixed together. Wait, you'll see, it feels so good."

Kevin dipped his fingers into the jar and rubbed a dollop onto Sam's calf muscle. She felt immediate relief.

"Excellent," she said.

"That's it. You only need a dab," he said.

"Thank you, Kevin."

He screwed the jar lid back on and put it into his drawer.

"Well, I best get started. Looks like Josh is a no show today. Call me if you need anything else, Sam."

"Okay, Kevin. Thank you." After a second she called him back. "Wait, Kev, why is Josh a no show?"

"Aw, I'm not positive. I think he went out last night on his ATV. You know, with the new group he's hanging with. Not the group I want to join, though they haven't invited me yet. Anyhow, I'm not sure, but I think they, well, maybe they're doing things that aren't normal if you know what I mean."

Sam stiffened her face.

"No, I don't understand. Are they doing something illegal? Josh wouldn't be into something like that. Besides, how would you know if you've never gone with them?" she said.

Kevin's face flushed.

"Well, I overheard them talking one time. These guys aren't the ones who do the role-playing games, like the group I want to join. Role-playing sounds like fun, and I even practiced my zip line skills, so I'll be ready for anything. I set up a few lines in the woods.

"But I overheard this other group member talking to Josh the other day. He hangs with them sometimes, they meet down at White Mountain. They ride the trails deep into the forest and do drop offs. I'm not saying it's anything wrong, but why would they always do it in the dark of night if not? These new guys he's been riding with aren't into the games, so they're doing something else. I can never make out what they're talking about, exactly, ya know. But they look like tough guys, like thugs."

"Really?" Sam was confused, this didn't sound right.

Kevin nodded and left, smiling. He seemed to be in a great mood. Sam couldn't remember the last time he had looked so happy, years it seemed.

Back to work. Sam looked through the files and realized they never picked up the lab report from Doctor Howard. He might have something new by now, like the toxicology results. She grabbed her phone and texted Kevin that she was leaving for a bit. She left a voice message for Josh, as well, just in case he decided to show up.

She would head to the lab, first. Then, she wanted to meet up with Zach and ask his opinion regarding Josh's night trips into the forest. What the hell had Josh gotten himself into?

Samantha decided to make a detour on her way to the lab. She drove her Jeep back to the Springs, compelled to see the crime scene again. She sensed there was something in the woods that they'd missed. She trusted her instinct but questioned whether the sounds she had heard and the feeling of despair that she had experienced just before the first victim's body was found, made any sense. She embraced her sixth sense and followed where it took her, willing to keep an open mind.

Sam jogged into the woods at a good stride. The temperature wasn't as hot as the past few days thanks to the rain, which made the trek easier, so she arrived at the scene in less than twenty minutes. Her pulse racing and her body sweating, she looked around while catching her breath.

Sam pulled the thoughts in her head into focus, but still, not a single valid scenario played out of how the body could have gotten there.

If there had been ATV riders who dropped her body, then where were the tracks? Thinking of ATVs reminded her of Josh, she wondered where he was and why he hadn't called back, he usually did. She hoped nothing was wrong.

She paced around and searched beyond the immediate circle still taped off, looking for anything they hadn't noticed before. Bending her head up to gaze at the sky, she wondered if a body could have dropped from a plane. But no, she dismissed it because the coroner would have found evidence of a fall. She scanned the tree branches as they gently bent in the breeze, the wind rattled the leaves, and she caught a shiny glint. Lifting the yellow tape, she paced another thirty feet or so and stopped.

Her foot hit something hard. Brushing the ground around with her feet, she uncovered a wire lying on the ground. Camouflaged, it was hard to see the gray color blended in so well with the rocky dirt. It was a length of three-eights inch thick galvanized wire, a twist of threads just like the line they had stored in the shed. She looked up at the trees and spotted something silver. Could it be an anchor, attached to the large tree?

Walking over to the largest tree, she noticed the round hook and it was easy to presume the line was meant to go through a loop in the anchor bolt. It was a zip line. *This could have been how Jessica got here. She could have been zip-lining in the woods and fell when the line broke.* But no, she hadn't been dressed for that kind of thing, though Sam didn't know what one would wear if zip-lining. Also a line this thick wouldn't easily break. Her phone rang disrupting her thought process.

"Hi, Zach. I'm so glad you called. I've got things to tell you."

"Hold on," Zach said. "I need you to drop whatever you're doing and get over here right away."

"Okay, but where are you?"

"We're parked in the same spot as yesterday. Detective Richards received a tip that something big was happening tonight. He's working with the DEA on this one, they think it's drug related. And I think the dead girls might have something to do with Keaton's dodgy business after all."

Sam swallowed hard. She had forgotten all about the other business of Keaton Hakes, but obviously, it was on Zach's top priority. Maybe Hakes was involved somehow.

"I'll be there in thirty minutes. No, sorry, more like an hour," she added realizing she had to hike back to her car.

"What did you want to tell me?" he asked.

"It will keep until I get there."

Sam immediately turned around, she could finish checking the woods another time. She jogged back then drove, and headed for Lost Nation.

28 - STAKEOUT

Sam parked her Jeep behind a trooper vehicle she assumed was Zach's. She'd been wondering what to expect the entire trip.

Her head had begun to hurt again, so she had taken a couple more aspirins, drank a bottle of water, and stopped at a gas station on her way to relieve herself, knowing there'd be no facilities in the woods to pee. She didn't want to take chances with all the cops around, assuming there would be many. She had been right.

Samantha counted eight vehicles. She got out and pushed her long hair into a hat then grabbed a windbreaker and her backpack that held essential survival items. Whenever Sam ventured into unfamiliar areas, she made sure she had it with her, and this time she had her better field glasses with her. *A good scout is always prepared*. Sam headed for the woods and was met on the trail by Zach.

"Good timing," he said. "You said an hour, and here you are. We got a solid lead. It seems there'd been drop offs noticed by the DEA. They had someone on the inside who gave the all clear for tonight. So we're helping with a stakeout."

"Sounds exciting," she said.

Zach stopped and looked down at her face.

"You know, I probably shouldn't have called you. I'm

sorry, I thought you'd like to be part of this, but I forgot, you're not a cop."

"No, I'm a Ranger. Nothing but a nature lover, right?" she harrumphed. "Listen, I'm a big girl, and I've had basic training. I'm a good shot, and I promise not to get in the way. Maybe I can actually help," she said.

"Believe me, I don't doubt that for an instant. But now I realize how selfish it is of me to ask you to help, it could be dangerous, and that's not something you signed up for. I'm sorry I wasted your time driving here."

"Oh, no," she said. "I didn't come down here to be shooed back home. I'm willing and able."

Samantha stopped and faced him. Zach smiled.

"You know, Sam, I care for you. A lot."

He said the tender words while reaching to touch her cheek. His expression looked sincere as his finger traced her jawline, then he let his fingers drop away.

Sam didn't know how to respond, so she nodded. Internally she yelled out that she cared for him, too. But the words never slipped through her lips. Perhaps it was her deep-rooted self-preservation sabotaging her chance for a happy ending. She wanted to kick herself.

Too late, Zach turned and led the way into the woods. They walked on the path a bit, then Zach veered off.

"We're to follow the green ties, see here." He pointed.

She nodded and followed him. They walked for a mile and came upon a flat area circled with huge boulders. A couple of men walked out from behind the stones into the open, one of them was Detective Richards, his cocky gait gave him away.

"Really, Zach? You brought in a Ranger to help with our

stakeout," Richards said.

Sam noticed he was twitching, reaching his hand down, and scratching his leg.

"She knows the forest better than most," Zach said.

"Yes, that's all well and good except this isn't Vermont."

"You know, Detective Richards, the woods here in New Hampshire are pretty much the same as those in Vermont," she said.

"Except, of course, here in New Hampshire a detective is running around in the forest, covered with poison ivy."

Samantha held back her laughter and glared down at his legs. The two men followed her stare.

Detective Richards wasn't the only one enthusiastic because of the better turn in the weather, they all wore camping shorts and short sleeves. However, he was the only one with exposed arms and legs spotted with the telltale signs of poison ivy. His skin was red and raw in blotches, and small blisters were already beginning to appear, popping from his skin in a random pattern.

"Dammit," Richards said.

"Leaves of three, let it be. Berries white, run in fright. Hairy vine, no friend of mine," she chanted. "No, no. Don't scratch, whatever you do, detective. The Urushiol from the plant is toxic, and the oil can easily rub onto other surfaces, making it much worse. Let me clean your arms and legs with an alcohol wash and then we can dab on calamine lotion to keep it from itching."

Sam lowered her pack to the ground and pulled out alcohol wipes from her first aid kit. She put on latex gloves then gently wiped the detective's arms and legs. The other officer, whose name remained unknown to Sam, mumbled a crude comment mentioning the detective's leg and how she was in the right vicinity for certain other services.

"Are we ten years old today," she said.

Sam returned her attention to the task and blocked him out, but in her peripheral vision noticed Zach, who pushed the other guy away with a shove. She smiled.

While applying the lotion, Sam listened to the detective and Zach discuss the plan. The first aid process was completed in less than ten minutes. Sam gathered the rubbish, placed it in a plastic baggy, and threw it into her pack.

"There, all finished," she said.

Zach held out his arm to help her up.

"Thank you," Detective Richards said as he pulled away and slipped on a thin jacket with long-sleeves.

"I guess it's good luck that we have a Ranger with us today." The detective winked at her, nodded to them, then went back to his position.

Zach cupped Samantha's elbow and directed her toward a large boulder on the other side. His unexpected hold sent a tingling sensation up her arm.

Flustered, Sam allowed him to lead her to their hiding spot, but she was embarrassed by her blatant reaction to his touch. *Could she ever get over him?* Once hidden behind the boulder, he let go then turned toward her. A ray of sun caught his hazel eyes, and a brief sparkle reflected there, taking her breath away. She realized he was speaking to her, so she nodded as if she'd been paying attention.

"When the helicopter lands we'll rush the pilot first, cut the engine as quickly as possible, then we'll chase whoever flees and try to arrest as many as we can catch."

"How many people do you think there will be?" she asked.

"At least two in the copter, but we're uncertain how many are meeting them for the drop-off." Zach pointed to the open area. "See over there, that's the trail they'll use to get here. It looks like there will be at least two ATVs, maybe more."

Sam grabbed his sleeve.

"Zach I have to tell you something about Josh. I think he might be involved. Kevin let it slip that he's been coming to this area with a new group he's been hanging out with. They ride these trails."

"Do you think he's involved? You know him better than I do," Zach said.

"I don't want to believe he could, and a week ago I would have said no way in hell, but recently I've noticed things. His behavior has changed, he's been moody." she said.

Zach gave her a thoughtful expression.

"Well, let's see who shows up before we make assumptions. There are lots of reasons for a man to be moody. Josh doesn't seem the type to be involved with drugs. I don't jump to conclusions or blame anyone until it's proved."

"Hmm. Seems you blamed Hakes right off."

"That's not the same thing at all. Keaton Hakes is guilty, we just get our evidence kicked out for stupid reasons."

Sam took a Clif Bar from her bag, tore it in half, and they both nibbled it along with a few almonds. They waited together in silence. Everyone on the team lay in wait as the late afternoon sun turned to dusk.

A noise stirred them to alertness. Off in the distance, they could hear the hum of the all-terrain vehicles, though it was hard to distinguish how many, it was certainly more than one.

Zach pulled out his Glock.

Samantha watched how he crouched, ready for action.

"Can I have one of those," she whispered.

Zach lipped, "no."

Then a roaring noise from the sky flew in closer, the helicopter was on its way. Things happened fast. The copter hovered and landed in the center of the circle of stones. The blades swept the air across the trees like a storm had hit with gale winds. Dried grass and debris was swept up in the waves of air, and particles stung her eyes. Blinded for a moment, her eyes smarted, the dirt scratched her eyeballs. Sam rubbed them and turned away from the landing area for a second, to clear her eyes. She turned back again, squinted, and wished she had carried goggles in her bag.

One man jumped from the helicopter, but the pilot remained inside with the vehicle still operating. There was no relief from the spinning blades. Sam knew the officers were instructed to rush as soon as possible, but the ATVs weren't there yet. If they intercepted now, they might lose the chance to get the perpetrators driving the all-terrain vehicles. The problem soon disappeared, and things unfolded in front of her.

Lights pierced through the darkness as two ATVs approached the circle. Four men got off the vehicles, carrying bags, jogging toward the copter. Things went berserk, and the troopers and DEA guys rushed out from behind the rocks and surprised the culprits.

The pilot panicked and tried to take off, the helicopter rising up a few feet. One of the team members jumped the pilot and took control. The copter returned to the ground, and the turboshaft engine was cut. The noise and the wind faded, and now Sam could hear other sounds. Men punching men. Calls out into the dark, freeze, stop, hands up.

They managed to round up everyone without a shot being fired. Sam stood by and watched from behind their assigned boulder, away from all the danger. Her back was toward the woods.

A sudden flash of light rocketed from behind her. Another ATV vehicle was approaching from a different path, unaware of what was happening to his buddies. Sam turned to see, the light blinded her. She raised her arms and covered her face with her hands. The vehicle stopped a few yards away from the spot where she stood.

29 - FIGHTING FIRE

The engine hummed, and a familiar voice called out to her.

"What the hell are you doing here, Sam?"

It was Josh. *Shit!* Without thinking she ran toward him and grabbed his hand.

"Come here," she demanded. "I need to talk with you, now."

Josh lifted the visor of his helmet, his mouth hung open, but his eyes traveled from her face to the action going on behind them. Sam saw the spark of discovery—he understood what was happening. Josh revved the engine and turned to leave.

"No, stop," she called out.

Without hesitation, Sam jumped onto the vehicle as it began to move, and pulled on his arm. Josh slowed down, twisted his head back and screamed something to her. Sam couldn't hear him because of his helmet but knew he wanted her to stop yanking so he could take off. She wasn't going to let him flee. Sam defiantly shook her head and yanked on his arm more.

The vehicle was going downhill and swerved with each of her tugs, as they continued down the trail. Relentlessly, she pulled Josh's arm, trying to force him to stop. The vehicle veered for another twenty feet or more until the ATV collided with a large tree.

Sam's head slammed into Josh, he hit the tree with his, and she thanked God he was wearing a helmet. There was a loud bang seconds after the crash, sounding like the pop of a gun, the noise reverberated in her ears. Sam reached under Josh's armpit with one arm and turned the key off while holding her ear with the other hand. The machine died with a sick noise and a final jerk.

Sam smelled gas fumes. She looked at Josh and watched his mouth moving, yelling at her, but she couldn't hear him. She felt disconnected from reality as if a temporary barrier was placed between herself and what was happening. Josh shoved her off the seat and Sam fell hard to the ground.

She looked up and saw Zach run over toward them. He knocked Josh off the vehicle and onto the ground. Zach pulled out cuffs and slapped them onto Josh's wrists. Then he turned toward Sam.

"Zach, hurry, get her away from here," Josh yelled. "The battery. It exploded and leaked sulfuric acid all over."

Josh jerked his head toward the vehicle, they all saw the flame creeping up from underneath the case covers that shielded the motor.

"Get her out of here. It's burning, and it's gonna explode the gas tank."

Josh got off the ground and started to run. Sam stood and ran with Zach up the hill, slipping and pulling each other forward to get away. A few seconds later a loud bang went off, and Josh's vehicle was in flames.

They plopped down on the ground and watched it burn.

"Thanks for the warning," Zach said.

"No problem." Josh dropped his head. "Can someone take this helmet off?"

Samantha obliged and then sat next to him.

"Jesus. The battery blew up. I checked the cell before I charged it the other day. I'm so sorry," Josh said.

The heat of the blazing fire burned against her skin. Her clothes felt like they were hot enough to burst into flames. She smelled the scorched oil and gas fumes, and the dark black smoke burned her nostrils. She looked at Josh. There were holes on his jacket where the acid must have sprayed.

"I'm sorry I made you crash," she said.

"So, why did you?"

Ignoring Josh, Sam was more concerned about the fire, it grew hotter by the second, and this wasn't a good place for a fire. Anger surged through her veins. *How could she have been so stupid?* It was her fault the vehicle hit the tree, and now the forest was in jeopardy.

"Are you okay?" Zach asked.

Sam was startled back to life.

"No, I'm not." She realized tears dripped down her face. "We have to call in for help before we have a disaster here. It's been warmer than usual, we can't afford a forest fire."

Detective Richards slid down the hill and bent to help her up.

"Let's all get back a bit," Richards said. "I called the fire warden right away. Don't worry, Sam, water is on its way. They're air lifting it. Meanwhile, a few of the guys ran back to the trucks, we've got a few Clean Agent extinguishers."

"Thank you," she said.

They climbed to the top of the hill to stand away. Sam was too angry to speak and didn't know what to say. Disappointed in Josh, she wondered how involved he was in this sham. What else had he done to mess up his life? All these years she thought he was a good guy, helping her stay sane. All along was he playing her?

She wondered if the men captured were responsible for the girls' deaths. *No.* Something in the back of her head answered her question. Her gut told her this band of hoodlums had nothing to do with the murder. They were too loud. The killer had been sneaky, had planned every detail, and left no clues.

No doubt, this would be considered a good bust. Breaking apart Keaton Hake's drug smuggling ring was a major accomplishment. Aside from the fire, everything went smooth. But she didn't believe any of the arrested men wasted their time killing young blonde girls.

The murders were deliberate creepy acts and not something motivated by money. The murderer had another agenda. One thing remained clear to Sam, there was a serial killer out there, and they had only dead ends to follow.

The officers dragged the arrested offenders back to the road, officially read them their rights, and drove them away in vans. The remaining DEA officers and Troopers hauled the fire extinguishers up the mountain trail to put out the fire.

Sam stayed with the men and took the first turn at fighting the fire. Stepping up to the flame, she held the weighty extinguisher close to her body and pointed the nozzle at the base of the flame. Her face burned from the heat but thankfully most of the smoke blew in the other direction with the wind. She fanned the spray back and forth and reduced the fire quickly.

They took turns and let the halogenated agent do the work it was intended to do. The argonite extinguisher was designed specifically for fires set by fuel, designed to be used for vehicle accidents. There would be no residue from the active ingredient left behind since it harmlessly evaporated.

The fire was contained by the time a helicopter arrived. The copter hovered a bit, then dropped its water load. Cold water splashed from the heavens onto the bull's eye and surrounding area, and the fire went completely dead. Two men had offered to stay behind to wait for the forensic fire team. They would investigate the cause and file the reports, and ensure no embers remained to possibly re-ignite.

Sam was relieved that no significant damage was done to the forest. Only a tree was scorched. The saddest part was the damage done to the ground from the fuel seepage, but at least that was contained. They gathered the junk and headed back to the vehicles.

As they trudged down the trail one last time, the troopers discussed the case. They called out, back and forth, their ideas of how best to serve up the evidence and the best way to present the case. One would think they wanted to be the lawyers. But this group thrived on the action and the rush of the siege.

Samantha had nothing to contribute to the conversation. She rubbed her itchy eyes and blew smoke from her nose into a tissue. Sam concentrated on what would happen to Josh. Even though he was arrested like the others, she wondered if he actually had anything to do with the group. Her gut had told her something was off with him lately. Mood swings and more sarcastic than normal, still her suspicions could have meant anything.

Once they made it to the country road, Samantha found Zach.

"Are you okay," he asked.

"Yes. I'm heading back. I need a good clean up and rest."

"Okay, then. Thank you, Sam. It'll be better next time, I promise."

He smiled. His hands rested on her shoulders, and it seemed as if he didn't want to let go of her. He glanced over his shoulder taking note of the other men. Then he looked into her eyes and gave her a little shake before letting go of his hold.

"Bye," he said.

She turned around and disappeared without another word, leaving the police to finish their work. Sam wondered what Zach meant by next time. Did he plan on asking her to more crime scenes or did he mean something more attractive, like a date? She shook those thoughts away. It was too painful to think of what could be, all fantasy.

30 – DRIVING IN THE DARK

D riving home Sam thought of Josh and about what Kevin had said to her. She wondered if there was more he knew but was sparing her the more worrisome details. She decided to swing by his house and speak with him before going home. It was a bit late, but she thought he'd still be awake watching the late show that he loved so much.

Kevin lived with his mother on a small, family farm, that had been passed down for decades. His father died or left them when he was still young. Sam never got the details and never asked. She didn't want to pry. She understood how hurtful questions like that could be, and Kevin had always been a shy and quiet soul.

His mother was a strange bird. As Sam recalled, she always wore a mean face, spoke harshly to everyone, especially to Kevin. Sam used to feel sorry for him when they were kids. She knew he was embarrassed whenever she had come to a school function. By the time they reached high school, his mother had stopped coming around the school activities, a saving grace for Kevin, she had thought.

Samantha knew what it was like to be embarrassed by a parent, she had often felt humiliated when Pop showed up to places, drunk as a skunk. People put up with him, but no one knew of his temper or how Pop had hit her, except Zach. He knew because she had told him. She actually hadn't minded the slap so much, at least it was honest and up front, and less painful than the emotional scars.

She recalled the comfort she felt, and the relief, the day she had told Zach everything that happened between her and her father. Zach explained that like many alcoholics, every time he quit and then drank again, he picked up right where he had left off. No slow crawl back into a bad habit, but instead directly into a full-blown addict, and Pop had kept down the dark path alone, all the way to the end.

Tears wet her eyes and her vision blurred. Sam brushed them away with her fist. She wiped her nose with her sleeve and concentrated on the dark road ahead.

Sam drove down the driveway of Kevin's family farm. It was set back quite a distance from the road, nothing visible until you got deep into the property. One couldn't find a more isolated existence, and Sam wondered if that was part of the reason his mother was so odd, socially. Sam parked in front and got out of her Jeep. No traffic could be heard, no lights from the road visible.

An owl hooted nearby, it sounded like it came from the woods behind the house. No lights were on, and Sam wondered if they were all in bed, then remembered Kevin had said that he watched TV in a room situated in the back of the house, said he liked gazing out of the windows into the woods while the commercials ran.

Sam walked up to the door and rang the bell. Ting-a-ling. It was one of those old fashioned school bells. They cleverly hung it near the door to use instead of installing the standard buzzer type doorbell. His mother invented things they needed rather than purchasing them the usual way. Sam had thought it was because they were poor and couldn't afford much. Perhaps she was wrong, and it was because the woman had a creative soul. After all, she did make a great rug.

The lotion Kevin shared with her the other day worked well to numb her pain. What did he say? She made it from herbs growing around the house. Samantha looked around and noticed a lot of plants. She couldn't see the color of them in the night's light, but they seemed to have blooms and she pictured in her mind a colorful landscape.

Sam rang the bell again and waited a few more minutes, but no one answered. From the corner of her eyes, she thought she saw someone at the window, the curtain moved. Then she looked again, but no one was there.

She would have to wait and speak with Kevin in the morning. Sam turned back to her Jeep, got in and drove away.

A strange concern overcame her. Sam's arm tingled as if snake venom was running through her blood. She pulled to the side of the road and waited a moment for her anxiety to leave. Counting to herself, she breathed slowly. Something was wrong, something was off. Sam had stumbled on to something, but she had no idea what that something was. A few minutes later, she felt normal again and continued on her way home.

The alarm buzzed. The annoying clock barely escaped getting thrown across the room. Sam got up, washed and dressed while only half awake. She went to the Riverside Market and picked up a steaming cup of strong coffee, just the way she liked it. Then she headed to Maidstone Lake for her morning pastime, to watch the sunrise appear from her favorite spot.

Samantha sat at the picnic table sipping her coffee, watching the sunrise, thinking of her Mother and Pop. Sam hoped they were together again, happy.

She hated to admit it, but part of her was relieved Pop was gone. She had watched him suffer for years, withering away right in front of her, and there had been nothing she could do for him. Pop refused to see what he had become, a drunk. Samantha understood now that he was angry with himself for losing his temper with her. But more than that, her father was angry with himself, blamed himself, for her mother's death. His guilt had gone beyond the tolerable.

She hoped he was at peace now, for assuredly Mother would forgive him for the argument that night; it was so long ago.

Breathing in the air, the forest fragrance filled her lungs. She was alert again with a new appreciation for life.

Sam watched the loons swimming away, going back to hide in their nests situated near the edge on the other side of the lake. This loon couple had yodeled their call weeks ago, reclaiming the territory where they had built a nest last year. The pair put on a great show and caught more than their fair share of fish. Good for them, she thought. Samantha must have done some good by educating the locals about keeping away from the nests, especially with their boats.

Loons had heavier bones than most other birds which made them great divers for fish. But the extra weight also made it more difficult for them to take off from below, and they depended on the lake to get airborne, needing the long take off area. If a loon made the mistake of landing someplace without a proper area to take off, they would be trapped and could die. Sam knew this place was well-suited for the loons just like it suited herself.

Sam took another sip of coffee. It was time to figure out a human problem. In the back of her mind, she had worried about Kevin not being at home last night. Maybe Josh had called him to bail him out? Why hadn't she thought of that before, of course, who else would Josh call?

Then again, Sam wasn't current on her friend's society as of late. She thought most of his free time was spent with the tribe in Swanton, and he probably didn't want them to know he was arrested. But she could be wrong, just like everything else concerning Josh. No, she couldn't believe he'd done anything wrong. Not Josh, not her friend.

Sam wanted answers. She decided to drive up to Coo County and speak directly with Josh. She had never visited anyone in jail before and didn't know the procedure, but hopefully, they'd let her visit him. With a sketch of a plan in her head, Sam went back to the office to leave a note.

Samantha went to the cabin only to find Kevin hadn't shown up to work. This only made her more confident that Josh had indeed called Kevin for help. She jotted a note telling where she was heading just in case someone showed up, pegged it on the door, and locked up. She drove north to the

Coos County Corrections Department facility that was a forty minute drive on Route 3. Although last night they had apprehended the group just east of Lancaster, she had heard the DEA officers say that the arrested men were being sent to the county's facility to hold until pre-trial.

31 - CONFESSIONS

The radio played while she drove which helped to clear her head, and she reached the facility in what seemed like no time at all. Sam thought perhaps she wasn't going to be allowed in and began questioning her judgment in coming here. She should turn around and go back to take care of her work.

Instead, she walked up to the reception guard and explained who she wanted to see and was instructed to wait. She worried that Josh might not even want to see her after she practically killed them and caused his accident. *Maybe he was hurt? No, he seemed fine last night.*

"Excuse me, are you Samantha Tremblay?" an officer asked.

"Yes." Sam swallowed her angst.

"Please, follow me."

Sam was brought into a bright room painted white on the upper half of the wall and baby blue on the lower half. The opposite wall had glass windows, and shiny stainless steel stools were fastened to the floor, one stool directly in front of each framed window. The other side was much the same. There were dark blue phone boxes hung on the lower section of wall, the earpieces were jet black. One for each window. Sam noticed Josh being brought in on the other side. She stood and waited to see which window he took then met him at the glass.

He looked red in the face, his eyes swollen as if he had been crying. But Josh never cried. It must have been from all the smoke the previous night, it had smarted his eyes. Or maybe someone punched him in the face last night.

His hair was combed back, still longer than usual and she wondered why he had been changing his look. She had noticed in the last few weeks that he wasn't grooming himself in his usual style. She wondered if he was letting himself go, or did he just want a more natural look? She had thought to ask him about it, *why hadn't she?*

Josh stared into Sam's eyes. His were wet. Yes, they were tinged with tears that he was refusing to let go.

She picked up the phone, and slowly brought the receiver to her ear.

"Are you all right?" she asked.

Josh nodded. "What are you doing here, Sam?"

"Why are you here, Josh? What were you doing up there on the mountain last night?"

"I wasn't there for the reasons you and your Trooper boyfriend think."

His voice sounded angry, and his eyes formed a single line so tight that Sam could scarcely see his warm brown eyes.

"First off, Zach's not my boyfriend. You know that," she said.

"Do I?" Josh snapped.

"Yes, you should. And don't change the subject. It's irrelevant. Do you realize the DEA had been planning that bust for a while, and you just happened to walk right into it?"

"How would I know? I have no idea what's going on. I was just there joy riding. I was supposed to meet up with a couple of new friends, but I got there early, so I took a drive. That's all there is to it. And don't give me that look. I don't care if you believe me anymore. I'll be out of here as soon as they check up on my story. Then the first thing I plan to do is quit my miserable job."

Josh's eyes opened wide now, glaring at her. If looks could kill, she would have been dead on the floor. Sam imagined her body melting through the tile crevices. His explanation sounded genuine, and she wanted to believe him. They'd been friends for so long, how could she have doubted him so quickly, she should have believed in him right off. Josh had never lied to her before so why would she think he was now?

"I'm sorry, Josh. It's just that you were on an ATV like the others, and showed up at the exact same time. I thought maybe you were into something new, something dangerous. I know how bored you get."

"Are you kidding me?" Josh put the receiver down a moment, hung his head, then he looked up at her again. "After all we've been through together, you think that little of me? That I would do something illegal because I'm bored." Josh shrugged his head away and stared at the floor.

He was right, and Sam was an ass. Seeing him this morning made her realize he never could be a part of a drug organization. He liked to have fun, but never indulged in drugs, though he did get drunk once in a while.

"Explain to me, please. How did you get that sore eye the other day? What are you into?" she asked.

He turned his head away again, and for a moment Sam

thought he was going to throw the phone's receiver at the window. But he kept his cool and turned back to speak.

"Okay, you asked, so I'll tell you. Kevin punched me."

Sam pulled her head back and drew in a deep breath.

"That's right," Josh continued. "Good, little ole' Kevin. He was hanging out with our ATV club, making a nuisance of himself, as usual. I told him to stop, and he slugged me without warning. That little mouse of yours has a mean streak."

"Did you call Kevin to come bail you out?" Sam asked.

"Why in the hell would I call him? I know you think we're friends and all, but in truth, we haven't been on good terms for years. But of course, you wouldn't know. Too busy licking your own wounds. Too caught up in your solitude and the fight to save the woods to notice us, imperfect humans."

Josh's words stung Samantha. She never realized he felt this way. She thought they had understood each other, but apparently, she misjudged everyone and everything.

"I'm sorry, Josh." She blurted the words.

Josh closed his eyes, breathed hard, and then put the receiver to his ear again.

"It's all right, Sam. I understand why you do what you do. Dealing with the attitude others dish at us is hard. People like you and me, we struggle to find our identity. God, we've been brainwashed to hide our true being, our heritage. You see, that's kind of what I've been attempting to straighten out with my new friends. The new group I'm hanging with are from a tribe. I thought maybe I could get back to my roots. You know, find my Native American heritage and reclaim my Abenaki identity. All the years in school . . . They all took that away from us. No more. I had hoped I'd be able to help you reclaim your lineage, too. I wanted to introduce you to the group once I got a handle on it all." Josh smirked. "I guess I was only fooling myself. Looks like we're both a couple of misfits."

"Misfits?" she repeated.

"Yeah, misfits. Why do you think your boyfriend dropped you like a hot potato years ago. Leaving without so much as an explanation. I mean, how could he have explained it, right? Zach is too polite to tell you that your native blood wasn't good enough for him."

"No, you're wrong, Josh, Zach isn't like that."

"Sure. And I'm the Easter bunny."

Josh looked at Samantha, and something softened. He smiled, his eyes warmed, and invited the rapport they had always shared to return, if just for the moment.

"You know, Sam, I've always loved you. I dream that someday my company will be enough for you, but I guess not. I realize now I don't have a shot in hell. But that's okay. At least I got to tell you my mind. I feel better now that the truth is out there. Now you know I love you. They'll let me out of this hell-hole in a few hours, but I won't be returning to Stratford. I've made my decision. I'll be staying with my new tribe."

"Where are you—"

Josh didn't bother listening to her question. He hung up the receiver and walked away as if he hadn't a care in the world. Sam watched him leave the room and felt a warm tear run down her cheek. She sat there frozen, wondering how she could have been blind to so much around her, for so long, and to so many.

Josh's heartfelt words jolted Samantha, and now she questioned all the truths she thought were real—maybe she had only fabricated things in her mind. Josh said he was in love with her, had been for a long time, and she hadn't even seen the slightest hint nor recognized his deep feelings, clueless of his intentions. How could she have been so blind? What a horrible person she must be, to be so close to people, and yet so far away.

Sam had never given the possibility a second thought—of the two of them—together. Even now, the idea seemed absurd to her, how could Josh even consider it? He was like a brother to her. Thinking back at his recent behavior and mood changes, Sam could see it was probably because he was jealous of the time she spent with Zach. *Of course, that was it.* Josh knew first-hand how madly in love she had been with Zach in high school. Sam was a heel. What kind of a friend is so careless of another friend's affections?

She walked back to the parking lot in a daze, trying to think of a way she could salvage her long friendship with Josh. But knowing now his true intentions, Sam knew the best course of action was to let him go. Give her friend the space he needed to get his thoughts together and find his identity as he had plainly stated. She knew first-hand how difficult it was to be so close to a person whom you loved and yet unable to do anything about it. You can't make someone feel something.

Samantha placed her hands on her face, rubbed her forehead, and tried to regain her decorum at least long enough to be able to drive back to the office. Her heart was spent. It was painful, coming to terms with her deficiencies, she was a horrible daughter and a selfish friend. She leaned against her Jeep and cried, letting it out slowly, but soon it was too much to hold in. The built up tension broke free, and she cried until she physically shook from her sobs. She didn't know how long she stood there weeping, but suddenly a hand touched her shoulder. She froze. Swallowed. Blinked her eyes.

"Are you all right?"

The sound of the familiar voice didn't put her at ease. The exact opposite reaction happened, sending pulses of terror through her veins. She didn't want to turn around and face him.

"Hi, Kevin." She sniffed and wiped her nose with her shirt cuff. "Yes, I'm fine. Just heading back to the office. I needed to blow off tension. First, you know."

Sam remained in place, unable to bear looking at Kevin right now.

"I saw your note on the door and came straight away. Is there something I can do to help? Why are we here, Sam? Did they catch the killer?"

Kevin seemed to be talking faster than usual as if nervous. She turned to face him, Sam wanted to see his expression, afraid of missing something important going on with one of her friends.

Kevin looked pretty much the same, the innocent misunderstood miscreant, his thin body slumped over with self-doubt. But when she looked closer into his eyes—for a split second she thought she spotted a gleam—some sort of givea-way he wasn't as he appeared. She immediately dismissed her thought, and chastised herself, recalling how she had doubted Josh and now their friendship was in ruins. How could she have harsh thoughts of Kevin? She recalled how she hadn't liked the way she thought of him so negatively before. *Be honest with him, direct and to the point, instead of assuming unfounded bullshit.*

"Kevin, where were you last night? I went to your house, but no one answered the door."

Kevin shuffled his feet and kicked at the tarred pavement.

"My mother said you came by. I'm sorry, Sam, I was passed out cold. I haven't been feeling well, you know. Must have caught something from working in the rain the other day. Anyway, I took one of those nighttime medicines and was zonked. My mother never answers the door at night. She's terrified of strangers you know."

"Oh, I'm sorry." Her face flushed. "Of course. I should have realized it was too late to drop by. I didn't mean to upset anyone. Please accept my apology and tell your mother I'm sorry. I've been messing things up lately," she said.

"Don't worry. It's' all good. I'll meet you back at the office then."

"Okay, Kevin. See you there."

Sam got into her Jeep, and looked over her shoulder, watching Kevin walk away. Something was off, and her instinct was screaming for her to stay away from him, but her reason refused to listen. It was time for her to open herself up, not shut down. She had a job to do. Sam drove thirty miles back to Maidstone, determined to get work done and forget everything that happened this morning.

The recent events had taken their toll on her emotionally. First, her father's heart attack then his death and later finding out what actually happened to her mother which in the end, only gave her more questions without answers Add to those traumas running into Zach again after all these years. And now, losing her life-long best friend's confidence. It was too much for her to deal with, it all hurt too much.

She drove with the radio blaring, trying to block out her thoughts.

32 - SENSE OF MACABRE

Later in the afternoon, Sam was stiff after hours of sitting behind her desk. She decided to stretch her legs and connect with nature again. She patrolled one of the trails that led deep into the forest. It was a familiar path. The breeze flowed between the trees and swooshed a beautiful white noise which mesmerized her. The soothing sway of branches in the wind helped Samantha feel more like herself again. The familiar pine scent soothed her spirit. A family of rabbits scurried across her path; she stood still and watched until they were hiding behind the foliage again. Everything seemed peaceful until suddenly that same sensation of deep sadness engulfed her.

The sky darkened, the chatter of the woods was replaced with a low drumming sound. The warm breeze turned chilly, flying her hair back, and stinging her face with a sudden cold. It was like the other day when she found Jessica's body up at the Spring.

An intense fear slithered down her back and rushed through her body, catching her breath. Surrounded by a shroud of sadness, she was smothered with terror. Goose-bumps pilled her arms, and she flung her hands up to rub them away. Then a screech blared so loudly, she threw her hands up to protect her ears.

Sam spun in a circle, looking, watching for something or someone. She lost her balance and swayed. Forcing herself to straighten up, she became acutely aware that she was on her own. She had to keep her wits about her. The sound ended as quickly as it began. Samantha suspected that there would be another body nearby, just like last time she heard that sound and felt that eeriness. What else could be the reason for the repeat performance and more importantly, what did it mean? Was the spirit world calling her just like in the old tales about the lodges, compelling her to do something for these poor dead girls?

Swallowing hard, she moved ahead taking measured steps. Scanning the area right then left, she searched for anything that looked wrong. Sam hoped her survival instinct would lead her to wherever she was supposed to go if that were indeed why she heard the sounds and sensed the macabre.

A noise. Stopping, Samantha heard a whimper to her right. Sam quickened her step and turned off the trail, into the woods. After ten yards or so, she found her.

A body lay on the ground, covered with leaves, only this time the pile moved. The girl was alive. Rushing to her side, Sam knelt on the ground and brushed the leaves away. Sam helped the girl turn over onto her back. The girl coughed and choked for a moment, gasping for air.

"There, there," Sam cooed. "You're all right now."

The girl had blonde hair and was wearing a pink angora sweater.

"What's your name?" Sam forced herself to use a calm voice, but her pulse raced, and her blood pounded against her ears. She knew the killer could be nearby, watching them. Time was of the essence.

"My name is Theresa. Theresa Pembrook."

Sam brushed leaves away from her fair face and smiled.

"What a lovely name. How did you get here, Theresa?"

The girl sat up moving jerkily. She couldn't have been more than eighteen or so. Her eyes opened wider, and she turned around, looking in panic. Her expression showed her confusion. Theresa reached up to touch her head, and then rubbed her hair a bit.

"I'm not entirely sure how I got here. Where is here?"

"You're near Maidstone Lake," Sam answered coolly.

"Oh. I didn't know where they were taking me."

Theresa's voice wasn't much more than a whisper.

"You see, we were playing this game. I met up with a guy who sounded kind of awesome online. I guess it was too good to be true."

Samantha guided Theresa to her feet. The girl staggered a bit and closed her eyes. She grabbed onto Sam's arm until she found her balance.

"Are you okay to walk?" Sam asked.

Theresa nodded.

"Good because we have to go—now."

They started back to the path.

"We hit it off at first," Theresa said. "The cool guy and me. I guess I was kind of stupid, huh?"

Theresa looked up at Samantha's face, she was searching for a response.

"Don't blame yourself for what someone else did," Sam said. "What else do you remember?"

"We drove around on his ATV, he even let me drive a little while. Then when we stopped to have a drink. The creep hit me." Theresa reached for her jaw and rubbed. "Then I felt this prick, and I guess, after that, I was out cold."

"Who hit you? Do you know this guy's name?" Sam was hoping she did, but Theresa shook her head.

"Well, you're lucky to be alive. Let's get you back to my office, and I'll drive you to the emergency room, you need a good look over."

Theresa was too weak to argue and allowed Sam to help her hobble out from the woods.

Samantha called Zach, explaining what happened while walking back to the office. The pace was slow, and by the time they reached the cabin, Zach was pulling up in his cruiser.

"Thank God you're here," Sam said. "Theresa, this is Detective Zach Gerard. He'll take you to the hospital."

"Of course, I'll get you all settled there. Best if we let a doctor take a look at you." He looked over his shoulder and said to Sam, "I called Doc Howard, he's meeting me there to collect trace."

Sam nodded, understanding full well this could be a big break in their case. If they could find any evidence on Theresa that the killer left behind, then they may be able to identify him. Whoever the murderer was, he obviously didn't get the chance to finish his job. *He was interrupted*, the thought gave Sam a shiver. Had she been the interruption? Perhaps the killer planned to return, to finish the job later. No matter, it was a slip-up and their best lead so far.

Zach closed the backseat door and turned to Sam.

"This is lucky. I don't understand why the killer left Theresa alive, but thank God he did. When I get back, we'll go to the spot where you found her—together. We'll poke around the scene and see if there's anything else."

Zach raised his finger, not exactly pointing at Sam but pretty close to it.

"Wait for me, we'll go back to the scene together."

Sam nodded.

"I mean it, wait for me." Zach hurried to his car and took off.

Sam waved as Zach drove away. The cruiser lights were flashing, Zach was driving as if out of time.

33 - In Over Her Head

Sam went into the office, sat at her desk, and opened drawers. Searching for something to do, she finally settled for a pen and folder then tried to concentrate on the paperwork in front of her, but she soon lost interest. The crime scene in the woods kept popping into her thoughts. The images taunted her and proved far more exciting than the report in front of her about the migration of waterfowl. The idea of going back into the woods to investigate the scene was too tempting.

Like a scratch that needed to be itched, the urge was too much to suppress her curiosity.

It would be hours waiting for Zach to return from the hospital, and by the time he did return, it would be dark. Worried the clues left behind might disappear, even by accident, she imagined all that could go wrong.

Scraps of material could be carried away by the rabbit family or a nearby bird who was nesting. The woods were alive, creatures moved and foraged, and critters certainly weren't going to wait until Zach arrived before resuming their survival activities. She talked herself into going back into the woods instead of waiting around for the paint to dry.

Samantha rose and nearly ran from the office, compelled to go back to the scene. On her way out the door, she grabbed a camera, rubber gloves, and plastic bags, prepared to collect any evidence she could find. She walked briskly down the trail barely glancing at her surroundings along the way. She figured she'd start at the beginning, the scene where Theresa Pembrook was found, then work her way back, taking a closer look on the return trip. It was crucial to document whatever evidence remained at the main scene.

She reflected on the day's events, regretting not having asked Theresa more questions. *First impressions are important.* Sam laughed at herself, how foolish her delusion of controlling everything. She was confident Zach would handle that part fine, he was definitely more trained at these things than she was.

She neared the spot where she had met up with the rabbit family. Sam stood still and listened, wondering if she'd hear the strange noise again or feel that strange bleakness. Nothing. She moved off the trail and tried to follow her tracks taken before. She stepped with care until she found the scene, the pile of dried leaves still in place.

Whoever had dumped the girl here must have brought tools with him to gather the leaves together so tidy, like a rake. A dreadful thought crossed her mind. The other girls had been drowned first, then discarded in the woods. *How come Theresa wasn't dead already?* The killer messed up.

Something had happened to interrupt his original scheduled plan, and Sam wondered if this would now make him more dangerous. She wasn't certain of the clinical definition of a serial killer or if this killer was one, yet, but he definitely was on his way to being a mass murderer. The Crime Unit usually had to take into account the motive which was a difficult task since they hadn't a decent profile. They knew nothing about the reasons behind the murders.

Samantha realized she was in way over her head, with no understanding of a killer's mind, motives or patterns. Hell, she didn't even watch televised detective shows. For a brief moment Sam wished she had, any knowledge was better than none. Why had she come out here alone? How reckless her decision had been, the killer could still be here, waiting, watching, returning.

34 - UNABLE TO BUDGE

She spun around to go back just as something went flying past her—a person on a zip line appeared in her peripheral vision. She heard the whizzing of the line, then it stopped, and within seconds a dark figure stood beside her. She had no time to react because simultaneously, she felt a prick on her chest.

Sam slumped to the ground. She batted her eyes, rolling her eyeballs to look around but she only saw the dried leaves, pine needles, a few cones, and twigs. What the hell just happened? Her throat constricted and for a moment she thought she would choke. She gasped for the air needed to fill her lungs with oxygen, they felt like flattened balloons.

Sam tried to move her hands up to her throat but they didn't budge, no matter how much she willed her muscles to move, they lay still at her side. She tried to mobilize herself and rocked her body until she was able to roll onto her side. Then she saw him.

A tall person stood a few feet away dressed in a type of costume. Tight fitting black pants revealed his hardened groin, proof that he was indeed a man. He wore a slim-fit zippered black shirt as well, looking similar to those worn by long-distant bikers. The entire outfit was dark, tense, and menacing.

Sam heard clicking sounds as the man unbuckled a harness attached to a line that hovered above them. She couldn't make his face out, he wore a rubber mask of a rabbit, and it reminded her of the folk tale character Ableegumooch, the trickster. But the mask covering his face looked more like a deranged rabbit, painted with blood stains around the mouth and eyes.

Panic poured inside her, all she wanted to do was run, to escape. Despite the fight or flight instinct, she was unable to budge, let alone career herself back down the path—she was helpless.

Daring to look closer she stared, searching for this creep's eyes that might show through the slits on the mask. She found them, they were sad brown eyes, like Kevin's eyes. No, it can't be. Impossible. Her denial sounded lame, pathetic even, as she recalled his prideful tone used when he had spoken of his training, and how he learned to use zip-lines. He had wanted to be part of the role-playing group. And what about the secret formula of his mother's concoction that numbed her pain, Had that been a test?

A sick feeling roiled up inside her gut. A fleeting memory passed her mind, and she remembered how she used to laugh to herself, thinking that Josh and Kevin behaved like Keoonik and Ableegumooch, two Abenaki characters from folk tales who tricked each other. Sam had thought of Kevin as the otter, the one who was the butt of the jokes, not the rabbit trickster. He must have seen himself as the ultimate cunning rabbit instead. Sam had to admit, he had fooled her.

Sam wanted to call out to Kevin to ask that he stop this sadistic ritual, to beg him to stop scaring her like this. She was petrified, but as much as she tried to open her mouth, she could barely produce a mumble of gibberish from her vocal chords.

Fear rushed through her veins, a deep panic welled inside her, and within seconds her face muscles stiffened more. Her mind was the only thing that remained under her control. She talked herself out of the mania with internal mantras of *stay calm*. If she could have closed her eyes to pray she would have, but she couldn't shut her lids, not even to keep out the dust of the ground.

"Samantha, don't struggle. It will only make your paralysis worse. Trust me I know."

Did he say paralysis? His voice sounded calm and in control, almost friendly.

"Have you figured out who I am yet? I wonder if you even recognize me. My voice must be giving me away, right?"

Sam tried hard to move but only managed a sharp look up as her eyeballs shifted toward the view of Kevin's face.

"So you have figured it out. Good for you, Sam. I always admired your smarts. You know, now that I've thought things through, this is all really your fault. Maybe you don't remember? Okay, twist my leg, I'll tell ya."

Kevin chuckled, but it wasn't a real laugh, more like a sinister giggle. The mask landed on the ground. Sam watched Kevin's eyes as he placed his glasses back on the bridge of his long nose. She saw an evilness there that she'd never noticed before.

With an urgent attempt, she searched the area, looking at the ground she managed to see, for anything that would be useful to defend herself if she were ever able to move again.

Maybe whatever Kevin injected her with would wear off? The thought gave her a spark of hope.

35 - ABUSE KILLS

"I'll tell you my sad, little story as I dress you, okay? You'll get a kick out of this, Sam. Promise."

Mortified, Sam saw Kevin reach down, but her vision was limited. He looked like he was busy with his hands, his shoulders moved up and down because of whatever he was doing.

Sam imagined he was undressing her, the thought made her sick. She couldn't feel a thing other than the slightest pressure. A panic surged up, and all she wanted to do was to push the creep away from her, but she was helpless to do anything.

"Well, a long time ago when we were kids, I invited you to my house. Do you remember that day? Of course, you don't, but I do."

Kevin turned his face and glared at her. Beads of sweat formed on his forehead and ran down his face. His menacing stare took whatever shallow breath Sam had left away. For a moment she thought she'd suffocate, but then Kevin turned his attention back to whatever he was doing, and her breathing returned, small short breaths working hard to find oxygen.

"Anyhow—I liked you. You always protected me at school when the kids teased me. But when I brought you to the house, my mother didn't like you at all. She said that you represented everything wrong with the world." He cottered his head while he spoke.

"Do you know, she beat me down after you went home, but I didn't care right off because you were my friend. After the first visit my mother beat me up real bad, and days later she flew into a rage again, just at the mention of your name. I was afraid to bring anyone home after that, we could only play and talk at school. But my mother still wouldn't let things go, such a bitch."

Samantha perceived pressure on her arm but still couldn't move it. She turned her eyeballs down as far as possible and saw that Kevin had tugged her shirt off, it lay on the ground near her knees. He was pulling something pink from a bag sitting on the ground.

"Hold still now." Kevin laughed again. The sound of his voice was haunting.

Wanting to scream, Sam couldn't manage even a whimper. The fast beat of her heart hammered inside of her, crushing her with a sense of doom. Her pulse pounded against her eardrum.

"Mother hated you and all the beautiful women from the tribe. Said you were all dirt. I stood up for you again one time and told her she was wrong, that you didn't belong to the tribe. But for some damned reason, she really didn't like you. I finally learned the truth one day."

He bent down to her face and stared into her eyes.

"Turns out your mama was the reason my father died, and my mother blamed you, too. I know it wasn't your fault, Sam, that your mother killed my father."

He sat back up and returned to his task.

"Oh well, that's what mother ranted. She said it over and

over again. Each time mother retold the story she'd hit me with her leather strap. Later, as I got older, she'd kicked me in the gut, sometimes burned me on my thigh or wherever she could reach to put out her cigarette. I would hear her say it, over and over again, you get the picture."

Kevin stuck his face in front of hers again.

Startled, a spike of terror shot through her insides. She would have jumped if she could. Sam stared back at his crazed eyes, they seemed to be from another world. He gawked at her, with bulging eyeballs stained with bloodshot. Kevin stared so closely to her own eyes that she saw his red veins pumping. He rose, out of view again, but she could still hear him.

"Like I said, she's a bitch. The only thing that made her happy was a picture of herself when she was young before she met up with my father and had me. She loved the way she looked in that photograph. Bright yellow hair with a big smile on her face and she wore a fluffy pink sweater. Just like the one I put on you."

Samantha tried to gulp but couldn't even do that, couldn't even feel the drool that had to have been sliding from her mouth. Her pulse raced, and she wondered if her fast heart rate would help wear off the drug he used sooner than he expected. She hoped so.

Kevin reached over and wiped her face with a handkerchief.

"I told you, you can't move. You're paralyzed, and all your slobber is just dripping from your mouth when you get excited. Don't worry yourself, Sam. I used my mother's Monkshood plants. Did you know that if you grind the root up, it makes a potent poison? Well, it does. But I use it for other things. Like the cream that I rubbed on your leg the other day. It didn't hurt you none, but it numbed the pain, right? Today I used a dose a little more potent injected with this special tool I made."

Kevin reached over and picked something up. He moved it in front of her eyes so she could see. It was a homemade tool of sorts, a wooden round disk about a half inch thick with at least a dozen tiny needles popping out of it.

"See that, it's my invention. Clever ain't it. I rub an extract on those prickly needles and voilà! Instant application. You can't move or fight against me, but still with the least amount of damage to you. I could have given you a lethal dose, you know. I've done that before."

Samantha heard muffled sounds but couldn't decipher what they were, then questioned if her mind was beginning to go as well.

"You've placed me in a pickle, Sam. You see I don't want to kill you, you're my friend. You're not like Mother at all. The other girls were selfish and mean to me. They went along with me on the role-playing, but then began saying bad things to me, calling me names. But you've always been real nice."

Kevin's voice grew louder with anger.

"You never should have taken Theresa away. First, you interrupt me at my house in the middle of the night then you wander along the wrong path. Now, I have to finish what I started somehow, so I guess it has to be you. You made me do this, Sam."

Tears ran down her face. Sam couldn't feel the wetness, but she tasted the salt against her dried lips. She wanted to vomit.

"Don't be like that."

Kevin stood, and she heard him walk away. Perhaps he couldn't go through with it. Maybe her tears reminded him of their friendship and that their rapport was more important to him than this sick ritual of his.

"Okay, I guess I need to dye your hair first. It's the only way, Sam. You have to at least look like Mother for this to work."

Hysteria flooded Samantha's thoughts when she smelled the chemicals. Kevin reached down, she watched helplessly as his hands grabbed her head and moved it side-to- side. He was right above her and Sam heard splashes of water hit the ground. Kevin turned her head, checking his work. She noticed his nostrils flaring each time his glasses slipped. He kept pushing them up with the back of a hand, she lost count how many times. Kevin drew forward a terry cloth towel and rubbed her hair dry. He hummed as he worked.

"You know, you kind of look like my mother now that your hair is getting lighter."

Sam thought her eyeballs were going to pop out of their sockets. Terror submerged her into a dark place, then she noticed a slight pinch. A muscle movement tugged her face. *Could she control the twitch?* She tried to rouse her mouth, split her lips, waggle her tongue, nothing.

This sick bastard dyed her hair. Kevin's next step would be to drown her, she knew it, and then he'd leave her here in the woods to rot. She couldn't accept that as her fate, nor the fact she was helpless. With all her strength she tried again to move. Nothing but the slightest pinch of her face. Her head was incapacitated, so she began testing the other end, her feet.

Concentrating, Samantha discovered that she could move her left toes and tried to move her left foot as well. There was some movement, and she managed to hit a rock with her shoe, this upshot gave her a surge of positive thought. She tried the same process on her right side. Sam managed to move both her feet.

"You know Sam, I have to confess. I enjoyed killing my mother. Yup, you guessed it, she was the first. It happened one day after I began the job. When she found out I worked for you, well, Mother was so angry. She beat her fists against my chest and yanked my hair out. Man, that hurt and I had to wear a hat for the first week. Remember?"

He tilted her head up and looked into her eyes.

"I guess not."

Her head fell back, and he resumed his work.

"I'm a grown man and told her so, told her to stop. But she laughed at me and walked her bitchy ass over to the kitchen sink and washed the dishes like nothing was wrong. All the while she called out bad things back at me, yelled names at me. She said I was weak and nothing but chicken shit. Yup, that's what she called me, her son the chicken shit. You know I'm not. I'm like the cunning rabbit in that story you told us. But mother found that out, too late."

More water splashed and the smell of ammonia combined with peroxide burned the inside of her nostrils.

"So while my mother stood at the sink, saying the nastiest things she could, well, let's say I couldn't help myself. I grabbed her filthy blonde head and pushed it down into the sink water. I pushed hard and held her down real tight." Kevin laughed.

"Ya know, bubbles formed all around her stinking face. She fought back like a wild woman, and it was fun, like tug-a-war. Do you like tug-a-war? I enjoyed it so much. Watching her wiggle in that damned pink sweater of hers. She thought she was so beautiful, *pfft*. Mother was ugly inside. That was the happiest day of my life."

Water got into Sam's eye and burned, she blinked. Her spirit rose, realizing that she had regained some movement in her lid. Whatever he had drugged her with was wearing off.

"I wanted Jessica to like me, but she turned out to be a bitch. Jessica was a bad girl and said nasty things to me, like mother. I hate that word, ya know. Chicken shit, it' ain't right. She got what she deserved."

Sam felt pressure on her skull as Kevin's voice sounded angrier; he must have been squeezing her head with his hands. Despite his torture, she welcomed the sensation. More hopeful than before, perhaps, she could find her way out of this situation after all.

"And ya know, the same thing happened over in the woods at White Mountain. Girls today are so mean. I had made arrangements to meet someone there, on the trail in New Hampshire, after I heard Josh was riding in those parts. See, I intend to blame all this stuff on him, cause he's a bully, too."

Kevin was out of her vision for a second then he held a comb in front of her eyes for a brief second.

"I'm combing away your snarls now. I know what you think, Sam. You think I'm a monster or something. But you see the real monster was Mother. She hated you, she hated me, her son."

Kevin pushed up his glasses.

"Oh well, it doesn't matter anymore. She's gone, but I relive that memory over and over again whenever someone is nasty to me. Mother will never come back again, I'll see to that."

Samantha decided she had to try to get away and now might be the best time while he was concentrating on her hair. Sam fumbled with her feet and found traction with a large stone between them. She pushed and was able to move it. Her jerking movement startled Kevin, and he sat back to look at her. His expression showed astonishment.

"Now why did you go and do that?"

Kevin stood up. His eyes pierced hers with such an evil that she dreaded to think of what his next action might be. Samantha saw him bend and pick up a large rock which he now held in his hands. He was going to knock her in the head with it, then all hope would be lost. With all her energy Sam forced herself to turn her body.

Miraculously, she rolled to the right and heard a thud as the stone hit the ground behind her.

"Dammit, you bitch."

He threw the rock at her, she endured pressure from the impact but still couldn't register the amount of force he used, or the pain. The rock landed on the ground next to her, she could see it in her line of vision, her blood stained the jagged points that jutted out of the rock's surface. His hands reached down, his fingers covered the spots of her blood, and then it was gone.

She would have to try to roll the other way this time. Not knowing how much time she had, she mustered every fiber of energy that remained and turned her body left.

Samantha rolled, and a pair of black boots came into her sight. One of the boots pulled back then slammed into her head. Samantha saw stars, bright flashes of light and rays shooting off in all directions, yellow, white, and then everything went dark.

36 - It's Different Now

Sam was caught in a dream. She desperately wanted to move but envisioned herself being pulled down as if she were drowning in air. Her hands and feet were bound somehow, tied to something anchoring her from far below. She looked up. The sky was dark purple, storm clouds filled the horizon. The clouds began to morph, they hastened away in fluid motion until they turned into nothing more than a foggy mist. Soft drumming sounds rose, the beat gave her strength, courage, and connected her to the earth's heartbeat. A lavender hue remained all around her as she searched for an object, the thing needed to keep her balance in the world. A voice sounded in song, rising up to the sky along with the drums . . . Samantha heard someone calling her name.

"Samantha, I'm here. Take my hand."

She recognized the voice but couldn't place a name to it. She turned toward the sound, but something held her back. Something tingled the skin around her wrist, so she looked down and saw a golden charm bracelet draped daintily around her slender wrist. It was just like the bracelet she had worn on her First Communion Day. Pop had told her it belonged to her mother and she had wanted her to wear it for protection from evil spirits. The sight of the golden chain warmed her heart.

Then she heard her mother's voice, calling to her softly from beyond the grave.

"We have been taught to love Mother Earth and to respect her. We are the Children of the Dawn, the People of the East. May the Great Spirit Creator bless us and smile upon us. Listen to the call from the lodge of nature, the knowledge is there."

The words repeated like a perpetual canon as her mother's sweet voice drifted away, fading into the surreal clouds of lilac. Joy filled Samantha's heart like she had never known before and she wanted to stay in that moment forever. But another voice beckoned her, calling out her name.

"Samantha, I'm here, right by your side. Take my hand."

Samantha decided she would take hold of the offered hand. There was more work to do for Mother Earth.

Samantha blinked her eyes, the light seemed harsh at first, so she closed them again. It took a moment for her to understand where she was. She heard a beeping sound and the pressure of something wrapped around her arm was taking her blood pressure. Then her hand was squeezed by someone standing nearby.

She was in a hospital. The idea seemed strange to her for a moment. She slowly opened her eyes again. A flood of polarized light from above blinded her, diffusing her sight in a whitewash. For a moment she could only discern the shapes of objects in the room. She looked at her wrist but only saw a hospital band. A tall man stood at her side.

"She's coming around. Thank God."

It sounded like Zach. Sam squinted, looked up, and saw his smile. The sight of his face comforted her.

A nurse stepped in front of him and asked her all kinds of questions. Sam took her time and answered them all, though they didn't make sense to her.

"Samantha Tremblay . . . Twenty-six . . . Grover High School . . . President Washington," she answered each.

"Good. She seems fine, folks. I'll come back in fifteen minutes to give a neurological test again," the nurse said. Then she left.

"You had us worried." It was Mr. Livingston, her boss, standing on her other bedside. He was tall, his hair wisped back as if he had just stepped in from a seaside stroll. His skin looked rugged and tanned against the light coming into the room from the window behind him, his smile friendly, and his tone fatherly. Sam hadn't seen him in weeks and wondered why he was there now, for that matter, she wondered why she was there, in the hospital.

"Don't you worry, Sam. Everything will be all right. As soon as you get well, you can get back to work. But until then, you stay in bed and rest. Take all the time you need, that's an order." Mr. Livingston bowed his head.

"Why am I here?" she asked.

Soft laughter originated from all directions of the room.

"I'm so sorry this happened," Mr. Livingston said as he patted her hand. "We found you, knocked out, in the woods."

Sam closed her eyes and tried to remember.

"Our best guess, you were at the same spot where you found Theresa Pembrook. I told you to wait for me, Sam."

Sam turned when she heard Zach's deeper voice.

"Sorry," she said.

"I'm sorry, Sam." Mr. Livingston reached and took her hand in his again. "I never should have asked you to get involved in this case. Now look, you're hurt and in the hospital. I'm sorry I put you at risk."

"Nonsense. I wanted to help. The victim deserves justice. None of this is on you. I make my own decisions."

Zach cleared his throat, and Sam turned in time to see his smile. She thought perhaps, he was proud of her. That meant a lot to her.

"Mr. Livingston, who's watching the office?"

"Don't you worry about that, everything is fine. I called Josh in to cover for you. And you know, he said he had quit."

Sam nodded. "Sorry to say he ran into a little trouble."

She looked up at Zach and saw him shaking his head and mouthing 'He's okay.'

"Well, I asked Josh to return at least until you're on your feet. Of course, he was upset you were hurt and agreed to come back temporarily." Mr. Livingston held his hands together, as if in prayer or looking ready to leave. The man had completed his mission. "Okay then, I'll get out of your hair and let you rest. Don't worry, Sam."

"Thank you, Sir. I'll be fine."

Sam watched as her boss left then noticed movement by another person, moving closer to the bed.

"Hi, Sam. When you're ready for real food instead of this hospital crap, give me a call."

It was Henry. Sam smiled up at him, happy to see his vibrant head of hair.

"Of course, maybe a sandwich or Nacho Special."

"Let me make you something even better. Chicken soup? No, I'll surprise you."

"Okay. I could use water right now, though."

"I'll step out and ask a nurse to bring in ice chips and water," Zach said.

As soon as Zach left the room, Henry went to her side, his expression looked concerned.

"What's the matter?" she asked.

"I have to tell you something, and it's important." Henry's face flushed.

"Well, what is it?"

"It's none of my business, but I know that something you think is real, is actually wrong. I mean, what you think is the truth is not the truth."

"What the hell are you talking about, Henry?"

"You think that Zach left without a word for no good reason. You think that he dated someone else in high school, too. I know this stuff because Josh talks a lot But he's wrong. You're wrong. It's not true. You've totally got the wrong idea about what happened back then. You believed the words of some jealous girl bullshit instead of listening to your heart."

"Oh, and how's that?" she said.

"Sam, I know what happened. I was there."

"Stop speaking in riddles. What the hell do you mean?"

"Just before Zach left for college he met up with your father, at the Riverside. I heard them talking."

Henry dropped his head, his face red enough to match his hair.

"Zach told your father that he planned on keeping in touch

with you, you know, while he was away at school. He promised he'd wait for you because you were special to him. But your pop got angry. I'd never seen him so mad, he looked crazy. He told Zach that if he really cared about you, he'd stay away, forever. They argued, and well, your father made Zach promise he'd never say another word to you." Henry's voice trembled. "Sam, you were under eighteen. Zach didn't have a choice."

Sam swallowed hard, not knowing if she was relieved to find out what happened, or disturbed that her father was responsible for Zach leaving her. How could her pop have done this to her?

"Why didn't you tell me before?"

Henry mumbled. "I'm sorry, Sam. I didn't see the point. Zach was gone. Your father was here with us, and your only concern should have been school. So I let it go."

"So why tell me now?"

Henry looked up, and Samantha saw the tears in his eyes. He wiped them back.

"Why? Because it's different now. Your father is gone, God rest his soul. Zach is here again. And he's taken with you, Sam. I can see he still cares for you, deeply. The way he stands by you, the way he looks at you. I wish I had someone who cared for me that way. I can't not tell you any longer. I'm sorry I hadn't said something sooner."

Sam reached and took Henry's hand into hers, and kissed it. "Thank you for the truth, Henry. I hate secrets."

He looked at her, smiling. "Friends?"

"Yes, friends. Always. Is the offer for a good meal still on the table?"

"You betcha," Henry said. "I'll stop back again tomorrow and drop something off before my shift."

Henry bent over and kissed her forehead, then left, waving as he passed Zach, who was returning to the room with water.

"Any more visitors," she said.

"Not for the moment." Zach laughed at this and drew closer to her. He reached down and took her hand in his. "Thank God you're all right."

"What happened," she said.

"I was hoping you would be telling me. I came back to your office after dropping off Theresa Pembrook at the Doc's, and you were nowhere to be found. So I checked the guide map of the trails and found the one you had mentioned. Then I went looking for you. I should have known you wouldn't wait for me, I'm such an idiot."

Zach thumped himself on the forehead.

"Anyway, after walking for a while, I heard you moaning. As I ran toward you, I saw someone running away. I could either chase him or help you. I decided on you. And then I found you like this."

Zach waved his hand at her up and down.

"What do you mean like this?" she said.

Zach went to the counter and picked up the hand mirror that a nurse had left and brought it to her. Samantha looked at herself and screamed.

"What the hell happened to me?"

"Seriously, you don't remember this?" he pointed at her hair. "The doctor said there was a chance of amnesia because you had a hard blow to the head. But how could this happen and you don't remember?"

Her face was bruised and pink, her eyes bloodshot. Sam rubbed her head and inadvertently touched a sore spot. "Ouch. And no, I can't remember how my hair turned yellow. This is a nightmare."

Zach cleared his throat.

"What?" she said.

"I'm going to make a few assumptions here, at least until your memory comes back, okay?"

Sam nodded.

"If anything sounds right or stirs your memory, let me know. First, I found you lying on the ground unconscious and dressed in a pink sweater."

"No way!"

He nodded and continued. "Yes. So, I'm assuming you ran into the killer out there. Thank God you're safe." Zach made the sign of the cross.

"My best guess is that he was returning to finish his business with Theresa Pembrook and found you there instead. Since you saw him, he had to change his plans and take you out—"

"You're saying he tried to kill me."

Zach nodded. "I think so. But here's the thing — you have jet black hair, not the preferred blonde, which is part of his signature. No problem, the killer takes care of things with dye and wallah! You have this."

Zach lifted the mirror in front of her again, holding back a laugh.

She grabbed it and looked at her reflection for a moment while trying hard to recall any details. She squeezed her eyes shut, but it was still a blank canvas. If she could just remember then, they'd be able to arrest the creep.

"Let's get a psychiatrist in to hypnotize me and get the answers we need."

"You are brave," Zach said.

He reached across the bed and brushed her hair back from her face, his touch gentle.

"No. The doctors told me to let you remember things naturally and not rush it. That concussion to your head could turn dangerous if we push things."

"So you've already been talking with the doctors about me," she said.

"Yes, I hope you don't mind. It's just, well we are working together. You're like my partner on this case, and with your Pop not being around . . . You remember that?"

"Yes," she breathed deeply. "I remember my father is dead and much more than I care to know." She harrumphed. "Let me try going back, to see what I can remember."

"Sounds like a good idea as long as we take things slow."

"Hmm." Sam closed her eyes and visualized the last things she could recall. "Okay, so I remember finding the girl, Theresa Pembrook, alive. I remember thinking how it was strange, you know, to find her alive. Don't get me wrong, I'm happy she's alive, I was just taken aback that she wasn't drowned. How is she doing by the way?"

"She looks better than you."

Sam reached up and punched his arm.

"Ouch. I guess your strength is coming back."

She smiled. "Yes, so watch out."

"Okay," he said with hands raised. "Seriously though, give yourself some time to rest. You've had a shock, and your mind needs to heal. When things come back to you, I'll be here."

"But I'm not finished yet," she said.

Zach kissed her head.

She tried to smile up at him, but she didn't feel optimistic at the moment. The dream was still crisp in her mind and filled her with questions. Sam wondered if the dream had meant something or was it a surreal wish created by a pent-up yearning to hear her mother's voice again. Sensibly she knew it wasn't a message from the grave. Her bracelet was still stowed away in her old jewelry box.

"Okay, Zach. I'll just rest for a bit. But when the floodgates open you better be wearing waders." She laughed, picturing him in high rubber boots trying to walk against a strong current.

A nurse entered the room and administered another test of questions to check her cognitive faculties. Once Sam passed the test, the nurse left.

Zach bent over and kissed her, this time on the lips. His mouth was warm and inviting. His gentle contact on her lips surged a reaction that made her feel lighter than air. It only lasted a few seconds and then Zach left, turning the lights down low on his way out. Sam fell back to sleep but didn't dream again. Instead, she felt so at ease her body completely rested, a first for her.

37 - REMEMBER THE NIGHTMARE

Sam woke feeling better, ate the breakfast that Henry dropped off for her, and passed her cognitive tests with flying colors. When the doctor stopped in to check on her, she pleaded to be released and convinced the doctor she was fine. Samantha promised not to work, but of course, her fingers were crossed. She needed to go to Confession, soon.

Zach picked her up at the hospital and brought her home then left to check on the lab reports of the newer crime scene. By lunchtime, she was bored and gave up on staying at home.

Sam drove toward Maidstone Lake heading for her office with a sandwich in hand that she had bought on her way. She unlocked the door and found it empty, lights off. Josh had paperwork open on his desk, but he must have been outside somewhere making rounds.

It wasn't a rainy day, but the skies were gray and the air damp. Sam was sore deep in her muscles and bones, so decided to stay moving instead of letting her body cramp up by sitting at her desk all day. She finished chewing her sandwich, scrunched up the paper bag, and tossed it into the basket.

Sam left the office intending to take a walk but soon found herself hiking toward the spot where she had stumbled across Theresa. She thought that she might regain her memory if it was nudged a bit, maybe recall details that could help unveil the killer. Hell, Sam wanted to remember any minutiae of what she had seen but had stowed away in her subconscious mind. She looked around but kept drawing a blank.

A thought flashed. She needed to know about the damned lab results, so she dialed Zach.

"Hi Zach, I was wondering, did you get the lab report back concerning the water found in the victim's lungs? The first victim."

"Sam, where are you?"

"I'm at the scene where I found Theresa, and don't even try to lecture me."

"I wouldn't dare." Zach was quiet for a second, then responded. "And the answer to your question is, yes. And according to the report, the water samples in both the first and new victim's lungs matched. Another fact linking them. It's been determined to be well water, zero chlorine present. And here's the weird part. The samples contained ingredients found in dishwashing soap. They're trying to identify which aquifer the water came from by the mineral content. That would narrow our search substantially. We should know shortly."

"Hmm. Sounds right, somehow."

"Do you remember something?"

"No, I guess it was just a fleeting image. Gone now," she laughed.

"Promise me, Sam. Get your ass back to your office and if you must go off again, have Josh tag along. Please."

Zach was still on the line, and she felt that he wanted to say something else but for some reason couldn't say the words.

"I'm heading back now," she said. "And I'm fine. Will I see you later?"

"I'll be heading that way shortly. Promise me, don't be alone."

"Okay, promise."

Samantha hung up and walked back to the cabin, easier since the slope was downhill. Sam entered the office and smiled when she saw Josh sitting at his desk.

"I'm happy you're here."

"Really?" He looked up from his paperwork, his mouth, and eyes horizontal slits. "Well, I don't think I'll be here much longer. No reason now that you're back. I meant what I said, Sam. Do you remember the other morning? The conversation we had at the jail?"

"Correction facility." She moved closer to his desk, slow so not to scare him away as if he were an injured animal or something. "I remember, but I don't want you to leave, Josh. You're my best friend."

He scowled. His eyes pinched together as if sporting a massive headache, which of course was herself. She had said the wrong thing.

"I'm sorry. Please at least stay here until I'm back on my feet. You're needed here. I shouldn't be working yet."

Josh smirked at this.

"Probably not. Knowing you, you didn't heed the doctor's advice. You look horrible as a blonde by the way."

She laughed.

"Thanks. I plan on a long hot shower and a dye job tonight."

"You know, you could have been killed." he said.

She heard Josh draw in a deep breath.

"Okay, I'll stay for a bit."

"Thank you," she said.

Sam jerked her head toward her desk and proceeded to her chair.

"Hey, where's Kevin?" she asked.

"I have no idea, nor do I care."

"Don't you think it's odd that he's not at work?"

Josh stopped what he was doing and looked across the room, his expression was not a happy one.

"I think the creep has always been a little too odd. Don't you? I'm relieved he didn't show up. Who knows, maybe his mother needed him. Who cares?" He thumped his fist on his desk. "Now, can I get back to work? Or do you prefer me to leave?"

Sam pulled her hair up and tied it back, then got ready to leave, grabbing her travel mug.

"No, please don't leave. Promise me."

"Okay, boss." Josh gave her a mock salute.

"I'll go check on Kevin, and you hold down the fort."

She walked over to Kevin's desk and opened a drawer then pulled out the jar of his mother's home remedy. She rolled up her pant leg, then unscrewed the lid, took a slather and rubbed in on the calf of her leg. The smooth texture soothed her pain. *What had Kevin said it was made of? Oh, yes, mineral oil, and it smelled sweet from rose water.* Kevin had also said it contained a secret ingredient from the plants surrounding his mother's house.

Sam wondered which plant, maybe she could try growing whatever it was, near her apartment. Or perhaps in Pop's backyard. She swallowed the lump in her throat, realizing her father was gone, for good. Yes, she needed to go to Confession, and soon. She had to ask for forgiveness for all the nasty things she had thought about her father. Even though it turned out that he was worse than she had known and he kept Zach away all these years, still she loved her father. She wished she had had more time with him, and felt guilty for all the time she had wasted by keeping away.

"What's that? Josh asked.

"It's a remedy for sore muscles, I guess. It's an ointment, one of those home cures Kevin's mother makes. He said this one has herbs, flowers, and stuff from the gardens around the house. When I stopped there the other night, I saw a lot of plants around their house, but couldn't make out what kind or see the colors in the dark. I think he said his mother had blue monkshood in the border gardens. I really didn't pay enough attention, wish I had. Oh well, I'll just have to ask Kevin when I get there."

Sam stood still a moment, her words echoed in her head. There was something important about this cure in a jar, but she was fuzzy as to what, exactly.

"His mother is a creep, too," Josh said. "You know she sells all those remedies at the Farmer's Market. At least she used to."

"No, I didn't know. Cool," she said.

"Remember Cynthia, my old girlfriend?"

Sam nodded.

"Well, Cynthia buys all that natural stuff. Anyway, Cynthia said Kevin's mother stopped selling there, a while back, and she can't get the stuff anymore, but she swears by them.

Who would have thought that Kevin's mom was ahead of her time?"

"Maybe it was all a throwback, from her hippie days when she was one with the earth," she said.

"Kevin always says she's an odd person. Probably she's too old to go there to sell these days." Josh said.

"Well, the stuff works as far as I'm concerned."

"Whatever rocks your boat," Josh said.

Sam left the cabin and drove to the Rasle's house. She thought about what Josh said, he had always teased Kevin, but she thought it was in good fun, never realized he actually didn't like the guy. Kevin was a bit creepy, but given his meek manner, and all the teasing he got over the years, who could blame him for being off.

Suddenly, a strange foreboding came over her and frightened her down to the bone. She hoped nothing was wrong with Kevin.

The dirt driveway was long and away from the road, not a sound could be heard. Sam parked the Jeep in front of Kevin's house. The place looked creepy, especially in the dim daylight. The sky was still gray waiting for the rain to give way. Sam stepped out of the Jeep slowly, she had a funny twitching inside her, the kind that made her skin crawl. She rubbed her arms and walked toward the front door.

She noticed lots of healthy plants along the front of the house. Even though the day was dark and dismal, or maybe because of it, the blooms of the largest plant grouping stood out bright blue. *Blue Monkshood.* Sam remembered that Kevin had mentioned the plant when they were working on the study for the University. He had said it was poison. *No, his mom wouldn't put poison in a remedy, or would she?* Sam was concerned about the secret ingredient in the ointment.

Frantically she scratched her leg where she had applied the cream. Ah, relief.

A sudden cold wind swept across the lawn.

She shuddered. At that moment she regretted her decision to come here alone, she should have listened to Zach. She wasn't Kevin's babysitter after all. And what if his mother answered the door?

The thought of facing Kevin's mother terrified her. Sam turned back toward her Jeep, then heard the front door as it squeaked open. She stopped in her tracks.

Samantha looked over her shoulder, thinking it might be Kevin at the door, but was surprised to find no one there. A gust of wind pushed the door open wider.

Spinning around she faced the house. The door's wood was weather beaten, the dark paint chipped and peeling. The steps were made from large pieces of granite that sunk into the ground, off balance to the right.

Curious, Sam dragged her feet forward and warily stepped up the granite slabs. She stopped in the doorway, peeked inside, not a soul in sight. She entered the threshold and swallowed hard. Something was wrong, very wrong, but she hadn't a clue what.

An intense, putrid odor assaulted her sense of smell. She rubbed her nose with her hand and called out.

"Is anyone home?"

No answer. Samantha listened for any noise, maybe Kevin was in another room or perhaps out back. Maybe he was sick and sound asleep, which meant his mother might come along at any moment.

Sam moved further into the house, into the living room on the right. Not a soul in sight, the room was empty. A fireplace centered the opposite wall, she smelled the old ash, there had been a fire lit the night before. The furniture sat sparse and shabby. The sofa and matching chair were covered in brown material, the arms worn thin and the stuffing showed through in spots. The carpeted floor featured an old gold color, something that hadn't been popular since the 70's.

"Hello, anyone home? Kevin?"

Sam felt uneasy, she shouldn't be in this place, something was off. The foul smell lingered, smarting her nose. She rubbed it with her fist again, while scrutinizing the room. Kevin might be sick, passed out somewhere and needing help. But would she run into his mother? She recalled what other people have said, how she was freaky. Town gossips said Kevin's mom had been crazy even in her younger days, but Sam didn't believe in gossip.

The floor moaned as she took a few more steps into the room, she turned toward an open archway. The kitchen was in full view from where she stood. Sam noticed the old sink, one of those metal base sinks often found in homes of the fifties and sixties, white with chrome door handles and built-in drain board. The tiles on the floor were black and white checkered made of old linoleum, scuffed on fifty percent of the surface.

"Hello."

Sam's eyes went back to the sink.

Someone had to be in the house or nearby. The dishpan was filled with water, the soap suds were overflowing. Zach had said something about dish soap in the well water, how it was found in the victim's lungs. Kevin's house was on a well, he had said so.

Sam fixated on the sink.

Frightening thoughts flooded her mind. She closed her eyes, but it was too late. Memories rushed into her brain, disturbing images gushed in, and she remembered it all. Residual pain, emotional turmoil, and dark shadows poured into her being.

Samantha's stomach rolled, and she gagged, she almost vomited but swallowed back the burning acids. She had to leave. *It was Kevin*. He had attacked her in the woods, and now she was standing in his house, a freaking target on her back, calling out his name.

38 - The Killer

Samantha gained total recall of the brutal attack. Kevin had paralyzed her, kicked her in the face, rendered her helpless. Not being able to move was the worst experience of her life. The loss of control over herself was a deep rooted fear that had been stirred up. She couldn't go through that kind of excruciating trauma again.

Her throat tightened, and alarm gripped her from the inside. She was still standing in the middle of Kevin's living room, staring into the kitchen at the sink, while she tried to think of what to do next.

The creep had drowned the women just like he had his mother. Where, here in the house? Or did he just carry extra water around? What had he said the day when they first went to the Springs? He preferred well water? The lab had said the water in the victim's lungs was from a well and had dishwater in them. Had he taken the girls here first, then dragged them into the woods paralyzed? Yes—the scratch marks on Jessica's hands — perhaps from rubbing against the wire of the zip line?

She had been so stupid not to have seen it sooner. Sam turned to run away from this forsaken place, the stench alone of something rotten, filled her with revulsion. It was the smell of death she had been breathing into her lungs, his mother's corpse was probably in the house, hidden somewhere like a Bates-like lunatic would do. She had to get away.

Panicked, she turned to run toward the door. Sam tripped and fell face first, onto the dirty gold carpet. Years of smoke and grime left a nasty lingering stench that assaulted her. She wiped her face, pinched her nose, and pushed herself up.

She saw him and froze. Kevin was sitting on the sofa, his legs splayed out. *The bastard tripped me.* Sam was angry and wanted to lash back, but remembered what happened the last time she had reacted on reflex. He had been tactical and quickly improvised at the scene. She had to keep her guard up and not fall again to one of his cunning traps.

"Kevin," she said. Her voice sounded shakier than she wanted it to. *Please don't stand,* she thought. Kevin was skinny, but he was taller than her, and she had noticed the other day he was more fit than he let show. His entire life had been nothing but a charade. He didn't have to be picked on, he wore it like a badge so people like her would feel sorry for him. *To heck with his crap.*

Sam switched her approach, something Kevin wouldn't expect of her right now, given the situation. She wanted to be the villain this time and couldn't wait to start playing the role.

"What are you doing here, sitting on your ass? You're supposed to be at work." She spat the words as loud and as angry as she could muster.

Kevin flinched. A half-beat later his face lit up like the red light district. His eyes pushed so closely together they looked cross. He jumped to his feet.

Sam fled toward the door.

He caught her arm and swung her down to the ground,

whacking her head again against the floor. For a split second she wished she had amnesia again, but no such luck. Sam saw his face above hers, growling down at her like a mad dog. His hair mangled and sticking up everywhere, the dangerous lunatic that he was.

No matter what else happened here, she wouldn't let him use that pricking tool on her again. Sam couldn't bear the powerlessness, the inability to move, like before. She eyeballed his hand but didn't see anything in it. With only a split second to think, Sam kicked her knee up between his legs as hard as she could, squirmed to her side, and pushed herself up off the floor. She darted for the front doorway, flung it open, jumped the three steps, and fled outside. Sam ran straight into Zach's open arms.

"Thank God!"

Sam's body was shaking. She sobbed on his chest and tried to catch her breath. She had to make him aware of what was happening before it was too late.

"He's in there," she pointed. "It's Kevin. He's the killer."

"Don't worry, we'll go in and get him," Zach said.

"No. You don't understand, he has this thing," Sam motioned to her neck. "He made this too, he pricks you with something, and it paralyzes you. He's dangerous, Zach. Don't go in there alone."

Zach squeezed her in a hug, kissed the top of her head, then moved her to his side.

"You wait here. It'll be all right, I promise."

He pulled his Glock from its holster and pointed it toward the house. He motioned his arm, calling someone forward. Samantha turned and noticed that another police vehicle had followed Zach's. The lights were flashing, and the other officer came toward them with his weapon drawn as well. The two troopers headed toward the house together.

Samantha watched them leave as she subconsciously backed up until she was near her Jeep. She stood there waiting, watching, then she heard a shot blast. The sound echoed and rattled nesting birds from the nearby trees.

It felt as if her heart was in her throat. Seconds lasted for what seemed an eternity. Sam waited for someone to walk out from the house, praying it wouldn't be a monster.

The two officers appeared, their faces stern, heads shaking. Sam recognized the other man now, it was Thomas. He had been there when they called in the first crime scene, and he had helped carry the victim's body, Jessica's body, from the woods.

"Sorry, Sam. We didn't pull a trigger. Kevin shot himself in the head as soon as we walked through the doorway. He had a strange smile on his face, and then pulled . . ."

Zach couldn't finish his sentence. He held out his arms and pulled Samantha close to him. She felt his lips kiss her forehead, his arms held her tight. For the first time in a long time, Sam felt safe.

Thomas jogged back to his patrol car to call in the incident. Sam heard the buzzing sound of the scanner.

Zach whispered, "It's going to be fine. You're going to be all right. We'll weather all this mess together."

Sam closed her eyes and let Zach's comforting words take her away from the tragedy.

Everything became a blur for Sam. She stayed rooted near

her vehicle and distanced herself from the goings on. People came and left the scene, cop cars, ambulance, and the ME. The doctor walked past her, but she couldn't manage a gesture of recognition.

One of the medics approached her and checked her head. Finally, she was taken home. Still unfocused from reality, she couldn't remember who drove, but she crashed and fell asleep as soon as she landed on her bed.

39 - WHO CAN TEACH ME

Sam woke up, scratched her head, and tried to straighten her tangled hair. The strands felt stiff between her fingers, and she cursed herself for not buying any dye and conditioner to restore her hair. She wanted to get rid of the blonde and anything else associated with the nightmare she had lived through.

Her heart tightened in pain at the thought of the other girls who never made it out alive. *Damn you, Kevin.* Sighing, she rose and headed for the shower. Her head ached, and she was dizzy at first, then her instinct flared.

She felt queasy in the pit of her stomach. *She wasn't alone.* She moved to the wall, slid to the end corner, and peeked into the living area. Josh was sitting in a chair reading. Sighing with relief, she stepped into the living room.

Josh lowered his book. "Good morning sleepy head," he said.

Sam nodded and sat on the sofa across from him, crossing her legs to keep them warm. She leaned back and pulled a crocheted blanket her mother had crafted years ago and draped it over her shoulders. She felt warmer.

"I hope you're rested? You've only been out for sixteen hours."

"I'm confused." She rubbed her nose. "I don't remember

you being here last night."

"I dropped you off. But you seemed so out of it, so I decided to stay, in case you needed me. I'll go right now if you want me to."

Josh leaned forward as if ready to get up.

"No, don't be silly," she said. "I'm a little fuzzy. I can't believe it was . . . I mean, how could he have . . . It was Kevin all along."

"I know what you mean, it's hard to believe. I knew Kevin was off, but I didn't expect this. I mean our Kevin."

Josh shook his head.

"He always talked about his damned mother as if she was alive. I guess it stemmed from his guilty conscience or something. The coroner said she's been dead for months, hell, maybe years."

Sam pressed her lips together and nodded.

"It's going to take me time to let this all sink in. I feel so lost."

She looked around the room as if the answers she groped for were hiding somewhere nearby. On the table, in the woven basket her mother had made, or behind a wood cabinet, the one her pop hammered together.

Josh closed the book he'd been reading with a thump and placed it on the table, then leaned forward to look at Sam. His sight was direct, staring into her eyes.

"Sam, you may not want to hear this, but I know why you're feeling lost. You're avoiding the truth. Forgetting your own people. You and I have been friends for years, and I think I can recognize a few of your tells by now. Remember when your mom died? You and I, well, we talked things out. Right?

You speak of how much you miss walking in the woods with her. That's why you became a Ranger."

Sam harrumphed. "Tell me something I don't know."

Josh raised his arm and pointed to a group of pictures on the walls.

"Look, everywhere you turn in this place there are all these reminders of who your mother was—of who you are, too. My favorite is the photo of you and your mother in the woods together. My second favorite is the bag hanging on the wall peg, the one with the beaded flower design. It's beautiful workmanship, your mother was talented."

"I know. I always wished I knew how to do that, too."

Sam turned to look at the wall, her eyes blurred.

"But there's no one to teach me. And I don't think I feel lost because I can't find a decent arts and craft club."

Josh stood, bent to pick up his book and headed for the door. Looking over his shoulder, Josh replied.

"You're wrong, Sam. Some people can teach you things. They can help you discover your talents and how to use them, too. We still have a tribe. If you let me, I'll take you there, introduce you to the tribe. There's a meeting tonight. You could see for yourself."

He reached for the door handle.

"You might be able to find the missing part of you, the piece of you inside you've been searching for all along. I can only speak for myself, the tribe helped me."

Josh left without waiting for a response.

Sam watched as he closed the door, she heard his car rev up and drive away. She suddenly felt very much alone. Josh might be right. She had tried all kinds of activities to keep her heart happy. Ceramics class was a bust. Then she tried singing with the Church group, but she ended up scaring herself with her off-tune voice. She shrugged, got up from the sofa, and headed for the bathroom to take a shower. Sam intended to go to work like always, it was the only place where she belonged for now.

40 - It Had To Be Zach

It was mid-afternoon. Sam never made it to the office but instead sat at her kitchen table, drinking coffee, one cup after another. She watched the sunlight streaming through the window, it made the dust floating in the air visible. The light moved across the sky, changed the color of the objects in the room, and the way the furniture looked. Any thought, no matter how trivial, other than the reality of what happened was a gift.

The recent events jumbled her mind, and she thought of how it all began, and how it turned into a killing spree. Could she have changed the outcome? She had avoided an honest look at herself for years. Knowing she had misunderstood Pop and Josh was bad enough. But she had totally underestimated Kevin—his vulnerability turned into the motive for his hate crimes. Should she have tried to help more, maybe take him away from his mother years ago? Blinded to his true nature, well, she missed all the signs. Sam had a lot of things that needed sorting, she had been off the mark on so many issues.

If she had known the truth from the beginning, then could she have changed Kevin's course in life? But how could she have known about the extent of his mother's abuse without him confiding in her first? After hours spent in repentance and self-reproach, she came to realize it wasn't her fault.

There was a knock at the door. Sam looked out the window and saw Zach standing outside it.

A lump came to the throat, she swallowed.

Embarrassed for Zach to see her like this, still blonde, she was tempted to ignore him. Too late, he had already seen her through the window.

Sam shuffled toward the door. She hadn't checked herself in the mirror since her shower but knew she looked a wreck. Earlier she'd noticed that her hair was still a horrible shade of blonde but now with greenish tints from too much of something. The cheap dye hadn't taken well to her black hair, and the phosphates in her shampoo had made things worse.

"Sam, open up. Hurry, I have some food from Henry. I know you're in there."

Sam opened the door wide and invited him in. Zach placed the food on the table and turned to look at her. A smile spread across his face, and she wanted to hide underneath the rug.

"I hope you feel better than you look."

He was joking with her, but she felt so embarrassed.

Zach stepped closer and held her by the arms.

"No worries, you're still so beautiful."

Bending his head toward hers, slow and deliberate, he planted the softest kiss she'd ever experienced on her lips. Her body felt hot and shivery at the same time. Submissive to the sensation, Sam wrapped her arms around his head, adding her vigor to the kiss. What began as a gentle suggestion soon turned into a blatant want.

Sam melted in his arms, and they continued to return each other's advances. She moved his hand up her blouse, giving him permission to touch her breast.

Zach tenderly caressed her bosom, her nipples grew hard under the touch of his fingertips. He kissed her eyelids, her temple, and then her ear. The warmth of his breath sent a new sensation through her body, and all Samantha could think of was embracing Zach as close to her as possible.

She held his hard body, and they walked toward her bed in an awkward dance then landed on the mattress. Letting go of all pretense they pulled off each other's clothes. Sam let herself go, and lost herself in his arms.

It was her first time to ever make love, but she wasn't afraid because she was with her only love, Zach. Everything came naturally between them, and they moved like water rippling across a lake in a gentle breeze. Samantha smelled his sweat, recognized his touch, and fell even more deeply in love.

An hour later, Sam turned and saw that Zach was looking at her, a smile on his face. "Enjoy that?" she asked.

"I've been dreaming of being with you for so long," Zach said.

His words filled Sam's heart with extreme joy. Zach had been in her dreams for years, she never stopped hoping that they would be together. Her love for him welled up from deep inside of her. She smiled and kissed his forehead.

"I love you, Zach."

She blew out a sigh, her body, and mind at peace.

"You've got my heart in your hands, Sam. I have to tell

you, that was a big relief," Zach said.

"Did you know that loons mate for life?"

She smiled and watched him, waiting to see if he'd be surprised by her random comment.

"No, I didn't," he said. "But that's a good thing, right. Just so you know, I mate for life, too."

He kissed her then lifted himself up and leaned over to see her alarm clock.

"Sorry I have to go. Please, don't think I'm an ass, I didn't expect this to happen, though I'm ecstatic that it did." His smile was wide and beamed down at her. "But, I've got to meet the coroner."

Zach cupped her face with his hand.

"Are you all right, Sam? I mean, did you want this to happen?"

Sam wrapped her arms around him and pulled him down in a bear hug. She breathed in his manly scent, his sweat blending with his cologne, the pheromone heavenly. She could get used to this.

"Yes. I've wanted this for a long time, too."

His expression relaxed again.

"Good. I'm sorry that I have to go running off. Maybe you can spend the afternoon catching up on your rest. I'll stop in again tomorrow. Okay?"

"Sounds perfect." Sam sat up and threw on an old T-shirt.

"Get dressed, lover boy. I'll walk you to the door."

Sam leaned against his hard body and stole one more kiss before he left. Looking out the window, she waved and watched him drive away.

Part of her felt elated that she and Zach were together like it was meant to be, she had no doubt of that. Especially now that they committed their bodies to each other, it had felt so right. She was radiant having been with Zach after waiting all these years.

Samantha was confident of two things in her life, her love for Zach and her love for nature. The intense joy she experienced with Zach was amazingly powerful. The pleasure she received through nature was because of her mother, her heritage. There was no denying it. But something still nagged at the back of her mind, and it worried her so much that it interfered with her afterglow.

The only way to satisfy this persisting ache was to step out of her comfort zone. Something had been calling her, and she couldn't avoid answering it any longer. Samantha had to find out more about her tribe.

41 - The Truth

S amantha picked up the phone and called Josh. She needed to sample what he had spoken of—a community of people like themselves—and the tribe might be exactly what she needed. If indeed she had heard messages from the ancients, and their call to nature, then perhaps the tribe could guide her, help her to interpret the signs. She shook her head. Was she crazy?

Crazy or not, she knew what she had sensed, heard, and felt in the woods. She had to do something to explain the intense mirage and her dream, and not for anyone else, but for herself. She needed to wrap her head around it all so she could find peace within her own mind.

If nothing else good happened by exposing herself to the tribe, at least she could salvage her friendship with Josh. Their friendship was worth the sacrifice.

"Josh. Are you still willing to take me to the tribal meeting you mentioned?"

"Hell, yes, there's a meeting scheduled for this evening, perfect timing."

"Okay, then, let's do this before I have time to change my mind."

There was no time left for her to change her mind. Josh picked her up half an hour later, and they drove toward Swanton. She sat in the front passenger seat, wearing a handmade knit hat to cover her hair. She turned to face Josh and noticed he seemed different, changed somehow. His face was energized, the smile improved his appearance and exaggerated his strong features—he looked robust and confident.

"You can ask me any question you might have," he said.

"How well do you know these people?"

"I've been meeting with the Vermont Abenaki for a while now," he said. "I tried to connect with another tribe in New Hampshire, but considering everything that happened with the ATV and all . . . Well, I think I'll stay away from them for a bit. Besides, I'm in good standing with this tribe. I don't need any other right now."

Josh turned to look at Sam, his eyebrows wrinkled. Sam nodded her approval, and he turned his eyes back to the road.

"You know, the Swanton tribe welcomed me and helped to research my family lineage. It's like we were told, we are Native American. We're Abenaki, we were here first, and we're still here. There's no more secret to be kept. No one is hunting us down or trying to sterilize our women anymore."

Sam jerked her head up.

"You mean the government actually did that to the tribe? I thought it was all hearsay."

He nodded.

"Sad but true. Your mother was one of the brave ones and called them out. Everyone in the tribe knows who she was, and respects how she had advocated for them. Your mother protested, but she spoke out with eloquence with no fear. There are those who say that's the reason she died."

Josh took another quick glance in her direction then focused his eyes back on the road.

"Did I upset you?" he asked.

"Nothing can bother me anymore." She harrumphed.

"Careful of what you say. Some things should always bother you. There are evil things in this world. Many things are upsetting, even scary. But no matter what happens, I will always be there for you, Sam."

The car was silent for a long time. The route they took brought them through small towns between the faster straights. Sam watched from the car window without seeing the villages. She still had doubts, part of her was afraid of being rejected.

Could she find solace with the tribe? She wondered what her mother's life with the tribe had been like years ago. Sam felt a twinge of anger and couldn't understand why her pop had never spoken about their heritage.

"You know," Sam said, "Mr. Simpson told me that my mother died in a car crash. He said my pop felt guilty because he left the Springs early that night. He was angry with her for wanting to stay longer or maybe for sticking up for someone else from the tribe. So, he left my mother there, and she had to find a way home on her own. Then the guy who drove her home had an accident. His car went right off the embankment and dove into the riverbed. She drowned."

A tear found its way to the corner of her eye, she wiped it away. Sam thought she had cried all she could for her mother, but apparently, she still harbored a few ready to shed.

Josh nodded. "I heard something like that. Do you know who was in the car with your mother?"

"No," she said. "I suppose I can go back and have a heart-to-heart with old man Simpson, though."

"You don't have to. It was your mother's half-brother."

"My uncle? I had an uncle?"

"Half uncle."

Sam turned and watched the side of Josh's face, trying to see if he was earnest, or joking. She wondered what else he knew that he hadn't told her before. He gave her another quick glance, his expression uneasy. Josh slowed down the car and pulled to the side of the road, and put the column into park. He sighed deeply, closed his eyes for a moment, contemplating his next words.

Sam saw indecision cross his face, his mouth a taut straight line. His forehead was so tight it could have shattered at the slightest touch.

"Sam, your uncle is . . . I mean was . . ." Josh finally blurted. "Your half-uncle was also Kevin's father."

Samantha jerked back as if she had been physically accosted. The words seemed horrific to her somehow.

"No," she spat. "It can't be so. First off, that means Kevin was my cousin. No, Pop would have said something."

"Would he have? Your father didn't like the guy," Josh said.

"Of course, he would have. Pop knew I worked with Kevin. Hell, Pop knew we all hung out together since we were kids." She closed her eyes and then opened them, only to stare at the windshield.

"Did Kevin know all along?"

Josh nodded.

"Oh my God. And he still tried to kill me?"

Samantha pulled her lips in and tried her best not to cry.

"He attacked me, Josh. I couldn't move, and he ranted on and on about things."

"I'm so sorry."

"Kevin said his mother blamed my mother for everything wrong in the world. Now it kind of makes sense in a warped kind of way. Maybe he blamed me for his father's death, too? Oh, God. I didn't think it could get worse, but it's heartbreaking."

"I'm sorry you went through all that, Sam. It's horrific."

Josh reached across the seat and placed his hand on her knee.

"I told you there's evil in this world. Strange things happen right in front of us. I'm sorry Sam, I had to tell you. The entire truth, how he's your cousin. And I had to say something before we meet with the tribe. You see, they all know and someone might have said something to you, and . . . Well, I didn't want you to find out from a stranger "

Sam turned. Josh's head was down. She admired his honesty especially given the sensitive situation.

"Thanks for telling me. I'm okay, honest. Now let's visit the tribe before I get cold feet."

Josh smiled, put the car in gear and they were on their way.

42 – Nawihla, Returning Home

Josh parked his car in a grassy field, and they walked across the matted ground, the straw crunched under their feet as they approached a building. It had a large open porch attached to a rustic, dark stained building. Rolling hills with blooming trees filled the scenery. The leaves were opened, some trees had fruit blossoms that remained, showing off vibrant spring colors. There were also many pines, the evergreen scent drifted in the breeze.

Sam stepped up to the porch, made way to the door, and entered into an expansive hall. People were moving around, setting up tables, opening chairs, and someone in the corner was making coffee. Sam could smell the brewed beans and her mouth watered.

An elderly gentleman approached them.

"Good evening. Josh, you're on time." The man smiled at his joviality. "The meeting will begin in ten minutes."

Josh shook his hand.

"Sam, this is Wayne. He's a tribal member and tonight he'll be managing the council meeting. Wayne, this is Samantha Tremblay."

Sam held out her hand, and Wayne shook it heartily. His eyes were a soft brown color, much like Josh's sable color, they looked warm and friendly. Wayne had a few crow's feet at the edges, magnified by the glasses he wore. His lips protruded a bit as if his teeth underneath were too big for his mouth. His hair was gray and shoulder length. He wore jeans and a buttoned blue and white Oxford striped shirt. He looked like an average man, ordinary in every way. Her internal voice chastised herself for imagining such a bigoted vision as if she expected all tribe members to be wearing feathers or something.

"I'm pleased to meet you, Wayne. I hope I won't be in the way this evening."

"Don't be silly." He smiled. "Did you know that your name, Samantha, means a child from the sun?"

Sam nodded.

"We all know who you are, Samantha, and you are most welcomed to be here with us, anytime. We loved your mother and father. We were sad he stayed away from us after the accident."

Wayne bowed his head. "Please excuse me, I want to help finish setting up chairs and get ready."

Other people in the room looked their way, turning their heads fast when she returned the glance. Sam wondered if they starred because of the catastrophe she had underneath her hat. She tugged at it to make sure it covered her hair, then nudged Josh.

"Let's get a cup of joe while it's hot."

Josh walked with her to the table set up with the coffee pot, filled a cup, handed it to her. Sam sipped her coffee and noticed that the others glanced at her still; when she looked back, they averted their eyes.

"Is there something wrong with me being here tonight? Can you see my dyed strands poking out?" she said.

"No," Josh replied. "You look fine. They're curious about you, just like you are of them, that's all."

Josh left her side to help with the chairs. Samantha watched him as he worked with the others, no banter or teasing, only cooperation as they set up for the meeting. This was the side of Josh she admired—the Josh she had always been friends with—his Abenaki side.

Memories came to her now of all the times Josh had stood up for himself, proud of his heritage even if it meant getting a punch to the face. She had done the opposite and ignored her legacy. But Josh had always been the brave one, proud, no matter how many jabs to his gut he endured, he had always remained faithful to his family's bloodline.

Samantha's face burned. She looked to see if anyone had noticed her shame. No, these were all good people, and even if they guessed her thoughts, they'd never say a thing. Kindness was all around this place. She decided to let her wall of solitude crumble, at least a little.

A soft touch on her upper arm startled Sam. She turned and saw an elderly woman standing by her side. She wore a pale blue dress decorated with bright beadwork. It was a similar design to something her mother had embroidered years ago. The woman's hair was cut short with bangs, and dark. But it didn't look natural, she obviously colored treated her hair to hide the gray. Her face showed wrinkles around her eyes and mouth. Even though Sam knew the woman was smiling, her skin still fell south, any attempt to defy life's gravity was lost. The woman's voice was soft and pleasant when she spoke.

"Hello there, my name is Arlene, I'm on the council. I

know who you are. Samantha Tremblay, right?" Arlene smiled.

Samantha nodded. "Pleased to meet you."

"I knew your mother very well. She was respected by all of us who've been here for a while. She helped our campaign to gain recognition. Rest her soul. Without people like her, we would have never made it this far. I'm sorry she isn't here with us today, but I am so happy you're here now."

Sam hadn't expected for anyone to actually know who she was, let alone remember her mother. Years had gone by, and no one wanted to speak of her mother. Now, twice within ten minutes, her mother was mentioned. Sam's interest in the tribe piqued. She was curious and wanted to learn more about them, and her mother.

"Thank you, Arlene. What else do you remember about my mother? If you don't mind my asking."

Arlene's eyes pinched up when she smiled. From the open window, the setting sun's rays stretched across the room and cast a ribbon of light on Arlene's face. At that moment, she looked angelic.

"Your mother was special. Her soul spoke to the earth, and nature sent back answers through her from a lodge. Maybe you know what I mean, I sense you have the gift, too. I'll be happy to tell you more, but let's save it for another day. The meeting is starting." Arlene patted her arm and left to take a seat.

Josh came back and escorted Sam to the group area. The chairs were situated in a semi-circle, making it easier to see everyone. They took a seat. Sam watched the others as they were seated and the meeting began.

Wayne stepped to the center of the semi-circle of people and declined the microphone handed to him by another man. He wrapped his hair behind his ear and slowly scanned the group, turning his head, greeting each of them with a nod and his smile of recognition when his eyes met each of theirs. Samantha's face sweltered when he looked at her. The intensity of his eyes felt like he was looking straight into her soul.

"Hello, folks. I think we're a small enough group tonight so that you can all hear me without the Mic."

The people in the chairs mumbled their approvals, acknowledging with nods. There were over two dozen people seated.

"Let me begin with an introduction. Our tribal brother, Josh, has brought Samantha to visit with us tonight so she can witness our council as we tell and share our fundamental truths."

Wayne raised his arm and motioned for her to stand.

Samantha's legs felt like rubber as she stood. Her face burned as her eyes swept across the room, seeing in return the peering eyes of the others. Her palm itched, and she urgently scratched. Everyone in the room nodded or said a muffled hello.

Sam nodded then sat down again. She spotted the door across the room, the neon exit sign glowed above it. It seemed so far away. She turned and noticed Josh grinning at her.

"It's okay," he mouthed.

His smile helped her feel more comfortable, and she relaxed. Besides, no one was looking at her anymore. Everyone was facing forward waiting to hear Wayne, who began speaking.

"Let me start by explaining what's going on here tonight. We're holding counsel, not for any issue that needs a vote. Tonight is a special meeting, its only purpose is to remind ourselves of our tribe's fundamental truths, how we live our lives, and our tribal beliefs. We do this occasionally, so that we will never again lose what was once lost."

Wayne bowed his head for a moment of contemplation, then continued to address the entire hall.

"In our tribe, we aren't judged by how much money we hold in our pocket, but instead we are measured by what wealth we give to others. This is our way of life. In return, all we ask of others is that they acknowledge that we exist. We pray they accept us as Abenaki. Not merely a footnote in a history book that says the Abenaki are an extinct Native American Indian group from the past. I say, no to this. Because I have news for them, we are alive and well, and living among them."

The people clapped, some shouted, "we are here."

"Yes friends, we are here. There are many tribes of Abenaki, we all like to have our clan."

Some of the audience laughed at this.

"We are the Missisquoi tribe, once known as the St. Francis-Sokoki Band of the Abenaki Nation of Missisquoi. It's a mouthful, I know. But it's important to know who we are and where we come from. The name *Missisquoi* means people of the flint place. Most of us originated from right here, in Vermont.

"Here's a history lesson for you folks. The Sokoki band was once called *Ozogwakiak*, which means breakaway people." Wayne moved his hands like he snapped something in half, and a few people giggled.

"You see, our descendants live in many places now. We were forced to leave—to break away—to hide among the others, especially here, in Vermont. We originated from *Wabanah-kik*, which means Dawn Land. It's the Eastern part of our entire Nation, Maine and up into Canada. But our tribe was compelled to move west, for safety, and survival.

"Now, we live in *Ndakinna*, that's the Abenaki word which means, our land. The clans band together; this makes us stronger, better to be noticed, better for our voices to be heard. And it worked. Vermont officially recognizes some of our Abenaki bands. This is great news, folks. The state passed laws in 2012 to acknowledge that we are here and we have always been here. I think we should celebrate tonight and every day. But never forget, it took years of struggle to be recognized once again as a tribe. We owe this to many brave people who refused to be intimidated."

Wayne hesitated, taking a few seconds of reflection. He closed his eyes as if praying. Others in the room looked off into the distance as if meditating, or searching for the future.

"Yes, let's celebrate our lives and our tribe. Together, we have fulfilled the prophecy. *Nawihla* is the Abenaki word meaning 'I am returning home' and we have returned home folks. Never forget that we are alive and well. We have returned home."

The group clapped, a few of the younger people stood and raised their arms in the air, swaying, with their hands clasped together with each other. The mood kindled the heartbeat of a revival. After a moment, the sound faded and Wayne spoke again.

"Now, let's explain our politics."

A few people in the crowd softly laughed.

"Our tribe is organized under the Tribal Council. They guide our group by the majority rule. Everyone has a voice at the table, as long as it is respectful," he said. "But let's not forget what we believe. The basic truths and our ways."

"Decisions and the addition of new members must meet our strict criteria and satisfy the three truths. First, will the decision we make or the new member we accept into the tribe bring peace, and therefore be good for the tribe? Second, is the decision righteous and morally correct? Third, will the decision or new member preserve the integrity of the tribe? To be more specific, we need to ask ourselves will the power behind the decision protect our heritage.

"We will live with the results of each decision in our daily lives, it will co-exist with us, so it must be a wise decision that protects us and ensures a healthy future for all tribal members. All decisions and all new members must be right for the current tribe and for the tribe in the future."

As Wayne spoke, his voice lowered in tone, simultaneously someone had turned the lights lower. The fire burning in the hearth behind Wayne was the only light visible.

Some people in the group chanted while remaining in their seats, a soft, warm melody, like a lullaby. One of them began tapping a drum, thumping smooth raps. Another joined, and the sound melded into a peaceful sound.

The drum taps grew louder then softened again like a gentle rain shower. The wave of harmony sounded like a song she had heard before. She recognized it as the same melody heard in her dream. The canon that had repeated itself and reinforced her courage. The same rhythm she had heard in the woods, a rapping drum gently beating, like the heartbeat of the world.

Samantha closed her eyes, thought of nothing else except the mystical sound. She smelled the burning pine log in the hearth and the heavy scent of the forest drifting in from the open windows. The fragrance of the earth surrounded them.

Her body and mind relaxed, perceiving only the tranquil ambiance. In the moment, she was all-knowing, sensed the presence of everything important. Her mother — her pop — and many more souls touched her heart with love.

The undercurrent flooded her spirit, released her inhibitions, and encouraged her to travel to another place. A place where self-awareness made her complete again. Samantha's mind was content, in sync with nature, and in the woods where she belonged.

THE END

NOTES

In 2012 the state of Vermont officially recognized the following Abenaki bands:
- ♦ Nulhegan Band of the Coosuk-Abenaki
- ♦ El Nu Abenaki Tribe
- ♦ Koasek of the Koas Abenaki Traditional Band
- ♦ Abenaki Nation at Missisquoi, organized under the Missisquoi Abenaki Tribal Council.

To date 2017, the state of New Hampshire recognizes that the following tribes are present in New Hampshire, as cultural resources but not acknowledged as a nationally recognized tribe:
- ♦ Abenaki Nation of New Hampshire
- ♦ First Nation of New Hampshire
- ♦ Cowasuk Band of the Pennacook New Hampshire Tribe
- ♦ Cowasuk Traditional Band Council of the Sovereign Abenaki Nation

Administratively attached to the Department of Cultural Resources, the Commission on Native American Affairs recognizes the historic and cultural contributions of Native Americans to New Hampshire, promotes and strengthens Native American heritage and furthers the needs of New Hampshire's Native American community through state policy and programs.

Flag of St. Francis/Sokoki Band of Abenaki

On 24 July 1991 the Abenaki Nation adopted a tribal flag. The flag has a dark green for the Green Mountains with the tribal seal in the center. The brown shield represents deer or beaver hide. The three symbols in the flag's center represent: a red sun at the top, blue waves for the rivers and Lake Champlain in the middle, and at the bottom representation for the green grass and forest lands of western Vermont.

Learn more at New Hampshire Folklife
https://www.nh.gov/folklife/learning-center/traditions/native-ameri-can.htm

More Info on the tribes:

New Hampshire's History Blog | New Hampshire's Native Americans: Hiding In Plain Website: http://www.cowhampshireblog.com/2006/08/10/new-hampshires-native-americans-hiding-in-plain-sight/

Information About Loons:

The Common Loon - Information via the Audubon
　　　Photos, Facts and bird song and calls
http://www.audubon.org/field-guide/bird/common-loon

The Loon Preservation Committee
Celebrating Over 40 Years of Loon Freservation in New Hamp-shire
The Voice of the Loon
http://www.loon.org/voice-loon.php

Learn more about the loon and one man's conservation fund-ing here:
http://www.audubon.org/news/the-lure-common-loon

From The Author

Thank you for spending time in the North East Kingdom. I enjoyed writing about Samantha and her journey to find a killer and the missing pieces of herself. I think we all get lost from time to time, but there is always hope and a trail to lead us back to ourselves, and of course, there's always room for justice.

I dedicate this story to my daughter, Kasandra. She's a kind, fun-loving, and quiet person, whom I love dearly. By profession, she's a talented stylist and a dedicated yoga teacher, who's spreading peace in the world as she journeys through life while discovering the strength within herself, all while helping others to do the same. Kasandra is a wholesome part of our world and she makes the lives that she touches better. When Kasandra was a young girl, she liked to read about the Native American culture, and she inspired my curiosity.

This story could never have been written without the constant support of my husband, Jerry. He gives more than takes, he is silent rather than accusing, and thinks before he speaks.

Many people claim to be wise, but rarer are those who truly are sagacious from experience—Jerry is one man who takes to heart all he has learned and never lost his faith or empathy along his journey. I thank him for his patience, his support, and I aspire to his example of compassion.

The story's setting of Brunswick Springs is inspired by the suggestion of Mary Lou Paquette, an active person who likes to paddle waterways in her kayak to find new nature haunts.

I've camped with her many years ago, and we've shared a few eerie experiences together, and I know for a fact, deep down inside, she's not afraid of anything. I thank Mary Lou for her years of dedicated service in the Airforce and Army, also for her continued work with other Veteran services. She gave her life's work to our country, and I salute her for her courage.

I'm thankful for my daughter, Kasandra and new daughter-in-law, Shelbie, as well as the men in my life: my husband Jerry, my three sons Sami, Nick and Stephan. I'm thankful for and proud of my grandson, Aden, a good person and talented artist who's beginning his career.

I'm lucky to be blessed with the best. My family inspires me, and remind me that there is integrity in the world, as long as each of us is willing to put in the effort required and keep people close to our hearts.

A cherished moment can bring light in our times of darkness.

THANK YOU FOR READING . . .

Thank you for spending your valuable time reading my story, In The Woods - Murder In The North east Kingdom.
Your support is important to me.

As an author, my goal is to take you to places that are far away from your daily routine and show situations that stretch your imagination. Your honest review is always appreciated, so please make a note on the store website where you purchased your copy or any other website where you might recommend books to your friends. Let others know what you think about the story, how it made you feel.

Your book reviews make a big difference and help make this book become more visible in an ocean of competing titles. Thank you.

Reviews are the best way to give back to any author.
Other books by Elisabeth Zguta:
Breaking Cursed Bonds
Exposing Secret Sins
Seeking Redemption
Dreamer: A Ukrainian World War II story

Visit my websites for more information about these books and other short stories.

EZIndiePublishing.com
ElisabethZguta.com

Keep up to date and find me on social media.

Twitter handle @zguta
Elisabeth Zguta, Facebook Author Page
Elisabeth Zguta Goodreads Author Page

Thank you for choosing to read
In The Woods - Murder In The North East Kingdom
Your review is appreciated. Until next time, take care.

Made in the USA
Middletown, DE
23 October 2022